JANE MORELL

COLLISION COURSE

Complete and Unabridged

ULVERSCROFT
Leicester

First published in Great Britain in 2004 by
Robert Hale Limited
London

First Large Print Edition
published 2005
by arrangement with
Robert Hale Limited
London

The moral right of the author has been asserted

British Library CIP Data

Morell, Jane
Collision course.—Large print ed.—
Ulverscroft large print series: adventure & suspense
1. Qaida (Organization)—Fiction
2. Terrorism—Great Britain—Prevention—Fiction
3. Suspense fiction
4. Large type books
I. Title
823.9'14 [F]

ISBN 1–84395–926–7

C409253732

Published by
F. A. Thorpe (Publishing)
Anstey, Leicestershire

Set by Words & Graphics Ltd.
Anstey, Leicestershire
Printed and bound in Great Britain by
T. J. International Ltd., Padstow, Cornwall

This book is printed on acid-free paper

Jane Morell was born in England but has spent most of her adult life abroad. An educator and poet, her work has taken her from the Peruvian Cordillera to the jungles of New Guinea, and for more than ten years to various parts of the Middle and Far East. She and her husband have a home in Mid-Wales, to which they return as often as they can.

COLLISION COURSE

An undercover operation, linked to Al Qaeda, has established a network of bases for the training of experienced terrorists dedicated to suicide missions against Western objectives. The activation of this network is imminent, with Britain destined to become a clandestine source for supplying skilled volunteers for terrorist 'spectaculars' in the West. But a top secret, covert counter-operation by Britain's Intelligence and Anti-terrorist organizations has been shadowing the terrorist network, only holding back from destroying it because in such situations there is invariably one optimum moment to go for the jugular. Now that moment is at hand and all depends on one man and one woman . . .

Books by Jane Morell
Published by The House of Ulverscroft:

THE SCORE
CRIME IN HEAVEN
SIDEWINDER

Prologue

The Catalyst

A clear and lovely night. Three-quarter moon riding high above rolling hill country. Swathes of natural woodland and conifer plantations slashed dark across moonlit grassland. Sleeping farmsteads here and there, midnight black on summer-sweet pastures.

And on the two-lane road slicing across the slopes 200 feet above the valley floor two cars are burning rubber, white Toyota in front and hell-bent on holding on to its narrow, hard-won lead but the chasing Mercedes on its tail and gaining on it inch by gruelling inch.

'The Merc back there — that bastard Traven — how long before he catches us up?' At the wheel of the Toyota, Rob Remmick clips it out. The excitement and danger of the hunt is on him, but they've just roared past a sign warning of hairpin bends close ahead and he's got minimal space to manoeuvre because on their right the hillside falls steeply down to the valley floor — and between them and the drop there's nothing but grassed verge and a wire fence.

'One minute at most.' In the passenger seat beside him, his brother Steve, peering into the side mirror, sees the Merc's headlights closing in on them, its compact black shape hugging the tarmac.

'Traven armed, you reckon?'

'Likely. Bad light for shooting, though — '

'*Faster*, Remmick! For love of The Almighty, more speed!' Behind the Remmick brothers the courier is kneeling on the back seat, he has cast off his safety belt and is glaring out of the rear window at his enemy. He is as fear-free as Rob Remmick but there is no excitement in him, there is only a cold fixity of purpose powered by a hatred that is both visceral and of the mind. He has been appointed to carry out this night's job in furtherance of the cause he serves, and his life is expendable if that sacrifice is called for; he has long known and accepted that. The Remmick brothers, as individuals, are nothing to him; they have no personal significance for him, and no call on his loyalty: they are not of his creed, and, therefore, exist solely to be used by his own kind as a means to the desired end. However he is well aware that the elder of the two, Robert, has a good and very private reason to hate him. 'Faster!' he demands again. 'Faster, for the love of Allah!'

2

But it's too late for that. They're into the first of the hairpin bends — Remmick takes it at 50, has to brake and then as they hit the straight again the Mercedes punches into them from behind — drops back a bit then accelerates and rams into them a second time.

Rob Remmick keeps the Toyota on the road, just. Steve's holding on to whatever he can, but across the back seat the courier sprawls unconscious, the belt he spurned lying over his head. Rob sees the next bend barely thirty yards ahead — a glance into the rear-view mirror shows him the dark shape of the Merc lining up for its third strike.

Traven's closing in for the kill! he thinks and, dare-devil eyes alight, sets himself ready to hold the Toyota against the coming impact *then go on the attack* — with a bit of luck he can send Traven and his Merc careering down that slope to their right. The Mercedes slams into them — drops back again. Rob feels the Toyota shudder; takes his foot off the accelerator, but even as he does so realizes he's misjudged relevant speeds and distances. He's too close to the bend! Hasn't got a hope in hell of making the turn — has to *brake*! Brake hard and —

Through a split second, Rob Remmick sees a moonlit world stark black-and-white swinging round him and thinks, Christ I'm going over the edge *I'm going to die.* Then —

Night owl a-hunt in fields and woodlands near that road would hear screeching of tyres across tarmac, would see the white car lose out to the skid and run out of control, surge across the verge, smash through wire fencing then jink away down the slope . . .

But there is no night owl hunting nearby: there is only the road. And on the road there is only the Mercedes — and Traven, at its wheel. In his way, he also is a hunter.

★ ★ ★

But at the time Traven was in trouble of his own and did not witness the Toyota's frenetic descent of the slope. Dropping back from the last impact he saw the Toyota slew across the road and break through the wire, but then he was up to the hairpin himself and going too fast for it. He wrestled the Mercedes round it but couldn't hold her, she skidded side-on, hit the rocky hillside bordering the carriageway and stopped.

He came to three minutes later. Shocked, bruised, and aware of severe pain in his left leg, he released his seat belt and, cautiously, methodically, assessed how much damage his body had sustained. He found that — bar his leg — all was well. A cracked bone there, he

4

judged, not a full break, thank God, and the pain bearable while it had to be. So get on with it, man! he ordered himself. Get back along the road and — no, wait! God knows what's happened at the bottom of that slope, so first thing to do is get on your mobile to Hewson in the control car stationed thirty miles south of here on the route our MI5 informer pinpointed for us — wrongly! — as the one the Remmicks and Shaheen's courier would take out of Swansea, put him in the picture so he can position back-up on alert ready to cover all possible outcomes to the situation here.

'Hewson.'

'Traven. I'm on a mountain road roughly thirty miles north of you, will give you map refs in a minute. Hear this: the Toyota's crashed. Gone down a hillside, has to be a wreck. My Merc's US too. I'm OK but my leg's injured; I won't be able to get down there. Ambulance and vehicle rescue services required, get them on the road at once.'

'Noted. What about the Remmicks and the courier?'

'I can't see the Toyota from where I am, it's on the far side of a bend. I'll go round there now, call you back soon as I've checked.'

'OK, understood. Give me those map refs, sir.'

Traven did so, then cut the call and, taking his night glasses from the glove pocket, slung them round his neck and manoeuvred himself clear of the Mercedes. Rested for a moment then, leaning on the bonnet, nauseous and slightly disorientated. Around him, moonlit hills and valley serene, quiet. But Traven was aware of no beauty there. Only the loneliness of the place came at him and he thought, those three men down there at the bottom of the slope — are they alive or dead? Rob and Steve Remmick, Shaheen's courier . . . But as he thought the courier's name his mind played tricks on him, and behind his eyes he 'saw' not the courier but the man's sister, Hanna. Just for a split second her face was there, smiling at him, and the long, dark hair blowing across her mouth the way it had done that day when —

Get focused! Traven exerted his will and the split second died its death, was gone. Pushing himself upright he gritted his teeth and, favouring his left leg, worked his way along the car to the boot where, he knew, two narrow planks of wood were stowed among the emergency equipment the Mercedes carried. Pulling out one of these — it was about the right length — he settled it firmly into his left armpit to serve as a crutch and, gingerly, experimentally, let his left foot take some of his weight. Christ, that hurts. Get on with it. Have to.

Moonlight throwing his shadow small and black behind him, Traven limped back along the road. Not far to go. Just round the hairpin, should be able to see from there. Ought to've brought a gun, like Jim said. Don't be stupid; those blokes at the bottom of that slope can't be exactly fighting fit. All three of them are involved in a terrorist operation that threatens all 'men of good-will' the world over so, to my mind, it will be no more than rough justice if the life has been smashed out of each and every one of them.

Yet when — standing by the ruptured, curling wire where the Toyota had burst through the fence — he focused his glasses on the crash scene below him and saw the distorted shape of the white car at the bottom of the slope, his first thought was *thank God, they didn't burn.*

★ ★ ★

Dismissing the thought, Traven called Hewson again as promised. 'I forced the Toyota off the road,' he explained. 'She's at the foot of a steepish slope, about 50 metres down, looks wrecked but is still on all four wheels. She's at the edge of a wood. I'd say she turned, or was turned by the driver, so that she struck the outermost trees side-on. No signs of life that I can detect.'

'She didn't catch fire?'

'No — not so far. Could yet happen, of course, if petrol's leaking and makes contact with electric wiring that's broken but still live.'

'How long between the crash and you getting a dekko?'

'Ten minutes minimum.'

'Any cover available near the wreck?'

'Plenty. The wood, hedgerows . . .'

'So one or all of those blokes might, just might, have got lucky — been thrown clear or something, then taken off cross-country?'

'By the look of it from here I shouldn't have thought it likely any of them were capable of taking off anywhere, but you never can tell.'

'So I'll implement close-search coverage?'

'Yes. Cover all possible escape routes from the crash site, night-vision choppers — '

'I know the drill, sir. If anyone got clear of that wreck, we'll have 'em. Rob Remmick's always been a lucky bastard, but from what you say that could be about to change. Hewson out.'

Traven did not return to the Mercedes. Perching himself awkwardly on a nearby culvert wall to take the weight off his injured leg, he used his binoculars to keep watch on the Toyota. The moon watched with him, but, naturally, it kept its own counsel. He saw no sign of life within or in the vicinity of the car tilted drunkenly against one of the tree trunks at the edge of the wood below him. But then suddenly he glimpsed an intense, red-bright flash of light inside the Toyota — and a second later saw her engulfed in fire. Lurid, coppery flames ballooned up into the night sky — swirled in luminous clouds among the treetops while the fire at the heart of the blaze consumed the car and all that was inside her. It ate her guts out, leaving only still-glowing metal bones at the foot of the moon-bright hill.

On seeing the first spark of heat-light within the Toyota, Traven, realizing what would happen next, pushed himself to his feet in horror, careless of the jolt of pain in his leg. And standing on the road above the wreck, watched the cremation of the car he had forced into the skid which had turned out to be its death. And the men who'd been inside her? What of them? The two Remmick brothers, and Shaheen's courier: terrorists, all three. 'God rot the lot of them,' he said aloud, as the fire slowly died. But he was still standing there staring down at the dull red glow of the dying fire when, some thirty minutes later, the first of the police vehicles arrived.

★ ★ ★

Rob Remmick regained consciousness half a minute after the Toyota struck the grey tree trunk passenger-side-on. His seat belt and airbag had saved his life, but the impact had thrown him heavily against the door and he'd hit his head. With consciousness returned he fumbled the torch out from under the dash and took stock of the situation. Steve's side of the car had slammed into the tree trunk and beside him he saw his brother slumped, out cold. The rear door on that wing was wide open, swinging loose on one hinge — and there was no sign whatsoever of the courier. God send me two things, Rob Remmick thought then. One, Steve *alive*. Two, that I can open that bloody door he's fallen against, it's not jammed. Releasing his belt he checked his own physical condition; found his face bloodied, right arm and side bruised and painful but — thank Christ! — both legs OK. So — get Steve, then clear out of here!

Luck had come back to him. The crash had damaged the catch of his door but as he pushed against it with his left hand it gave a little. He pushed harder, got it half open before it stuck fast. Easing himself through the gap he stumbled round to the passenger side — and found luck still with him. Steve's door was virtually undamaged except for broken glass. Opening it, he found his brother obviously concussed, and his left leg at a funny angle, almost certainly fractured. Standing back, Rob conned over the plan he'd been building up inside his head. I'll sling Steve over my shoulder, take off cross-country — then the first road we hit I'll contact Mike on my mobile and he'll come pick us up. He's at that pub ten miles south of here, knows this country — I can count on Mike, he's never failed me yet. Yep, that's it. So — get going! Traven's up there on the road, if he can he'll come down after us and he might be armed so — move, Rob Remmick! Hell, no, hold on! What about the courier? He must have been thrown clear as we came down the hill. Maybe he's dead? But with him being the bastard he is, I need to know whether he is or is not; that matters to me, it matters one hell of a lot.

Rob Remmick found Shaheen's courier a few yards uphill from the Toyota: he was lying splayed out alongside one of the boulders scattered across the slope. Catapulted out of the car when the door burst open, he had hit

11

the rock head-on: one whole side of his face was a bloodied horror, cheekbone stove in, jaw hanging loose. But when Remmick felt for the pulse in the flaccid wrist he found life there. A flicker only, but life, no doubt of it. And looking at what was left of that only-too-well-known-to-him face, he recalled the business that still stood unresolved between the two of them. Straightening up, he stood quiet under the moon and, *bearing in mind the situation between them*, debated which of the two courses of action now open to him he should take. His eyes were on the crest of the hill rising behind the road off which Traven had forced him, but at that moment he was not aware of it, or of Traven either. Inside his head he was living another time, another place — and only himself and Shaheen's courier there, locked together in a closed, steely circle of mutual hatred and contempt.

Decision came quickly, and undisturbed by either doubt or guilt. Robert Remmick put back his head and smiled up at the clear night sky. As things stand here now, it's in my power to break that circle, he thought. Maybe there's a slight risk to me in doing so, but what a gain! I can break this bastard's hold on me for ever and no one will know that the breaking was *a deliberate act*.

Renewed strength surging within him at that infinitely pleasing prospect, he hauled the half-dead courier back to the Toyota then manhandled him to lie with his head and shoulders propped against the open rear door. Then, placing the thumb and fingers of his left hand on the man's neck in the positions taught to him years earlier by instructors in the art of the swift and silent kill, he applied sufficient pressure for sufficient time to ensure the courier's death.

That done, he went back to his brother. Won't be easy, this next bit, he thought. Bloody difficult, in fact, with one arm a bit beat up — not out of action, though, is it? — so get on with it, never mind the pain, get the two of you out of here! And a few minutes later, with his still unconscious brother slung across his shoulders in a fireman's lift, Rob Remmick set off cross-country, travelling southwards. But in his haste to put distance between himself and the crash scene he had not paid enough attention to distributing the unconscious man's weight evenly across his shoulders. Becoming aware of this he stopped, shifted his burden to a less strain-inducing position, then turned for a last look at the wreck, picked out the blurred white shape of the Toyota at the edge of the wood — and at that moment saw the car explode into a ball of fire and flame.

'*Christ!*' he breathed, watching. But then he grinned. Couldn't have done better if I'd torched it myself, could I? he thought. Now the courier's body won't have any stories at all to tell, let alone the true one. The true one'll be burned to ashes inside the bastard's greedy, scheming brain.

And turning his back on the courier's funeral pyre Rob Remmick went on his way, keeping in cover as he carried his brother Steve to safety across the moon-dark hills.

1

Two years later: summer 2002

'Oh come on, Jilly! We've been through all this before! I know I'm a bit of a dull stick with women but — '

'How right you are!' On her way to the front door of his flat the girl stopped and swung round, blonde curls flying, her pretty, blue-eyed face not even angry, just faintly exasperated. 'You know what, Steve Remmick? Just lately you've begun to bore me out of my socks!' She laughed. 'Don't argue any more, darling. Let's just agree: we've had a good time together but now we've exhausted each other's feel-good factor about it, so it's best to call it a day. OK?'

'*Not* OK! I'd rather you stayed.' Frowning at her across his beige-carpeted hall, Steve Remmick was dismayed, but uncertain how to deal with the situation.

Slowly, Jilly Court walked back to him, stared up into his eyes. 'Let me tell you something, one-time lover,' she said quietly. 'At first you and I were good together, in fact we were very good, the sex especially. But

— this is what I think, anyway — that was only because there at the start of it each of us was *in need* of someone. We happened on each other, and we clicked. But now, I've grown out of my so-called need, whereas you're still in the process of working your way clear of yours. You're *still* all wrapped up in your brother, him getting killed like that not long before we met. So I want out of it now, Steve. You're too quiet a bloke for me, now I'm back to my normal self.' She put out one hand and, briefly, laid her palm against his cheek. 'You and I, we've lost it,' she said.

'I'm sorry I bore you.' Yet in an odd way Steve Remmick felt relieved that she was leaving him. I'll be free, he thought. Whatever that means. If it means anything now Rob's dead.

Again, the girl laughed. She looks even prettier when she laughs, he thought — then realized that, for the first time since they'd met, it didn't matter to him one way or the other how pretty Jilly Court was or what she thought of him.

'You know what?' she said. 'You should find yourself someone dark and intense and into books and art and all that stuff. Me, I'm looking for a good time — dancing, dining out, *fun!* So 'bye now, Steve darling. Thanks for the good times, and — I wish you well.'

16

Then turning away she made for the door again, went out of it without a backward glance, and closed it quietly behind her.

For a moment, Steve stared at the shut door; then he shrugged, muttered, 'I wish you well, too', and went back into the living-room of his flat. The curtains were closed against the night and the predominating colours — tawny yellows, russet browns and a rich cream — seemed to him a welcome in themselves. Well, they would, wouldn't they? he thought. I chose them because for me they sang the right song. After a moment he grinned wryly, thinking, if I'd said that to Jilly she'd have burst out laughing . . . Ach, to hell with it. Besides, she was always tidying the place up. Christ, I need a drink.

Mixing himself a whisky-sour at the small built-in bar he carried it over to the armchair in front of the fireplace — his favourite chair, it had a low, shelved table either side of it, telephone and magazines on one of them, books and newspapers on the other, opened mail scattered over both. As he cast his tall, wiry body wearily into the chair the telephone beside it rang, so he put down his glass and answered it. The call was from Rebecca, his brother's wife. Somehow, even now, twenty-two months after Rob was killed, he could not think of her as Robert's 'widow'; in his

17

mind she still lived as Rob's 'wife.'

'Steve, so glad you haven't gone to bed yet. Is your girlfriend with you?' Rebecca did not like Jilly, and never used her given name if she could avoid it.

He laughed, pleased that she had rung. 'She's just left. And — this'll make your day, I guess — this time she's gone for good.'

'Did she say why?'

'She said I'm boring — and she's probably right, at that!'

'You don't sound heart-broken.'

'I've just discovered I'm not. But I'm sure you didn't ring to talk about Jilly — '

'No way!' Rebecca laughed, and as her laughter came to him down the line, Steve Remmick saw her face in the eye of his mind: strong cheekbones, pointed chin and cornflower-blue eyes all framed by the thick, straight, blonde hair — naturally blonde, he knew that. However, as she went on, her voice was serious. 'Steve, there's something I have to give you,' she said. 'I should've given it you ages ago but . . . Well, anyway, this afternoon I was clearing some junk out of the attic to throw away, and I saw this metal box Rob left for you.'

'*Rob* left for me? But it's been all this time. You should've — '

'Yes, I know, and I'm sorry, truly sorry.

Twenty-two months. Yes, it *is* a long time, don't think I don't know that . . . But there was so much to do, then. I just . . . forgot, I suppose.'

Her voice had gone small and desolate and hearing it like that Steve thought, if you set my grief for Rob alongside Rebecca's, mine was and is a thing of quite ordinary stature. 'I had no right to take that tone with you,' he said. 'Forgive me.'

'Nothing to forgive.' But she waited for him to speak next.

'This box — what's in it, d'you know?' he asked.

'I've no idea. It's locked. I guess it's probably something to do with the stuff you and he were into with Shaheen's lot. And as you know I've always kept myself well clear of involvement in that. One of Rob's kind is enough in any family. See where it got him.'

'You don't *know* that what happened to him was anything other than an accident. You really do have to get your head round that, Rebecca. Police reports never — '

'Witnesses can be bought easily enough in the circles Rob moved in . . . Anyway, back to this box. Would you like me to bring it over to you?'

'Is it big? Heavy?'

'Not particularly. It's made of metal and

about nine by ten inches, probably contains papers, I'd say.'

'And it's locked?'

'Padlocked. Look, I'm so sorry about this. I only remembered when I saw the thing: Rob told me it was for you.'

'When? When did he tell you that?'

'God, I don't know! It must have been soon after that time Traven rolled the two of you and Shaheen's courier off the road. It doesn't *matter* when, does it?'

'Not really. Leave it.'

'So I've got the box here, but — now please, don't be crosser than you already are — I can't find the key. I don't remember having it but I suppose I must have — '

'I can force it open easily enough I expect. Shall I come over and fetch it?'

'That'd be great,' said Rebecca, having got what she had hoped for. 'Come tomorrow around midday and stay for lunch.'

That settled, they chatted a little longer and then ended the call. Replacing the handset, Steve picked up his whisky-sour and relaxed, letting the restfulness of his own place sink into him, thinking about Rebecca. How well do I really know her? he wondered. To this day I'm not quite sure how she truly felt *while Rob was alive* about the way of life he and I were into then — had been

20

integrated into during our teen years, drawn into it by that IRA talent scout who'd marked Rob out as gold-standard potential within days of first meeting him. And — like it'd been ever since we were kids growing up together — wherever Rob led, I followed without question; my older brother always the star, events seeming, to me at any rate, always miraculously subject to his will.

But, for me, all that altered fast following Rob's death. *I changed*: discovered for myself a new reality — and then, with Traven's help, a whole new world. I switched allegiances, joined what had until then been the opposition. And when I had finally convinced Traven that I was levelling with him, he gave me the chance to prove both my commitment to my newfound credo and my worth to him as his double agent for MI5. He took me on trial then, three months after Rob's death, and *because* he was dead: never could or would have happened while he was alive. But with him dead I ... became myself, I suppose. It's as simple as that — yet as complicated as all hell, too. Ach, forget it. You made the break, made the choice — now go wherever the new path leads you. Strange, how things work out: me working under cover *for* Traven *against* Shaheen now. I wonder what's in that box Rebecca's got for me? It's not like Rob to do that sort of thing. It has to mean he must've thought he might die soon — and that wasn't his style, not his style at all. Besides, whatever did he have in his possession that he needed to hide away so securely — yet wanted me to have in the event of his death?

To hell with it! Suddenly, Steve shivered, and broke free. The thing's probably got a pile of unpaid bills inside it, he thought; then finished his drink, poured himself another, and settled down to read.

★ ★ ★

The next day Traven reported in to Michael Gray, arriving at his London office at 10 a.m. as requested.

'You still have total confidence in Steve Remmick's bona fides? His commitment to us?' Traven's boss at MI5, a bullet-headed, authoritative man, was sitting easy behind his desk. 'There's great risk to us in this: if we entrust him with the mission we have in mind, it'll put him in a position from which he could wreck Operation Double Talk, leave it dead in the water.'

'I'm aware of that.' Running a hand through his straight, grey-streaked hair, Traven stopped pacing up and down in front

22

of Gray's desk and faced him. 'Although he and his brother carried out contracts — drugs deals, and worse — for Shaheen's cadre together for so long and so effectively, in their personalities they were poles apart. Robert was a born natural for clandestine and subversive operations, but Steve . . . Steve went into that life simply because Robert did — '

'And proved himself just as brilliant an operator. Yes, I know. You've told me all that before. Answer my question.'

'Willingly. Yes, I have absolute confidence in Steve. I've had him on trial for a year and a half now, and I'm sure of him.'

'So all right — we'll go ahead. Instruct him to concentrate on Shaheen's — '

'How much of the big picture do I reveal to him?'

'Give him most of our information to date. Some of it is new to you at this moment but we'll rectify that shortly. Reports came in an hour ago from Anti-Terrorist Branch, I want you to see them. Remmick will need to be aware of the full scope of both the operations in progress, Mansoor and Shaheen's Desert Wolf as well as our counter-op Double Talk, if he's to pull off this final job.'

'And we don't have a great deal of time left.'

Gray favoured him with a wintry smile. 'Indeed we do not.'

'To date, Soheil Shaheen sees no threat in Steve.' Traven's dark eyes were sombre. 'Robert and Shaheen, they were two of a kind and, therefore, quickly came to understand each other and then, in time, to trust each other fully. With Steve, it was different. I believe Shaheen perceived him as a born *follower* — a disciple, even, if you will — of his dashing and highly charismatic brother and, because of that, after Robert's death, gradually allowed Steve to move into Rob's place as his friend, or as near to 'friend' as men like Shaheen ever have. Which was Shaheen's mistake. Steve may indeed have lived in the shadow of his brother Robert, but inside himself he was no shadow. He is intrinsically the better man and, since Robert's death, he's become his own man — which is, *our* man . . . That was an act of great courage on his part,' he added quietly.

Gray leaned back in his chair, eyeing Traven sardonically. 'Staying with the old firm in order to be in a favourable position to inform on it to its enemies, like Steve Remmick's done — that's the act of a traitor, some would say. However, you aren't here to philosophize, Traven, are you? You're here firstly to get my OK for Remmick to move in as close as he can to Shaheen, the leader of the cadre Mansoor is using in Operation Desert Wolf and, according to our latest reports received, intends to use to provide security etc for the controllers and their forthcoming mission over here in England. And, secondly, for me to brief you on what you may tell Remmick re the situation we want him to get us info on, via Shaheen. You've just got my OK to use Remmick, so now sit down and listen while I proceed with the rest. This could take a while. Care for a drink? Coffee? Something stronger?'

With a shake of the head and a quick 'No, thanks', Traven sat down in a chair facing his boss across the desk. 'Go ahead. And the full story please.'

'OK. Following on the 11th September terror strikes in the US and the action in Afghanistan, certain militant Islamic fundamentalist and anti-West organizations regrouped with the aim of co-ordinating and extending their influence while, at the same time, updating and diversifying their subversive potential and strike power. They appointed an executive council, and it set about establishing, in certain designated countries, covert networks which would first facilitate and then ensure the continuance of terrorist strikes on Western targets. One such network is in the process of being set up here in Britain; that's the objective of the op code-named Desert Wolf.' Gray waved away what he had just said with a dismissive hand. 'Both you and Remmick already know this, but I'd prefer to build up the picture from its roots, so bear with me,' he said.

'I will — mixed metaphors included.'

Gray carried straight on. 'In Britain, Mansoor is top gun of Desert Wolf. That op's mission here is the establishment of an extensive 'feeder' network which will provide internationally active terrorist groups with suitably trained and qualified personnel for their strikes. To that end, a number of carefully selected places of instruction have been vetted and prepared, at which zealous volunteers — drawn from various terrorist groupings in Europe, the Middle East and the US — will enrol and take training as aero-engineers, pilots and the like, or in skills that will enable them to infiltrate police, military or political organizations etc. When their training is completed these volunteers will be posted to wherever their particular acquired talents may be put to best use in terrorist activities.' Gray fell silent, his eyes fixed on the blue, sunlit sky beyond the tall windows facing him.

' "Wherever their acquired talents may be

put to best use'.' His head down, Traven repeated the words and then, sombrely, added his own. 'As in Omagh, in New York, and in a plane flying the night sky above a town called Lockerbie.'

Gray's mind slipped back into gear. 'The groundwork for Desert Wolf is almost completed,' he went on. 'Six venues for the instruction of the volunteers have been selected, and are prepared for them. Shaheen and his cadre have done a very thorough job for Mansoor so far. We've had the whole thing under surveillance for the last eight months and their preparations for the first intake are excellent. Thank God we're on to them . . . So, on to the job we now want Remmick to do for us — '

'The entrapment of the controllers, and the ensuing destruction of the Desert Wolf network. The controllers: hardline terrorists to a man; all three of them on the wanted list of many governments — not all of those in the West, either.'

'True, but at the moment immaterial. Those three men are the key to the success of Desert Wolf — and are the prime target of our counter-op Double Talk. Like Shaheen, they're dyed-in-the-wool terrorists, hands-on activists. Their leader, due to his political clout and his international contacts at the highest levels, is Khaled Mansoor, Egyptian by birth — and an ex-Taliban adviser. His speciality is armaments, together with the logistics, tactics and strategies of all types of warfare and civil conflict. Second to him, we have the Syrian, Bakhtiary. A professor of biochemistry, and the oldest of them at 53, he's experienced in the construction and use of weapons of mass destruction, and also in the acquisition, safe transport etc of the required materiel. In recent years, he's been closely involved in research into antidotes to diseases resulting from mass-contamination scenarios. And third in the hierarchy we have Zayani, an Iranian businessman who is an aviation expert and who happens to have — among his many trading interests — a controlling vote in the import/export textile company in London which has long had Shaheen on its books as one of their representatives.'

'They're all three in Paris at the moment, I believe?'

'Not so. Mansoor arrived here three days ago, in advance of the others, in order to check up on Shaheen's arrangements for the controllers' inspections of the training sites and, of course, to organize their final meeting — which is the one we want Remmick to infiltrate, it's the definitive one.'

Pushing back his chair, Gray stood up, placed his hands palm-down on the desk, stared Traven in the eye and laid on the line the deadly situation confronting them.

'Once all three controllers are in England they will disperse and carry out their inspections of the sites for Desert Wolf's feeder network which, under Mansoor's direction, Shaheen has been preparing. They will be working to a ten-day deadline. Our surveillance teams and undercover men report Shaheen's network fully in place, and well organized in all respects. Our assumption has to be, therefore, that at the end of that ten-day period of inspections the controllers will give the OK and Desert Wolf — should we fail anywhere along the line in our covert counter-op Double Talk — will then move into its active mode, triggering into action the two things we aim to prevent: one, the terrorist network will become fully operational: two, the controllers themselves, splitting up at once, will again escape our trap.'

'Like they did five years back.'

Gray straightened up, nodded. 'Those three are major players in international terrorism, and we've got a chance here, via Steve Remmick, to nail all three of them together with incontrovertible evidence of their terrorist activities. And that's a chance not likely to come our way again, Traven. So, when you're briefing Remmick, make absolutely sure that he understands, fully, what's at stake here. To date, we've been hamstrung, unable to get our hands on any concrete evidence against a single one of the controllers, but what Remmick's achieved so far has put him in a position from which it might be possible for him to procure such evidence for us. It's a high-risk assignment — '

'Steve knows that. Don't underestimate him because of what he was before his brother was killed. He can handle this — provided he gets the opportunity we're hoping he will.'

Gray favoured him with that wintry smile again. 'I've heard it said that the turncoat, because he can never entirely overcome a feeling that he has something more to prove to his new comrades, is in the event frequently braver — in all courage's many facets — than any of them. Well, here's Remmick's chance to prove it. He'll be working in close contact with highly dangerous men, while all the time his final objective is to cut their balls off. So fire him up good, Traven; fire him up good. He's got a job on his hands.'

30

2

That day, at about the same time as Traven left the building in west London where Gray had his offices, Steve Remmick took a bus from his apartment block in Ealing to Streatham, south of the Thames. Alighting at Streatham Common he walked across it to Wychwood, Rebecca's house on its far side. He had been thinking about his brother ever since he got up that morning: about Robert and Rebecca; Robert and the strong-box he'd left; Robert and the way he'd died twenty-two months ago, and the circumstances of the car accident he'd been killed in eerily reminiscent of the crash that Traven had engineered the night he was in hot pursuit of the Toyota and forced it off the road. That night, Rob hauled me clear of the wreck then carted me nearly five miles across rough country to ultimate safety, Steve thought now, walking on springy turf towards the house in which his brother had lived so happily with his wife Rebecca. But the night Rob's car was run off the road by a still untraced hit-and-run driver, he was driving alone. If only I'd been with him then! *If only* — ach, Christ! Cut it out — it's pointless to think along those lines, cut it *out!* Think Rebecca, think strong-box — yes, that'll do. Strong-box. Odd in the extreme that Rob should do a thing like that. He was not a bloke to brood on the possibility of his own death. If the subject came into his mind at all he'd simply have dismissed it and redoubled his precautions against that particular possibility becoming a reality.

Wychwood: once Rebecca and Robert's house, now Rebecca's alone. Built as a verderer's cottage around 150 years ago, over the years it had been added to, deconstructed, reconstructed, given face-lifts, modernized at least twice — and now was a sprawling, full-of-fascinating-surprises place to live.

After lunch, Steve and Rebecca took their coffee into the sitting-room and sat down either end of the cushioned window-seat overlooking the garden.

'I wish Rob and I had had kids.' Rebecca rested one forearm along the broad window-sill beside her and frowned at the roses outside. 'A son, I'd have liked. With luck he'd have taken after Rob and been good at sport. It'd have been great to watch him grow up . . . You and Rob, you were both so good at ball-games. Me, I was always an absolute duffer at all that'

'You were a pretty good skier.'

'That came in my late teens.' Rebecca turned to him, smiling now. 'And you know why I got so keen in the first place? Because I thought the clothes you wore for it were fabulous. But then when I got out on the slopes I soon found out it wasn't enough just to *look* good, you have to actually *be* good — else it's all just show, and I dislike that. Always have.'

Steve smiled back at her: he invariably did; Rebecca's smile seemed to reach right inside him and demand its answer. Now thirty-two years old, she was gifted with striking facial bones, deeply blue eyes and a generous, full-lipped mouth. Her golden-blonde hair, shortish cut, framed her face and when, like now, she was smiling, the left corner of her mouth tip-tilted upwards a little. Rob had loved her very much . . .

'So, the girlfriend's walked out on you?' Rebecca asked after a moment.'

'She has.'

'Repairs needed?'

'Nope.'

'I'm glad she's gone. She was taking you for a ride.'

'I know it. I enjoyed the ride, though.' He drank the last of his coffee then got to his feet, looked out at the garden, across lawn and flower-beds; the conifer hedge he and his

33

brother had planted together soon after Rob and Rebecca had moved into Wychwood stood tall and dense, gold-green brilliant in the sunlight. 'Actually now it's happened I'm quite glad Jilly's gone,' he went on. 'It wasn't that great between us any more. I'd have made the break myself if I'd had the guts.'

Sitting quiet, entirely at ease in the silence between them, Rebecca studied her brother-in-law. She had liked him ever since they had first met twelve years ago: a mutual and immediate liking that had grown deeper and stronger over the years until she had come to love him as, she supposed, having no siblings herself, sister loves brother. God, how glad I am Steve's broken with Shaheen and that cadre of his Rob and he were working with, smuggling drugs and God knows what else for them, she thought, eyeing this tall, leanly built man on whom she had come to depend, seeing him as her comrade-in-arms against the alien world she'd been pitched into by her husband's sudden death. Steve's so like Rob in many ways, she thought, yet in the matter of committing himself to serve a terrorist organization like he and Rob did he's somehow *different* from him. Rob — and I knew this perfectly well when I married him, but it didn't have a chance of challenging the sheer emotional and physical imperative of my wanting to have and hold Rob for always — allowed no moral qualms to stand in the way of him getting to live the kind of life he desired to live. Rob did whatever he had to do in order to acquire money, a certain kind of power and — this above all, for him — the challenge and thrill-delivery of being a clandestine and hands-on mover and shaker in events; *hands-on* as in violent and dangerous. To my way of thinking that's a dreadful way to live your life. I knew it was, and kept well clear of involvement in it, but I *accepted* it, didn't I? Because if I hadn't, Rob would have . . . gone. He'd have left me. I knew that if I put it to the test — gave him the choice between me, and Shaheen and the cadre — Rob would walk out of my life, and *stay* out. And I'd have died if he'd done that. Steve, though, he's different. I've known he was for a long while, but it's only since Rob was killed that it's become clear to me — to Steve too, I believe — to what a huge extent he's different. Basically, it seems to me, Rob had a killer instinct, whereas Steve hasn't got that. I don't think he'd ever put the boot in the way Rob used to if it served his own interests.

But then — suddenly, as she was looking out over her summer-drenched garden — Rebecca shivered. No, I'm wrong there, she thought. I believe that, in certain circumstances, Steve *would* put the boot in. He's fanatically loyal, and if loyalty and love called for it he'd go for his enemy tooth and nail and he'd fight to the death. *To the death.*

'Y'know, that conifer hedge needs trimming,' he said, swinging round to her. 'How about I do it now?'

'But you came for the strong-box — '

'Huh! I don't reckon there's priceless treasure in there — old bills, more like. I'll do the hedge then take the box home, force it open later. OK?' He was already heading for the door. 'You relax. I know where everything is.'

Rebecca let him go. But when she saw he was fully engaged in his hedge-trimming she turned her back on Wychwood's garden, hunched herself into one corner of the window-seat and put her face in her hands. She was not weeping; she was simply grieving for Rob.

★ ★ ★

Khaled Mansoor chaired the preparatory meeting of the controllers at a house put at their disposal for that purpose by a director in one of Zayani's export/import companies. Situated in Kent, it was a residence of modest but pleasing exterior and luxurious interior. After a lunch at which no mention was made to the purpose of their meeting, the three controllers repaired to the library. Seating themselves round the oval table in the centre of the room they got down to business immediately, conversing in Arabic.

Mansoor opened proceedings. 'Our objective here today, as all of us are aware, is to ensure that the feeder network Shaheen has set in place here in Britain is ready to function. Until now each one of us has been concentrating on his own particular field of responsibility within the international plan that will be activated as soon as we declare Operation Desert Wolf satisfactory in all respects, fully prepared to provide us, in time, with a pool of volunteers trained to the various skills germane to our requirements. Therefore, in order to clarify the overall picture here, I will now detail our individual assignments within the framework of the inspection as a whole.' Handsome in a hard-featured way, immaculately suited in grey Italian silk, he looked enquiringly at his fellow controllers. 'Have you any questions, before I commence?'

'Yes!' Facing him across the black onyx table, Zayani's harsh voice came fast on the question and his brown eyes, angry and suspicious as always, challenged those of the Egyptian. 'Are you, personally, completely certain that Shaheen is worthy of the trust that has been placed in him?'

'Were I not, he would have been replaced as cadre leader. Have you proper reason for asking this?'

'Sufficient in my eyes.'

'Then I would appreciate being informed of it.' Mansoor's face and voice were devoid of expression.

The Iranian complied without demur. 'Soheil Shaheen is a man of mixed blood — '

'And to some extent *because* of that, a true fanatic to our cause!' Mansoor's interruption was dagger-sharp, as he leaned across the table and gave Zayani stare for stare. 'Shaheen was indeed born to an English-woman, but he was *fathered* by a Palestinian. And — Hussain, my deeply respected comrade — have you not heard that it is frequently the half-breed who becomes an exceptionally ferocious zealot in the service of whatever 'cause' or 'ethos' he commits himself to? Reaching manhood as he does, always aware of two seriously different mindsets and ways of life — in Shaheen's case those of his English mother on one side, those of his Palestinian father on the other — he is racked by opposing forces, and realizes he must commit himself to one of them alone if he is to give real meaning to his life. And once he has made his choice, then, he has to spurn everything he has rejected with an active and abiding hatred lest it seek to win him back.' Mansoor was sitting tense in his chair, his eyes never leaving Zayani's. 'Shaheen is such a man, and he is beyond price to us,' he concluded, low and hard. 'His love of Islam is driven by the duality of his blood, and it is sublime: in his life, all things are subject to it. There will be no further discussion of the matter.'

'Unless — permit me to point this out — it should happen that, in the course of our inspections, we discover some fault in the preparations Shaheen has made.' The third man at the table, the Syrian Bakhtiary, spoke softly and reasonably, spreading his soft-fleshed hands on the brocaded arms of his chair, a smile hovering at the corners of his full-lipped, well-defined mouth. There had been previous occasions when he had had to smooth the water between the other two controllers, and he was a master in the art of being all things to all men — while at the same time concealing his own position in the matter being argued. 'However, in the light of Shaheen's previous success as director of two similar operations, that would seem to be a highly unlikely development. Also, we should take into consideration the fact that although he is such a fanatic he experiences no difficulty in working with Westerners. He set up the drugs line over here with Robert Remmick, and the majority of the men in his present cadre are Brits; he has won their loyalty —'

'Enough.' Zayani cut in sharply, his dark face set. 'I accept Khaled Mansoor's decision.'

'Then we will proceed,' Mansoor said. 'I shall outline my own responsibilities first. I have three separate duties. The first is to inspect arrangements for our volunteers who will attend the IT courses, those in Advanced English, and those covering English for Special Purposes — which are in London, Manchester, and Oxford respectively. My second duty is the provision of security for yourselves, via Shaheen, throughout our mission in this country; also to receive from each of you regular progress reports, to edit and collate them and, subsequently, to store them in our secure database. My third duty is to arrange all matters pertaining to our summit meeting, nine days from now, at which we will make our agreed depositions that will' — pausing, he smiled at each of the others in turn, then ended with grim pleasure — 'will as it were *switch on* our covert operation Desert Wolf, which will shortly begin providing us with gifted, dedicated and highly trained men sworn to our cause . . . Gentlemen, I shall be at your disposal at all times for information and, should it be required, assistance — as you are well aware, I have overall command of widely dispersed, armed and highly trained agents I can call on. You already know the codes and numbers for contacting me at any time . . . Questions?'

Zayani gave an impatient shake of the head; he was a man who — even when sitting in discussion, as now — gave the impression of being driven by a restless energy, a need for immediate action.

Bakhtiary responded with a polite 'Your designated areas of responsibility are clear to me.'

Satisfied, Mansoor moved on to outline their individual duties. 'So, to the aviation courses. Inspection of the arrangements in place at these will, naturally, be in the hands of agent Zayani: he is our expert in that field. We have six of our people enrolled for these. All of them are, of course, qualified pilots, but in order to infiltrate Western airlines, as will undoubtedly be required of them, they need further and specifically targeted training. The courses selected are at private flying schools and clubs at Cambridge, Oxford, Taunton and Guildford.' Mansoor paused, his eyes fixed on Zayani. 'You are to ensure, in particular, that each and every aspect of our precautions in relation to the *security* of our volunteers at those places is rock solid.'

'I shall be satisfied with no less.' But the Iranian was giving nothing. The cut planes of his face and the brooding intensity of his deep-set brown eyes spoke of an intrinsically harsh and unforgiving spirit. He had seen savage fight-to-the-death action over the years, whereas neither of these two he was liaising with now had seen hands-on action for the cause recently; for many years now they had been behind-the-scenes players, and in some obscure, visceral way Zayani hated them for that — despised them, even, could not bring himself to regard either of them as his true equal.

Mansoor turned to the Syrian. Darkly suited, compactly built, Bakhtiary sat totally relaxed, pale eyes alert in his olive-skinned face. A professor of biochemistry, he was equipped not only with degrees and research laurels in his field from Europe and America but also with considerable experience in its darker aspects, its use and abuse in the service of armed insurrection, oppression and terrorism. His speciality was weapons of mass destruction, together with the covert acquisition and safe transport of same. His present research centred on the development of antidotes to diseases caused by chemical warfare.

'Your assignment, sir,' Mansoor said to him, 'covers two installations, at each of which one of our agents will be active. At the most vital of these two places, the nature of the work in progress there has initiated enemy security of extreme severity. Should you therefore need more time to carry out your inspection, you are to inform me. I shall then adjust our schedule to accommodate the delay.'

'God the Almighty and the All-seeing fights at our side. With His help I shall meet our deadline.' Bakhtiary's voice and face were devoid of expression as he spoke.

Mansoor knew he did not mean a word of his pious but banal statement and, frowning slightly, went on, 'The agents concerned, scientists of some repute, are scheduled to take up research positions with our target pharmaceutical companies, both of which are situated in counties in the South-East here. Their mission is the acquisition of knowledge as to the state of research, throughout the

43

western-aligned nations, into the development of antitoxins to combat epidemic diseases resulting from chemical attack.' Mansoor's eyes challenged the Syrian's. 'It is my understanding that you know these two agents of ours personally through your own academic work, and also that you are familiar with the manner in which such establishments conduct their business,' he said. 'So tell me, in all honesty, have our scientists a good chance of success in their mission?'

Bakhtiary took his time to reply; nevertheless, when he did so, he did not commit himself wholeheartedly one way or the other. 'The two agents concerned have twice before operated successfully in similar situations,' he said. 'But whether they will gain what they seek here . . . that perforce depends less on them than on the quality of the opposition they encounter as they pursue their secret assignment.'

Mansoor nodded, then moved on. 'The second element of your operation will be simplicity itself compared with that first one,' he said. 'We have four volunteers enrolled in a one-year course in Advanced computer studies at a college in Cambridge: you will vet the arrangements made for them.'

'It is understood.' So politely spoken, but a certain mockery in the Syrian's world-wise

— but far from world-weary — eyes.

Mansoor ignored it; he was as subtle an operator as Bakhtiary, and both of them were aware of it. He proceeded with the agreed agenda, and as soon as it had been dealt with reminded them that in nine days' time the three of them were to convene for their final conference and the taping of their Declaration of Completion; then he ended the meeting.

Parting with all the conventional phrases of politeness, these three men who lived and had their being at the heart of an international network of terrorism then went their separate ways. Zayani, however, manoeuvred matters so that he had an opportunity to speak privately with Mansoor before he left the house, hanging back beside him inside the front hall when Bakhtiary went on out, heading for his parked car. Putting his dark face close to Mansoor's, he asked him the question he did not want the Syrian to hear. 'The man Robert Remmick, that Brit who assisted in our drugs trade over here, the one who died a while back — is it indeed true that Shaheen counted him *a friend* of his?'

'It is true.' At that moment, Mansoor could see no reason to hide the fact; some days later, he was to regret not doing so. 'Why do you ask?'

'Because I find it a strange thing — and suspicious, given Shaheen's hatred of the West.'

Briefly, Mansoor held him eye to eye. Then he said, light and hard, 'Soheil Shaheen and Robert Remmick had in common a love of the challenge and ravishing excitement of violent action; and each possessed that wild yet controlled courage that draws such men together and makes each one, whatever the ethos of his life, comrade to the other.'

'Then is it the same with Robert Remmick's brother, who still works with us? Does Shaheen extend the same comradeship to him?'

'No. There is not the same brotherhood, not the same . . . closeness of selfhood between them. But he places unreserved trust in him.'

'Is he right to do so?'

'I trust Shaheen's judgement in all things. And we have no reason to doubt Steven Remmick; he has served us well in the past and continues to do so.'

But Zayani thought he detected a slight, a very slight hesitation in Mansoor's voice, and he tucked his perception of it away in his mind as something it might be wise to remember.

46

★ ★ ★

Pushing aside the day's newspaper, Steve Remmick put the square metal box down on his kitchen table. It sat squat to the blue-and-white checkered cloth; dark green-enamelled, its padlock of solid brass. As he stood gazing at his brother's legacy to him, grief stabbed deep into him, but with an effort of will he drove it out. Rob was dead, and with his death the world had become a cold and lonely place to dwell in. Not hostile: simply lonely.

So get on and live it, Remmick, he told himself. Open this damn thing, because something 'of' Rob must be inside it, something he wanted you to have — or to know about, perhaps? — if the impossible happened and he lost out.

Fetching a hacksaw from the garage he sat down, cut through the hasp of the padlock, slipped it free and lifted the lid, looked inside Rob's strong-box. Two things only lay in there: a four-inch thick package wrapped in brown paper that fitted neatly into the bottom of the box and, lightly Sellotaped into place on top of it, an ordinary white envelope with 'Steve' scrawled across it in — unmistakably! — his brother's bold handwriting. Easing the envelope free, Steve took it out

47

and, turning it over, found it copiously sealed at the back. Breaking the red wax, he drew out the single sheet of notepaper folded inside and smoothed it out flat on the table. There was no date on it, no salutation or greeting: only several lines of writing and, below them, Rob's signature.

Thought you had a right to know this, Steve. Besides which, I *want* you to know — in fact I think you really *need* to know, because there's something I did that might make trouble for you in the future, so you've got to know truth from fiction so that you can deal with it if it surfaces. In the Toyota that night in the hills, with Traven up there on the road above us, I killed the courier. As the Toyota ran wild down the slope he was thrown clear just before we hit the trees. He was badly injured all right, no argument there, but I reckon he'd probably have been OK if he'd been got to the medics in time. But that courier was trouble for me, Steve. Real bad trouble. So the way I saw it was that fate was giving me a chance — she'd put right there in front of me a chance to win clear of the deep, deep shit I was in because of that bastard courier. And, as you know, I've never been a bloke to turn down a good chance. So I lugged him back to the car and put certain of my old skills to good (for me, anyway!) use — you know, the lethal pressure-point manoeuvre.

Later, when I saw the Toyota torch herself, I realized I needn't have bothered. But — you'll understand — I had to make sure.

Reaching the end of it, Steve sat staring down at the words his brother had written on the white notepaper. Murder, cold-blooded murder — *Robert*, guilty of such a thing? Killing, yes. Both he and I were involved in actions that resulted in deaths, and to my certain knowledge he killed at least twice in shoot-outs with the deliberate intention to kill. But — an injured comrade, and *in cold blood?* Rob, a *murderer?* And what was that 'deep, deep shit' he was in? *Christ.* What's it all about, Rob?

Burying his face in his hands Steve thought back — to Rob, the courier and the car crash that night . . .

But within a couple of minutes, realizing he was in danger of drowning in memories and regrets, he pushed himself to his feet and got on with his life. First, he went back into the garage. On a shelf there lay a small bundle of candles and a box of matches kept to hand against power cuts. Picking up the matches he went back into the kitchen and burned Rob's letter to ashes. Then he cleared the ashes away, made himself a cup of coffee and sat down at the table again. After a couple of scalding hot sips of it he put it aside, reached into the strong-box again and lifted out the thick, brown-paper package. Handling it, he saw that its wrapping was in fact a large manila envelope, folded over but not sealed. Running his fingers over the contours of its contents he felt the individual rectangular shapes inside shifting under his touch — and he knew then. 'Shit!' he murmured, and upending the envelope, shook out what Rob had stowed inside it.

Banded blocks of banknotes: tumbling out anyhow on to his blue-and-white tablecloth, they fell softly and settled in a sharp-angled heap. 'Shit!' Steve Remmick said again — only louder this time because he could see the face of some of the notes and the value of each was £50.

He tidied the money into piles, checking the number of notes in each block as he did so, then did his sums: £30,000, it came to. Shaken to the core of his being, he picked up the envelope again thinking to put the cash

50

back inside it, but as he opened it a sheet of notepaper dropped out and fell on the table. The writing on it was Rob's so he picked it up and read it:

The lolly's for you, Steve. Thought I'd put a bit aside in case the opposition get lucky while I'm still young, you never can tell. If you're reading this it has to mean they did — so have yourself a good time with this little lot, mate. And by the way, knowing what a stupid straight-up sort of guy you are in such matters, I swear to you this stuff is absolutely *clean*. Clean both ways: no blood bought it; no crime was committed in the getting of it. Cheers. Rob.

Well aware of the danger of keeping anything that might ever be used in evidence against himself and his brother, Steve Remmick burnt that note also. Then he slid the banded banknotes back into the envelope, and stowed that at the bottom of his sock drawer. While doing these things he pondered what he should do with the money. Thirty thousand quid! The obvious thing to do was bank it. Why not? demanded pragmatism. But inside him a stubborn little voice spoke up differently — and stood its ground. No, you should not do that, it said quietly. It simply *isn't right* to do that. It refused to give him any further reasons, or any alternative instructions; but then quite suddenly it abandoned this negative stance, not to advance reasons, rather, to spell out for him the positive action he should take: give the money to the nearest living relative of the man you — and probably you alone in the world — know your brother murdered, it commanded.

Hearing this, Steve Remmick smiled. How splendidly, setting-the-mind-at-rest simple! Rob, by his own admission, killed the courier for some sort of personal gain for himself: therefore, any money he has to give away should, by moral logic, make recompense for the taking of that life. The decision made, all that remained was to implement it. He'd have to find out who was living next-of-kin to the courier, then take the money to that person. Surely no great problem in doing both those things, he thought. Traven would either know, or be able to find out for him, the identity of the person sought. And there couldn't be many blokes around — not in the circles in which the courier had lived and had his being. No way! — who'd press for a great deal of information on where the cash came from if £30,000 was theirs for the taking.

3

Soheil Shaheen: as a child nicknamed 'Red' on account of the dark-red hair that, straight and thick-growing, lay smooth to his well-shaped head. He was a sombrely handsome man, of mixed blood. His father, a Palestinian, had worked at the Kuwaiti Embassy in London, and his mother had been employed there as a translator. Born and brought up in London, Shaheen had severed all contact with both his parents when he was seventeen, and taken off for the Arab world his spirit yearned towards, joining a terrorist group in Lebanon. Highly intelligent, informed and articulate, ruthless and fanatical in support of the use of terror tactics to advance Islam in world affairs, his career progress had been rapid. Now, at the relatively early age of thirty-four, he commanded the cadre he had been assigned to on his recruitment — the cadre which at that time Mansoor had been in the process of enlarging and upgrading for service as prime tool to his hand, for the organization and subsequent prosecution of the UK dimension of Operation Desert Wolf. As the groundwork for the mission went forward, Shaheen's outstanding aptitude for covert subversion had caught Mansoor's eye, and within a couple of years he was appointed leader of the increasingly able and trusted cadre.

Now, with the groundwork for the training of the volunteers completed and all three controllers already arrived in England to carry out their inspections of the complex arrangements made by the cadre, Shaheen had summoned certain of his most senior lieutenants to a meeting in order to run through their plans, since during those inspections he and the cadre were responsible for the security net covering the controllers. And for Shaheen much was at stake in this. The inspections would naturally be rigorous in the extreme, and only if the arrangements he had put in place were judged to be absolutely comprehensive, appropriate and secure, would the controllers — hard men all, and each highly experienced in his field — give the order for Desert Wolf to move forward into its active phase in Britain. He was also aware that should his preparations fail their examination, he would be savagely disciplined and permanently downgraded.

Determined that such a humiliating failure in the service of all he believed in should not come to pass, he had impressed yet again on his four senior lieutenants at the meeting that day — the fifth, Steve Remmick, had been unexpectedly called in by Mansoor — that throughout the period of the coming inspections they must be hyper-vigilant in regard to the security surrounding the controllers and their activities. This instruction delivered, he glanced at each of them in turn, anticipating tacit nods of agreement; only one of those present was important to him as a personality, the others he considered to be no more than highly competent and useful followers who happened to excel in certain spheres of covert operations. The nods came readily from all except one — and he normally was one of the followers, so Shaheen was surprised.

'Why the drama? You heard something special, or what?' Sandy-haired Liam Kidd crossed his arms on the table round which they were sitting and stared his leader in the eye. He resented being called in if all it was in aid of was yet another lecture on the importance of security. Shit, all of us here already know everything there is to know about that, man, he was thinking; blokes like me and my mate Cooper were brought up to see it as the basic necessity for long-term individual, and group, survival.

Shaheen eyed him in silence for a moment,

dark eyes intent. 'Traven's good, and he's got MI5 and MI6 on his side,' he pointed out then. '*So far*, he and they remain ignorant regarding Desert Wolf. But he is a very subtle operator, and likely to make unexpected moves.'

Kidd nodded and sat back, wishing he had kept quiet.

'You haven't answered Liam's question.' Relaxed in his chair, facing Shaheen directly across the table, Brad Cooper — burly and broad-shouldered, gifted with piratical-Spanish good looks — smiled his buccaneer's smile. He enjoyed a bit of verbal sparring; besides, Liam was his oppo, and as such was not to be put down by anyone.

'Leave it, Brad,' Kidd put in quickly. 'Doesn't matter.'

'Ah, but it does, it does.' Cooper pushed back his chair and stood up. The broad shoulders were a true guide: he was a big man, and at thirty-eight his body was, quite clearly, strong and agile. He eyed his leader with a touch of malice. 'Do you have suspicions of a traitor among us?' he asked.

'Of course not.' Shaheen's head was down; his bony, lean-fingered hands lay palm-down on the table.

'So, as Liam here has just said, why the drama? None of us here are novices. We don't need continually reminding of the importance of security; it's second nature to us.' Cooper was watching the Palestinian's hands — and saw the brown-skinned fingers tighten on the wood they were resting on, then clench into fists.

Shaheen looked up into the eyes of this lieutenant of his: Cooper, and the absent Remmick, were the only two of these aides of his whom he considered worthy of his respect as men in their own right. Steve Remmick's loyalty he had always taken for granted, seeing him as Robert Remmick's shadow even after his brother's death. But Cooper — Cooper was the only man in his entire cadre whom he felt he did not fully understand. But since he was also the one he would most like to understand, he told him the truth — on this occasion. 'For a short while recently, I have had a feeling that in some way all is not quite as well as it should be with Desert Wolf. There is in me an unease, a sense of . . . *foreboding*.' He spoke the last word in Arabic because it seemed better suited to his meaning, and he was aware that Cooper spoke that language fluently.

Cooper repeated it, savouring it on his tongue. 'Foreboding. Yes, the Arabic conveys more,' he said, with an appreciative nod. 'And

I have a strange thing to tell you, Shaheen. In what you have just said, our instinct — our sixth sense, if you like — is the same. But in my case it's more than just a feeling: I have a name I associate with it. I was going to bring up the subject today, anyway. And now we know the two of us feel the same way — well, the conclusion's obvious, isn't it?'

'Obvious indeed. Since you have a name to put forward, action on our part should be immediate — '

'What the hell are you two talking about?' Tom North, sitting facing Liam Kidd, interrupted sharply. A taciturn man, and at over fifty far older than the others, he was the cadre's bomb-making specialist. That was the only aspect of terrorism that was of any real interest to him. Unlike many of the other cadre members, North was no conviction terrorist; he was simply a man who had discovered a niche in life in which he found that the work in which he was so highly skilled won him not only monetary rewards but also esteem and — in his case, this above all — a certain status and comradeship among his fellows.

'Traitors, North.' It was Cooper who answered. 'We're talking treachery and those who engage in it.'

There was a brief silence; during it, tension

gathered in that room in the safe house in Tottenham Court Road. And when Shaheen broke it his eyes were still fixed on Cooper and his voice was quiet but steely. 'Name your suspect.'

Cooper made him wait, making great play of sitting down again and getting comfortable in his chair.

For Christ's sake, watch your step with Shaheen, mate, Liam Kidd thought, eyeing him nervously. You think it's quite a joke to mock him like you're doing, you get a kick out of it, but he sees it as an insult — he won't react here and now, maybe, but you can bet your bottom dollar he'll get back at you for it somehow, sometime.

Finally the big man leaned across the table towards Shaheen, grey eyes slitted, glinting with pleasure in anticipation of the personal, hands-on action he hoped and expected his revelation would win for him.

'Rebecca Remmick,' he said. 'Rob Remmick's widow.'

Shaheen's face betrayed nothing, but his body tautened in concentration as his mind assessed the implications of Cooper's accusation. Obviously, if there was truth in it, if the woman was indeed informing on them, then the threat to the success of Desert Wolf — although almost certainly peripheral, given the relative paucity of any information she was likely to have acquired — was nevertheless dangerous and, possibly, imminent. Yet —

'But Rebecca Remmick was the subject of an in-depth and hostile investigation by a team of our own,' he said quietly, 'and it was established that, although she accepted her husband's involvement in terrorist activities, she herself neither played any part in them nor knew anything about them. Consequently she would have nothing to betray.'

'That was years ago — '

'So presumably you have new evidence against her?'

'Nothing concrete. But the information I've had from my source, though only anecdotal, seems to me significant enough to warrant the woman's . . . interrogation.'

'And the name of this source of yours?'

'You know I'm not going to tell you that.' Cooper grinned at him. 'Golden geese like that one don't take kindly to publicity — probably give up altogether on laying golden eggs if they find it forced upon them.'

Ignoring the verbal decoration given it, Shaheen accepted the principle. 'Very well,' he said. 'So it is your opinion that she should be investigated again?'

'Yep. I believe that since Rob died she's decided to cash in on his past — made contact with blokes he used, been given info, and sold it to the opposition.'

Shaheen eyed him warily. He knew that what Cooper suspected could be right, and that, therefore, the safest course was to let him have his way. After all, Shaheen himself had nothing to lose by doing so — whereas to antagonize Cooper by doubting him now, with the cadre deeply involved in the controllers' make-or-break inspections of the Desert Wolf network, could only too easily have counter-productive results, given Cooper's hubris and his volatile temperament. 'I agree with you,' he said finally. 'It is best that we determine her guilt or innocence.'

Cooper smiled. It was what he had hoped for; he enjoyed carrying out interrogations, especially of women — and in Rebecca Remmick's case even more so, for it would give him an opportunity to get back at her for the humiliating way she had rejected his advances after Rob died.

'I'll get on to it at once, then,' he said. 'I've been to her house quite a few times so I know both it and the locality fairly well. Steve won't like it, I suppose. Still, no sweat — I'll keep the whole thing quiet till it's over and done with. Anyway, we all know he thinks she's fair rubbish himself on account of her refusing to work with him and Rob — '

61

'We make no move against her yet. With the controllers present here in Britain, the decision regarding action in such a matter — and as to who is to undertake the interrogation if it is to go ahead — is theirs to make, not mine.'

'Whose call is it, then? Zayani's?'

'Mansoor's.'

'Good. From what I've heard he's one ruthless bastard.'

'I have met him many times, as you know. He is not a man to ignore any possible threat.'

'So you reckon he'll give me the go-ahead?'

'If he says we interrogate her, we shall do it: if he says not, we shall not.' Shaheen's voice as cold as his eyes: he knew Cooper for a frequently gratuitously violent man. 'Remember that. I will not tolerate unilateral action of any kind in this or any other matter,' he added, colder yet.

Cooper held back the anger rising in him. 'We'd better move fast.'

'I shall proceed without unnecessary delay. When the decision has been made I will inform you of it.' With that, Shaheen moved on to the next item on his agenda for the meeting.

★　★　★

Soon after Steven Remmick had made his cautious but successful approach to Traven offering his services as MI5's mole inside Shaheen's subversive cadre, the two men had by chance discovered a mutual leisure interest: they both enjoyed a game of squash. That had been within a month or two of Robert Remmick's death, and now, over a year and a half later, they still met occasionally for a game, using safe private courts and signing in under assumed names.

On the evening of the day Cooper pointed the finger of suspicion at Rebecca and demanded that she be interrogated, Steve and Traven played best-of-seven-games, showered, then went for a drink in a quiet nearby bar, settling down either side of a table in a secluded corner.

Steve had a personal question to put to Traven; he had called him to arrange the game with the express purpose of asking it. But his prime concern was with the MI5 mission against Desert Wolf, to which he had committed himself. Deeply aware of the things he had done in the past in service with Shaheen's cadre, there was in him now a fierce determination to 'black out' those past actions, if possible to obliterate them. Somehow, to achieve that. Inside himself he was aware that it wasn't really possible to do so: those things had been done, so it wasn't humanly possible to *undo* them. Nevertheless he found great comfort in the knowledge that every piece of counter-terrorist information he was delivering to Traven was contributing in some measure towards the approaching, planned-for destruction of the terrorist op Desert Wolf in which Shaheen's cadre was playing a major part — a destruction which he, Steve Remmick, could then set as a small piece of 'white' against the terrible 'black' uglinesses in his past. A small contribution, yes, but — useful. Hopefully.

So now, his glass of lager half-full on the table in front of him, Steve asked how successfully the massive surveillance MI5 had in place to keep track of and report on the controllers now arrived in Britain was progressing.

Traven took his time to answer, looking across at this mole of his. With his steady, watchful eyes, regular features and straight fair hair, Steve Remmick could not hold a candle to his dead brother Robert for looks and sheer charisma, he thought, but by God he's by far the better man. And oddly, it didn't take long to convince me — convince me beyond doubt — of that fact; after a mere couple of weeks I called off the watchdogs I'd set on him when I took him on trial. And

64

since then he's worked himself ever deeper into Shaheen's trust and confidence — and therefore been in a position to provide me with some alpha-plus intelligence. But Steve's greatest coup — as he knows — is, we hope, close at hand. During their final conference, the controllers will commit to tape their individual declarations, which they expect to be the signal for Desert Wolf to move into its active phase — but which will in fact, to us engaged in counter-operation Double Talk, be the signal for the poised Special Forces of MI5 and MI6 to close the net simultaneously on all three controllers and on all Desert Wolf's separate and widely dispersed activities. And Steve Remmick is the man who — provided our plans go right — will make a secret copy of the tape of those declarations and deliver it to me, thus giving me incontrovertible proof of the leading roles played by all three controllers in acts of terrorism: internationally big fish to a man, those three.

'We're right on course,' he said quietly. 'As you know, Mansoor has been under surveillance for some while, since he spends a great deal of time in England and has a residence here.'

'Things are working out as I hoped.' A glint of excitement in Steve's eyes. 'Like I told you yesterday, I'm definitely assigned to do the recordings. I'm to tape the declarations, then make two copies; that'll give them three tapes in all, counting the master tape — one for each of the controllers.'

'But, in fact, you will run off three copies. And the third one you will conceal on your person and covertly bring to me: it will be the rock-solid evidence on which the case against the controllers will be based.' Traven spoke sombrely and then sat lost in thought until — suddenly — he smiled, broke free of his vision of future triumph and picked up his glass. 'Jumping the gun more than a little, aren't I?' he observed wryly. 'The most critical part, the most dangerous part, still lies ahead: you making that extra tape and getting it to me.'

'Nearly three years you've been working on Double Talk. That's a long, long time to keep such a complex mission clean.'

'Not entirely clean. We lost Spencer last year — and were remarkably lucky to succeed in masking the truth as to how and why he got killed.'

'What sort of bloke was he? I remember Rob talking about him-'

'Steve.' Traven's interruption was quiet but incisive. 'Give me credit, please. When you rang me to set up this meet you had more than a few games of squash on your mind; I hadn't been with you five minutes this evening before I realized that. You've got something important to either ask me, or tell me. So do it. Whichever it is, get on and do it.'

For a few moments Steve eyed him in silence, suddenly assailed by an overwhelming sense of gratitude towards this man. Traven — Traven, of MI5, of all people — has become my friend, he was thinking. *He set me free from Rob.* Rob — and this is something I've only come to understand recently — never ever truly *saw* me — he wasn't ever really interested in doing so, I suppose. He simply wanted me to stay in the place in our lives that we'd got used to as we grew up, and which suited him — namely, to be as it were a sort of echo of himself. Well, I'm not that now and it's Traven who made that possible.

'Sure, you're right,' he said hesitantly. 'There's a couple of questions I want to ask you.'

'Fire away.'

'It's about the courier, the bloke who was in the Toyota with me and Rob that night you came after us into the hills and ran us off the road.'

'What about him?'

67

'Who's his next-of-kin, and how can I get in touch with them?' As Steve blurted out his question he was looking directly at Traven and to his surprise he saw an immediate change come over the MI5 man's face, a frozen sort of look as if Traven had exerted his will and ordered all expression — out! Out *now!*

'Why do you want to know?' Traven asked.

'It's a bit of a story.'

'So drink up, fetch us another lager, then tell it.' Already smiling and at ease again, Traven drained his glass and slid it across the table. 'As you should know from your considerable experience, I'm a good listener.'

Steve hesitated for a moment, still wondering why his question had disturbed Traven. Then he stood up, collected the two glasses and eyed Traven warily. 'If I tell it, will you answer those two questions I asked?'

'That will depend on the story which, presumably, will reveal to me your reason for asking them.'

Steve fetched the fresh drinks, then sat down again and told Traven about the £30,000 that Robert had bequeathed to him, and what he intended to do with it. However, he made no mention of the note to him that his brother had left in the strong-box, in which he confessed his guilt in the death of the courier.

Traven heard him through without interruption. When the story was told, he sat forward, smoothing one hand over his grey-streaked brown hair. 'Thirty thousand — a very useful sum of money,' he observed. 'Why give it away to someone you've never even met?'

'Rob and I survived that night: the courier didn't.'

But somehow I think there's more to this than that one simple fact, Traven thought, reading the angst in the younger man's eyes. 'No blame to you or Robert for that,' he said, a hint of challenge in his voice.

'Nevertheless, I'd like to offer . . . some sort of recompense to his nearest living relative.'

'I don't see why — '

'The courier *died*, for God's sake! Rob couldn't bring out the both of us so he had to make a choice and he chose *me* — and the courier *died* back there! . . . I just don't want the money,' he added, a stubborn set to his mouth.

'Very well. I understand that.'

'So find me the name and address of his next-of-kin. I don't imagine he'll be as loath to take the cash as for some reason you seem

69

to be to give me — '

'As a matter of fact it's a girl. A young woman, rather: the courier's sister.'

'Funny, I never thought of it being a woman. Is she into terrorism and the drugs scams to fund — '

'Never! The opposite, if anything — ' But there Traven broke off sharply, sat back and went on more quietly. 'As you know well enough, the courier was a conviction terrorist. His sister never touched it. They were both Lebanese, and born in that country. But he was brought up in Lebanon, whereas she was brought up over here. The two of them were never close.' Reaching for his glass he drank some lager then went on, his voice bland now. Watching him, Steve thought, he's disengaged himself from those two people he was talking about — but then he wondered why Traven had been engaged in the first place. 'Her name is Hanna Tregorian,' Traven said. 'She lives out at Chesham. I'll give you her address and telephone number.'

Steve frowned. 'So you know her — know her personally, I mean? D'you think she'll agree to see me? Odd, isn't it, how I'd assumed it'd be a man. That would've been a sight easier; I'd have been able to deal with that.'

'I'll speak to her first, if you like.'

'Go see her, you mean? Speak for me, pave the way a bit — '

'No, not see her. I'll phone her and tell her you're — ' Traven broke off, grinned, then went on light-heartedly (yet Steve guessed at some sort of slow burn of longing in him). 'I'll tell her you're tall and young and handsome, and altogether a good bloke and well worthy of any time she might see fit to give you. How would that suit you?'

'Couldn't be better, and thanks. What's she like? Tell me about her so I — '

'No. That's for her. Hanna Tregorian will tell you as much, or as little, as she wishes you to know.'

★ ★ ★

That evening Brad Cooper and his buddy Liam Kidd were playing billiards at their local pub when Shaheen contacted Kidd on his mobile.

'Shit.' As yet unaware of the identity of his caller Kidd put up his cue then took the call.

'Shaheen here. Are you alone?'

'Nah. I'm with Cooper. Public place, but only the two of us in earshot.'

'Then hear this: permission has been given for the interrogation discussed earlier today

71

to be carried out. You, Kidd, are the agent appointed to do the job. It must be dealt with within the next two days, and you will report results to me immediately it has been completed. Questions?'

Hell, Brad'll hit the bloody roof when I tell him, he was counting on it going to him, not me, Kidd thought. But what he said was, 'Two days ain't much — what if the Remmick bint simply ain't home, got visitors or — '

'In that case the job must be put on hold until after the final conference.'

'Understood, I'll get on to it pronto. There's one thing I guess I'd better get clear, though.'

'What is it?'

'How far do I go with her? I mean — '

'I know what you mean.' Shaheen paused for a moment, then asked, 'Is Cooper right there with you?'

'What? Yeh, sure, Brad's here, d'you want to talk — '

'Then ask him, Kidd.' Shaheen's voice came down the line loaded with mockery and a certain contempt. 'Ask Cooper how far you should go with Rebecca Remmick. I know what his answer will be; consequently I have no doubt whatever that, provided you have the necessary will to follow Cooper's recommendations, you will by the end of your interrogation have extracted from her proof of either her innocence or her guilt. Depending on your report on her, I shall either order direct action against her or . . . offer her our sincere apologies for any, shall we say, inconvenience, she may have suffered during your visit. Have you further questions?'

'Nah. I'll get on to it — '

'Your report is to be with me no later than eight thirty on Thursday morning. I have one further instruction to give you: in the interests of security you are to carry out this job entirely on your own. You will employ no back-up at any time during the operation — no back-up whatsoever. Understood?'

'Understood, but — '

The line went dead in his ear, and he switched off his mobile.

'The bastard! The fucking *bastard!*' Standing at Kidd's shoulder Cooper spat out the curses, anger boiling up inside him. 'That job should've been mine! It was me put him on to the danger; he's got no right to sideline me now — '

'Hey, easy, man! Take it easy.' Kidd swung round to his mate and, as he did so, a group of youths erupted into the pool-room, five or six of them barging in loud with the drink in them, shoving each other round a bit, swapping foul-mouthed chat but both language and behaviour relatively good-natured. 'Time to move on, I reckon,' Kidd muttered.

'Scum.' Cooper stood eyeing the new arrivals darkly, his hands balling into fists at his sides; he despised those who drank to excess. 'Mindless scum.'

Seeing him spoiling for a fight, Kidd laid a restraining hand on his arm. 'Come on, let's be on our way,' he said, 'we've got more important things to get stuck into. Too right, this job Shaheen's just handed me ought to've gone to you. But orders are orders, I gotta do it. You're a sight better than me at the sort of stuff it calls for, though, so I need your advice — '

It did the trick. Cooper turned away from the horse-play developing and headed out of the pool-room, already dreaming up interesting possibilities for making the most of the interrogation his mate had just been awarded. 'Rebecca Remmick: long time no see. Yeah. We'll work it together, Liam. Break any resistance on her part — no sweat, a pleasure, in fact.'

'Not *we*, mate,' Kidd interrupted nervously. 'I ain't allowed no back-up; Shaheen said I got to — '

'Shaheen's one rotten craphead! But to hell with him: I'm going to have a hand in the questioning of Rebecca Remmick, Shaheen or no Shaheen. You and me will plan the tactics of it together, Liam. Blow by blow as they say, eh? I'll obey orders and not go anywhere near the bitch's house, but in my mind I'll be with you every step of the way, believe you me, mate.'

Cooper rented a service flat in Edmonton, north of the Thames. Driving there now he and Kidd settled down and talked late into the night, discussing the questions to be put to 'the Remmick bitch', and the methods Kidd should employ to persuade her to answer them in the event that she was unwilling to do so of her own free will.

4

Hanna Tregorian's detached house on the outskirts of the town of Chesham stood at the end of a road bordered on both sides by similar 1930s-built homes. Each set centrally in its own quarter-acre of land, the two- or three-bedroomed dwellings were of pleasant aspect but displayed little individuality when seen from the outside. As Steve Remmick walked along the road, the banknotes his brother had left him packed into the briefcase he was carrying, he admired the succession of well-kept, colourful gardens he was passing and was conscious of an ambience of . . . tranquillity? Perhaps.

Number 31 he was looking for. Home to Hanna Tregorian who, according to Traven, was twenty-four years old, a well-qualified assistant working with an upmarket consortium of architects and interior decorators whose offices were in central London . . . And she's sister to the man whom I but no other living person know was murdered in cold blood by my brother Robert. On the thought, Steve came to the wrought-iron gate displaying the number 31, found it standing open so walked down the paved path to the house and knocked on its front door.

As the door was opened to him, his world, through a totally silent few seconds, stood still in order that he might devote all of himself to looking at her. She was almost as tall as he was, and she was slim; her black hair was drawn back from her face into a chignon and her eyes, long and darkly brilliant beneath strong, curved brows, were looking straight into his.

'Hello,' she said to his silence. 'Traven said you would be on time, and you are. But then he's invariably right — and not only about the little things, either . . . Would you like to come in, or are you going to say whatever it is you've come to say standing on my doorstep?'

Steve rejoined the world. A world not quite the same now, for him; he knew that and for a moment was afraid — but then the fear was gone and he went forward into the newness with wonder. 'Thanks, I'd much rather come in,' he said, stepping across the threshhold and into her house. 'I've never been much good at talking on doorsteps; it's an acquired art I suppose.'

Closing the door behind him, she turned and faced him, and now he noticed she was wearing a severely cut skirt of some richly blue material and a long-sleeved, high-necked blouse patterned with tiny, multi-coloured flowers. 'You're not what I expected,' she said.

'Didn't Traven tell you? So you'd know it was me?'

'No. I asked, but he just said if a youngish, tall man knocked at my door at eleven o'clock this morning it would be a good idea for me to let him in and listen to what he had to say.'

'You mean you don't even know my name? Who I am?'

She shook her head. 'No. He said you would tell me — said it would be better if you told me yourself; that I heard it from you, not him.'

'Traven — you must trust him a lot, then.'

A small and somehow secretive smile came on her smooth-skinned, oval face. It spread into her eyes and then she said, 'I would trust him with my life.'

I would give a lot to hear this woman say that of me, Steve Remmick thought. 'Then he's a lucky man,' he said.

Her smile faded. 'Not altogether so lucky, I think.' Then she turned and led the way on into her house. 'Would you like some coffee?' she asked. 'Now that we've established that you're not here to sell me double-glazing or insurance, we can have it in the sitting-room and you can tell me why you have come.'

Yet nearly half an hour passed before they got round to talking about that. In her kitchen they made coffee together — Lebanese coffee, so the making of it proceeded under her strict instruction, and took time. As she was about to put the pot of coffee on the tray she had set ready —

'Couldn't we have it in here?' Steve asked.

Pot in hand, she looked across at him. 'Would you rather?'

'Yes. I would.'

'Why?'

'Because what I have to say to you isn't easy to say.'

'So why will it be any easier in here?'

Steve had a strong feeling that she intuited the true answer to her question perfectly well, and he felt elated that she nevertheless wanted to hear him say it. But then when it came to the point he chickened out and said only, and feebly, 'Here in the kitchen . . . well, it's probably the place in your house where you're most relaxed.'

That's what you *say*, Hanna thought, but what's in your *mind* is that this is where I come down in the morning in my dressing-gown and with my hair loose. And she found herself happy at the tenor of his thoughts — and also with the way he managed to only *half* conceal them from her. 'So we'll stay in

79

here,' she said smiling.

Sitting facing each other across the table, they tasted the coffee and congratulated each other on its excellence. Then Hanna Tregorian said quietly, 'It's time now.'

Meeting and holding her eyes, Steve told her. 'My name is Steven Remmick — '

'*Remmick?*' Her eyes were hard and cold. 'Then you are brother to the man who was driving that car — the night my brother died?' She was on her feet, glaring down at him. 'I hate and despise all terrorists. If you are of that breed, get out of my house *now*! I don't want to hear anything you've got to say!'

He stood up, faced her. 'At that time I was that kind, yes, obviously, since I was there in the car with your brother and mine. But I'm out of it now, out for good, I mean, and I only wish I'd never been in.' He paused then, thinking, how can I make true sense to her of how I've changed since then? She is special to me and I want to keep her in my life, somehow I know I *need* her in my life. But then recognizing his own turning — achieved as it had been despite a tearing sense of loss of a whole piece of his life, and only with Traven's help and constant support — as too big a thing to be encapsulated in a spur-of-the-moment sentence or two, he fell back on the trust she had in Traven and had already revealed to him. 'I'm sworn enemy to terrorism now,' he said to her. 'Traven should have told you — ' He broke off: it was not for him to reveal that particular truth, that was in Traven's hands, not his. 'Traven knows. He knows I'm no terrorist now.'

Traven's name seemed to win Steve's case for him. Hanna eyed him in silence for a moment and then looked down, her fingers moving idly on the bare wood. 'You are right,' she said quietly. 'Traven would never have vouched for you if he had had even the slightest doubt ... I'm sorry. The name Remmick took me back to the dark days when my brother was trying to force me to join him, to work with him in the service of the terrorist network here in Britain, at that time 'Robert Remmick' was a name always on his lips ... Yet I never quite understood the relationship between those two. My brother seemed to swing wildly between hating him, admiring his expertise on the job, and referring to him in a peculiarly personal, almost gloating way.'

'But you do believe me? That I'm out of it now?' Steve's voice was rough and demanding — he wanted her with him, not claimed by memories of other men.

Hanna's fingers stilled, and she sat down

again, frowning. 'I believe you, but something equally important has just occurred to me,' she said.

'Tell me,' he prompted.

'It's that — bearing in mind that I was sister to your courier — you have an equal right to challenge me about terrorism as *vice versa*. And you have Traven to vouch for you, I can't name anyone who's in a position to do the same on my behalf.'

'You don't need, anyone — '

'You believe me simply because I say so?'

'I'd believe anything you told me.'

Her eyes darkened. 'That's a very big thing to say to anyone, and I don't have an answer to it.'

'I haven't asked you a question. I've only told you how I feel.'

'Then I would like you now to tell me why you've come here,' she said.

And now Steve found it easy. Concisely, he told Hanna of the money his brother had left to him — though not of the letter Rob had written to him — and said he would like her to have the £30,000, he had brought it with him and would like to give it to her now. Yet even as he said those last words it dawned on him that Hanna Tregorian was going to refuse the money — her face and her body language were telling him so.

She did. 'I want no part of anything even remotely connected with my brother and the way he lived his life,' she said, as he fell silent.

Steve made no attempt to persuade her otherwise. But he did not want Rob's £30,000, either; it belonged in a past he had disowned — besides, he'd be getting the money under false pretences since it was a dead cert that Rob wouldn't have left it to him if he'd known he, Steve, was going to work with Traven against Desert Wolf! 'The same goes for me,' he said — but then suddenly he laughed. 'To hell with the money. I'll give it to the Red Cross or something. There's more interesting things to talk about. D'you think I could have another cup of coffee?'

Hanna also was eager to move on, to leave Robert Remmick and her brother in their shared and violent past and go forward — possibly with this young man she'd met barely an hour ago and under such strange circumstances. Yes, quite possibly; for there was a maturity, and diffidence about him that attracted her strongly, the rapport between them was strong and she did not want him to leave; she wanted to get to know him. Smiling to herself, she poured a second cup of coffee for each of them. And as they sat drinking it and talking together they discovered a common interest in films, books, and — strictly at layman's level, as both hastily agreed — archaeology and how it ties in with historical research.

Looking at her as she sat slim and graceful in her chair, Steve found himself consumed with a desire to know more about her, and when a slight pause came in their conversation, he said, 'Traven told me you're Lebanese, but your English — well, it's perfect, and you've hardly any accent.'

'That's not surprising: from the age of five I was brought up in England.'

She had closed up against him a little, he saw that. But her eyes . . . something in them, it seemed to him, was telling him she wouldn't mind him going on with what he'd started. 'I'd like to know about it — about you,' he said.

'Why?'

Steve grinned. 'Could be because then I'd feel free to tell you about myself?'

For the first time that morning, Hanna Tregorian laughed. 'Typical male reasoning — I must remember to ask you to do so!' Then turning sideways in her chair so that as she spoke she could look out at her garden through the picture window on the far side of the kitchen, she told him a little about

herself. 'My parents were Christian Lebanese,' she said. 'They met when both were
working for the British Council in Beirut, he
as PA to the British Representative there, she
teaching English. When events turned really
bad in the mid-70s and Council activities
were run down, they stayed on and kept the
premises ... well, *safe*, making sure the
property wasn't commandeered by any of the
militia groups as a base or a checkpoint. And
naturally, doing that earned them big kudos
with the Brits ... I was born to them in
1977, when my brother was six years old. But
then in '83 all the family got caught in the
street during a mortar duel between two
groups. We had to run for cover. But my
parents ... didn't run fast enough. My
brother and I were younger and quicker — or
maybe just lucky: he made it uninjured, I
suffered leg and arm injuries.'

Hanna's voice died away, and she sat quiet.
After a few minutes, Steve invaded her silence
because he sensed her slipping away from
him back into those days she was speaking
about, and he did not want to lose her like
that. 'So you and your brother were orphans,'
he said, and saw her — as she sat in profile to
him, dark hair gathered into thick, silky swirls
at the back of her head — lift her chin a little.

'They were very good to me then, my

parents' English friends at the British Council,' she said. 'Beirut was still what the journalists call war-torn: it wasn't much of a place for a wounded little girl, hospitals overcrowded and medical expertise and supplies — well, you know, I expect. Anyway, the Representative and his wife took charge of me, and at the Council's expense I was flown to England for treatment. Then, as soon as I was well again, I went to live with a couple in Oxfordshire who were neighbours and close friends of that Beirut Rep. and his wife. And that's where I stayed. My new parents brought me up — ' Hanna broke off with a shake of the head. 'No, that's a long, long story. Suffice it to say that within a few years they adopted me, and I grew up as one of their own children. They're farmers; I often spend weekends with them,' she said, and Steve saw one corner of her mouth lift as she smiled.

However, although she fascinated him, there lingered at the back of Steve's mind a slight but persistent misgiving. Hanna was, after all, sister to the courier who'd been running drugs for Shaheen's terrorist cadre when he died; so the question had to be asked. 'But — your brother? Did you lose touch with him, then?'

Hanna got to her feet and stood looking

down at him, studying his face, her arms straight at her sides, her hands clenched into fists. ''Give me a child from the age of seven and I will make him mine for life', she said, imbuing the quoted words with a bitterness that startled Steve — and caught at his heart, also, she was surely too young for such . . . alienation? 'I don't recall who it was who said that but, whoever he was, he spoke a dreadful truth.'

'Go on. You can tell me.'

She nodded. 'I know that,' she said. 'My brother was older than seven — but not *enough* older, I suppose. After our parents were killed by that mortar round, a certain uncle of ours — my father's brother, so he had the legal right to do it — laid claim and took the orphaned boy into his own household, brought him up as his own, with his own blood-sons. And that uncle was a Hizbollah activist.'

'He didn't lay claim to you, though?'

Hanna's mouth lengthened, but no way could you call it a real smile, Steve thought. 'A *girl*-child?' she mocked. 'No, my uncle didn't lay claim to me. The young boy, yes: useful clay to the moulder's hands. By his middle teens my brother belonged heart, mind and soul to my uncle's terror group.'

'Your brother, and the rest of your family

— they were kept away from you? No letters, no phone calls — ?'

'In Lebanon he ran a very tight ship, did my uncle. He saw to it that I was . . . *erased* from the family consciousness, from its life.'

'And they accepted that? All your relatives, they allowed it to happen?'

Again, Hanna smiled, but this time it was a true smile — and beautiful to see, Steve thought. 'There was one aunt; she and her husband were brave enough to resist his will. For a while they wrote to me regularly — even visited me once, came over here to England,' she said.

'And you're still in touch with them?'

'No. Both of them died four years ago. An accident on a boat.' They were silent for a few moments. Steve did not know what to say. Finally he fell back on something that would pull Hanna's mind away from Lebanon. 'How did it happen, your brother coming to Britain?' he asked.

'He was planted in England in the mid-90s by Hizbollah agents, to work for an organization affiliated to Al-Qaeda. That was intended as a first-step-on-the-ladder job; he was marked for higher things but — ' Frowning suddenly, she broke off, turning away. 'Enough of all that, I'd rather we talked of something else. Let's go outside, I'll show you my garden — if you like?'

'I'd love to see it, but I'm afraid I don't know much — '

'Good! In that case even the little I know will impress you, so come on.'

However, gardening did not figure greatly in their conversation as they walked in the garden then sat down on the beechwood seat in the shade of a flowering cherry tree. Mostly they talked trivia — while all the time eyes and body language, together with an occasional brief touch of hand on hand or arm, communicated on a more personal level. And when Steve was leaving her house — a good two hours after he had been invited into it — and asked her to meet him for dinner the following evening, Hanna Tregorian nodded and said she would very much like to do that.

★   ★   ★

Rebecca felt a great affinity for Wychwood. This was mostly because she and Rob Remmick had lived and loved in it together since their marriage, but also on account of its own — to her way of thinking — intrinsic aura, a lustre somehow lived into its fabric in the course of the years it had provided comfort and safety — or was that simply wishful thinking on her part? she'd sometimes wondered since Rob died — for those who resided in it.

The day after Liam Kidd and Cooper planned her interrogation together, Rebecca came home from work later than usual — she and her manageress had been stock-taking at the sports-and-leisure-wear boutique Roberta's which her husband had bought for her six years ago — and also much wearier. Deciding against changing out of the dark-blue trouser suit she was wearing — coffee first! — she went straight across the hall into the kitchen. Putting her mobile down on the table she took off her jacket, slung it over a chair and picked up the cafétière — only to put it down again as her front door bell rang.

She recognized her caller the minute she opened the door to him: he was Liam Kidd, an associate of Rob's who had been to Wychwood a few times in the past on errands for Soheil Shaheen.

'Oh. Good evening,' she said, frowning, eyeing the wirily built man standing on the step, his dark windcheater open over a sweatshirt and Levi's, his short, sandy hair smooth, an ingratiating smile on his foxy face.

'The name's Kidd, Mrs Remmick,' he said politely, 'Liam Kidd. I don't suppose you remember me, but I've been here a few times before on business for Mr Shaheen — '

'I do remember you.' He seems a bit nervous, she thought — anyway, I'd better go along with this for the moment, the sooner I know why he's here the sooner I'll be able to deal with it and get rid of him. Besides, it's best not to rile Shaheen in any way, now Rob's not around any more. 'What can I do for you?' she asked.

'There's a couple of things Mr Shaheen wants me to ask you about.' Kidd licked his lips, then smiled again — it did not reach his eyes, but Rebecca didn't notice that. 'It's to clear up something about the crash when your husband got killed; new stuff's just surfaced . . . D'you think I could come in? It ain't a good idea, you being seen out here talking to me.'

New information about Rob's death? Kidd had Rebecca's interest on the instant. Could be something had come up showing it hadn't been an accident?

'Your husband would've wanted you to co-operate, wouldn't he?' Main thing is — *get inside the house quick as you can*, Cooper had impressed upon him; once you're in there you can do as you like and she's got no come-back. 'Rob, he was one of our mates, y'know; we'd like to be sure the coppers read that crash right.'

91

Rob. Ah, Rob, I miss you so. And I want it right, too; I've always had my suspicions. 'Come in,' Rebecca said, opening her door a little wider. 'I'll give you all the help I can.'

Liam Kidd stepped into Wychwood, into its big front hall. It was much as he remembered it: polished oak floor, rugs scattered about, and on the far side two long, dark settles standing one either side of the door into the living-room — and beside the one on the right a door that opened into the kitchen, he had been in there once.

Soon as you're in, don't waste time, Cooper had said, get stuck into the bitch straight off — show her the gun, smack her about a bit to show her who's boss, then rip her top off and wade in good and proper. So as the woman closed the door behind him he drew his handgun from the pocket of his windcheater, then as she turned to face him, cocked it and levelled it at her midriff. 'OK, stop right there!' he ordered.

Caught totally off guard, Rebecca froze, mind empty, body rigid — and Kidd closed in on her fast and pistol-whipped her across the face. Staggering back against the door, she clawed at it for support, willing herself to stay on her feet. Reaching out with his free hand Kidd grabbed a fistful of her blouse and ripped it open. He drew back a little then;

92

stood studying her, a looselipped grin on his face. 'Nice,' he said. 'I like women with good boobs on them . . . You going to answer a few questions now?'

'What is it you want?' Her words did not come out as firmly as she wished, there was blood inside her mouth and her face hurt; nevertheless she straightened up as she spoke, pressing her back against the door for support, pulling the edges of her blouse together with one fumbling hand. You slimy little prick she thought grimly. I'll stick this out somehow, see you off yet!

But Kidd was pretty sure of himself by now — after all, he had the gun. 'I want answers to certain questions, luv — and they ain't about that fucking accident,' he said. 'I put the question, you give me the answer. OK?'

'You're not making any sense! I don't know anything that could be useful to you — even when Rob was alive I didn't know much, so how could I know anything at all now he's dead?'

'That's what we gotta be sure about, see. There's been whispers going round as say you've been grassing us up on the sly.'

'But like I said, I don't *know* anything — anything about the cadre, and what Shaheen's doing!' Dear God, he's not going to believe me! she was thinking even as she spoke, but she said it because it was the truth. 'Those rumours, they're lies; they have to be lies! I *can't* be grassing you up, I don't know anything *at all* about Shaheen's plans, I've no way of knowing.' But Kidd stood there, silent. That grin was on his face again, but now it was slightly different — something in his eyes said *he* was different, too, said I'm enjoying this, and for me it's going to get better yet. Looking into his eyes, Rebecca felt real, gutwrenching fear for the first time that evening. 'You have to believe me!' she cried desperately. '*I don't know anything*!'

Kidd read the fear in her, and his smile broadened. 'You *say* — but then you would, wouldn't you? Trouble is, it ain't that easy, luv. Ain't no good me going back to the boss and saying 'she says she doesn't know anything', now is it? Mr Shaheen, he wouldn't like that — ' But he broke off, suddenly realizing that he was letting things slide — which was just what Cooper (knowing him!) had warned him to avoid at all costs. Get on with it, Liam me boy! he urged himself. Show the bitch who's boss! 'You're trying to play me for a sucker, you little bitch,' he said angrily, and, grabbing her arm, jerked her away from the door, got behind her and pushed her in front of him across the hall. 'Get into the kitchen — go on, go! Go!' he ordered, jabbing the muzzle of the gun into her back on each 'Go!'

But fear had galvanized her mind. This'll be the only chance you'll get! it shouted at her. Once he's got you in the kitchen he'll tie you up and really go to work on you, so bloody *do something* before we get there! Your mobile's on the kitchen table so go for him *now* — smash the gun aside, shove him off his feet then dash into the kitchen, grab the phone, dial 999, yell out address and shout *help!* Damn all else to do, so —

Whirling round, she hurled herself bodily on Kidd, left arm lashing out sideways against the gun in his right hand, the other clawing stiff-fingered for his eyes as she drove her whole weight in against him. 'Bastard!' she was screaming, not aware she was screaming. 'Rotten bastard scum, I'll gouge your bloody eyes out!'

Taken by surprise, Kidd reeled back under her assault, lost his balance and almost fell — then she was on him, tried to knee him in the groin, failed to connect so kicked out hard at his legs. The edge of her shoe caught Kidd on the shin. 'Shit!' he howled, then in trying to favour his hurt leg keeled over and went down, arms flailing wildly — and the gun flying out of his hand as it hit the floor. Landing flat on the polished boards it planed blithely away from his frantic hand.

Rebecca was on it cat-fast — picked it up, closed her fingers firmly around the butt. *Who holds the gun, rules,* it said to her — and with shock, then terror, then a thrilling sense of power she realized that the death in its mouth was in her giving now, not Kidd's. Turning on him, she aimed the gun towards him as, on the far side of the hall, he began to scramble to his feet.

'Take one single step towards me *and you're dead!*' she said, hearing her own voice hard and confident, seeing him straighten up then stay rooted where he stood, his face working with suppressed fury as he fought back the gut-instinct to charge her. 'We'll go into the kitchen now,' she went on, when he was still. 'You go first. I'll be right behind you with the gun centred on your back. My mobile's in there. I'm going to call the police.'

'You ain't, you know. I reckon . . . I reckon I wasn't thinking right, a moment ago when you told me you know nothing about the cadre.' Liam Kidd was back in business again: his face was now as calm and friendly as his voice, as he set out to lull her into a sense of security. 'Looking at it fair, how could you know anything, when Rob's dead? Those rumours — ain't no sense in them, is there? And if you call the fuzz now — hell, think of all the hassle that'll come from it! Hassle for you, I mean; for you gotta admit that the widow of Rob Remmick ain't a gal who's exactly whiter-than-white with the coppers, is she now?' He gave her a quick grin. 'Added to which, if you turn me in, who knows what stories I might come up with about you and me, and why I'm here? I could make a lot of trouble for you, lady. So you better give me the gun, and we'll part friends. I can work it with Mr Shaheen — '

'Shut up *and stand still!*' Her last words sharp with panic — for she saw that even as he was speaking Kidd had begun to edge his way towards her! Slyly, he was sliding his feet one after the other across the polished floorboards, was inching closer — and whatever the words that were coming out of his mouth might be saying neither his eyes nor his body language were sending the same message. His eyes were brilliant with the fury and violence in him and she saw his entire body tense, ready to attack, strike — kill. '*Stand still*, I said!' she cried again. 'I'll fire if you come any nearer — '

'Don't be stupid — you're *not* stupid, I know that. I'm on your side now, ma'am, I'll make it OK with Shaheen.'

Rebecca did not believe a word of it. Nevertheless he had halted, she saw. But the grin was back on his face again — and he was less than ten feet away from her now, if he came any closer he'd be near enough to go for the gun! He'd grab the gun! He was *not* her friend, he was enemy all the way through and —

'Link your hands behind your head!' she ordered, cramming down panic. 'Do it now! *Now*, I said — '

Kidd jumped her then. Launched himself at her in a low, shallow diving tackle, his arms hooked out in front of him to grab her and bring her down. She's not trained to the gun, he'd reasoned; she won't be quick enough to change aim so even if she fires the bullets'll go over my head.

But Liam Kidd was wrong in that. Trained to the gun or not, Rebecca's reactions were ski-slope fast. Her first bullet took him in the chest, the second in the head as he went down.

★　★　★

'Steve. It's Rebecca. I'm sorry if I've interrupted you in anything, but — '

'Never mind. Something's wrong, isn't it? Your voice is all trembly. What's up?'

'It's . . . it's to do with Rob. Well, Rob and me. This man came round to Wychwood a bit after I got home from the shop. A bloke named Kidd, Liam Kidd, he's been here before, to see Rob — you know, the cadre, Shaheen — '

'I know Kidd. Go on.'

'He . . . he had a gun. I didn't know he had, or I wouldn't have let him in, but I didn't and . . . there's been an accident. He — '

'*Are you hurt? Rebecca, did he hurt you?*'

'Sorry. It's difficult, over the phone like this.'

'Are you OK?'

'Yes, I'm all right, but . . . '

Her silence deepened the fear already in him. 'But what? Tell me what's happened!'

'I can't, over the phone. I can't, Steve. I'm frightened, I — '

'I'm coming over right now.' Never before had he known Rebecca so — so lost, so absolutely desperate. 'I should make it within an hour. If I'm a bit longer, don't get worked up about it, I'll be with you soon.'

'Oh Steve, that's so good to hear.'

'And Rebecca.'

'Yes?'

'Play safe till I get there. Listen carefully, this is important. Don't use the phone yourself, and don't answer it if anyone calls you. Lock front and back doors; don't go out, and don't answer if anyone rings. When I get there I'll give my special knock so you'll know it's me. All right?'

'All right. Now I know you'll be with me soon, all right . . . Drive carefully, though!' she added, her voice suddenly loud as fear hit her again. 'For God's sake don't go too fast!'

'I won't,' he said, then cut the call: the sooner he got to her the sooner he'd find out what had happened between her and Kidd, and the trouble — plainly, it was *trouble* — could be sorted. Hopefully.

5

As he drove to Streatham, Steve thought over what Rebecca had said, and its implications for himself and, possibly, for Traven and Operation Double Talk. Liam Kidd: Steve knew him as one of Shaheen's junior lieutenants, and Cooper's close mate although a lesser man than he — a fact which didn't bode well for Rebecca since Cooper was given to violence and had quite a reputation for dealing out extremely rough justice to anyone he even suspected of causing Kidd grief, seeing himself as the man's role model and protector. Also, Steve thought, since Shaheen's cadre was Mansoor's prime tool for the implementation of Desert Wolf, to find Kidd calling on Rebecca conjured up some very ugly possible scenarios in the mind.

Parking well away from Wychwood, he walked along to the house, noting on his way that although there was no car parked directly outside it there were several kerbside at intervals along the road.

She opened the door to him but stood blocking his entrance. 'Stay on the step there for a minute,' she said, standing stiff and still in her dark blue trousers and a black sweatshirt, her arms hanging limp at her sides. 'Something very bad's happened,' she began, but then suddenly her shoulders sagged. 'Oh God, Steve! You've got to help me, please help me, it's horrible — '

'Tell me, then. Just *tell* me.' Her eyes had a dazed, appalled look to them, he saw — and her lips were swollen, the skin either side of her mouth flared bruised, red and angry, and her face had a sickly, sheened pallor to it. She was in shock, he realized, and had almost certainly taken a beating.

'Come on, darling,' he said to her gently. 'I'm Rob's brother, remember? Whatever's happened, whatever you might've done, I'm on your side and I'll help you in every way I can.' Reaching out, he touched her arm and then took her hand in his. 'Just tell me.'

Briefly her hand tightened on his, then she pulled it away. And as she spoke her words came hard and clear. 'Liam Kidd, he came here with some rubbish story that I'd been grassing the cadre up, and he'd been sent by Shaheen to question me about it.' She paused, blinking. 'I got the gun from him and I shot him dead.'

For a couple of seconds, Steve stood rooted to the spot, staring at her, his mind refusing to accept the truth of what she had just said. Statements like 'I shot him dead' did not belong in Rebecca's world — both she and Rob himself had fiercely resisted Shaheen's attempts to involve her in the cadre's work. But then he thought, nevertheless I *do* believe her — Kidd's there inside her house and he's dead.

'I'll come inside and we'll deal with this,' he said harshly, and pushed past her into the hall. He saw the man's body at once: it lay sprawled just short of the door into the kitchen, on its back, one arm outflung, the other bent up under the head. Crossing to it he leaned down and peered into Kidd's face — what was left of the face, what could be discerned through the mask of blood and tissue — then as nausea surged in his guts he straightened, fumbling a handkerchief to mouth.

'The first bullet hit him in the chest but the second got him in the head,' Rebecca said coldly, standing behind him. 'He's dead, isn't he? Must be.' But then as Steve turned to her he saw she was looking at him, not at the dead man: she was staring at him, brother to her beloved Rob. 'Dead, like Rob,' she said.

'*Not* like Rob.' She's got to face what's here in front of us, he thought. There's no good served by allowing her to run away from it. 'You've got to look at this like it is,' he said to her. 'You told me you killed Liam Kidd, said you'd shot him dead.'

A narrow little smile came on her bruised mouth. 'As you know I've always believed Rob was murdered,' she said.

'Rob was not murdered.'

Rebecca nodded. 'So they told me. That's what they do when — '

'So are you saying that this — Kidd lying dead in your house with a couple of bullets in him — are you telling me this was an accident?'

'An *accident*?' The little smile was gone, and Steve saw she had broken free from the memory-world she had momentarily escaped into to avoid present horrors. 'Oh no, this wasn't really an accident,' she said, and then words came pouring out, and she told him how Liam Kidd had died. 'He kept coming at me,' she ended. 'He wouldn't stand still, he kept coming towards me and I had the gun by then so I said for him to stop. I pointed the gun at him and *shouted* that he must stop but he didn't, he kept creeping closer and I knew what he'd do to me if he got me so — I shot him.'

'Christ. Rebecca — '

'There didn't seem anything else to do,' she said, reasonably. Then she moved a little nearer to him and touched his arm. 'There still doesn't,' she said. 'There still doesn't, Steve.'

He put his hands on her shoulders and looked into her eyes. 'We'll go into the sitting-room now,' he said, 'and we'll sit down and decide how to deal with this. I'll have to ask you a lot of questions because I have to know everything that was said and done by the two of you.'

'I'm not to try and hide anything, you're saying?'

'That, yes. But I'm also saying it's important you give me even little things, things you might think to leave out because they seem too trivial to have any real significance. That's so especially in regard to the actual words Kidd said to you. I'll need you to tell me the whole thing again, in detail. You must get it right, and you must get it complete.'

'That won't be a problem; I remember it word for word, action for action, like it's written down inside my head ... My only problem will be to unremember it,' she added softly, as she turned and led the way into the sitting-room.

★　★　★

Seated stiff-backed and tense on the edge of the windowseat overlooking Wychwood's

105

garden, Rebecca told him all that had happened that evening between herself and Liam Kidd. And when she was done, Steve interrogated her. There was no other word for it: deeply concentrated, he prowled up and down in front of her — never moving far from her, though — and questioned her about her account of the killing of Kidd comprehensively and invasively, not pulling his punches.

Finally, he released her. Halting beside her, 'You were brave,' he said gently.

'And guilty of murder.' Whispering it fiercely she stood up and faced him, shaking, suddenly on the verge of collapse. 'I see that now. Oh God — '

'But not first degree murder. This was a killing in self-defence, and totally unpremeditated.'

'Rob would have been proud of me, wouldn't he?'

Rebecca's words came to Steve loaded with terrible bitterness — also, he thought as he looked into her eyes, with a sense of dread and . . . loss. 'We have to dispose of the body,' he said firmly, to bring her back to the urgent realities of the present.

She turned away, flinging up her hands in a gesture of despair. 'And how in the world do we do that?'

106

Steve had already roughed out a course of action in his mind — a *possible* course of action, and the only one he had been able to dream up that stood any chance whatsoever of winning a way out for Rebecca. Grabbing her arm, he swung her back to face him. 'Get a grip!' he said sharply. 'This must and can be dealt with, but we have to move fast, and we need some luck.'

'But what'll we do? There's a dead man here, how — ?'

'Through Traven, if he will. He has . . . there are ways — clandestine ways, special units that can be called on in a situation of this nature.'

'For MI5's own, I expect you're right. But neither you nor I exactly fit into that category, do we?'

Now watch what you say to her here, Remmick! Steve cautioned himself. She's not privy to the fact that these days *I do* qualify as 'one of Traven's own' — and I'm on oath not to reveal that state of affairs to anyone else. 'Nevertheless, I think he may be willing to help us in this,' he said.

'But why should he?'

Rebecca wanting to believe, but *afraid* to believe: Steve saw that, and reached out and touched her shoulder. 'We don't have time to go into that now,' he said. 'Take my word for

107

it, love — trust me, I'll explain later. For now, simply *trust me.*'

'I do trust you. I always have.' The doubt was gone from her eyes and her voice was soft.

'Then I'll ring Traven at once. Provided I give him a full explanation of the *circumstances* of Kidd's death I think — I *hope* — he'll see it's right for him to use those special powers he can call on.'

'It's our only hope, really, isn't it?' Rebecca's bruised mouth twisted in a cynical little grimace, and Steve perceived a certain brittle hopefulness come to life in her at the prospect of a way out for herself. 'Oh Steve, if you . . . if only you can swing this! Look, use the phone in here. I'll go make us some coffee and bring it in,' she said, and without waiting for his agreement went off into the kitchen.

Left alone in the sitting-room, Steve stood still for a few moments, weighing his chances of convincing Traven to intervene, to help out in the situation here at Wychwood. He had made a point of being fairly confident of success to Rebecca, but was well aware that in fact the odds were evenly stacked.

Nevertheless, Kidd was a member of Shaheen's cadre. And as at that moment Traven had a big mission going against that cadre, it was on the cards he would welcome

108

any opportunity to cause confusion and disruption among its personnel — which, surely, was exactly what Kidd's unexplained disappearance would do at this stage in their operation. So by disposing of Kidd's body, secretly, Traven could hope and expect to throw the cadre's smooth working out of kilter at this climactic moment for Desert Wolf . . . Yes, if I put it to him like that he might buy it, Steve thought. There could be advantage to him and MI5 in doing so — unless there are other factors involved which I know nothing about.

* * *

In the kitchen Rebecca set about the familiar, comforting process of making coffee with relief, forcing herself to relax. And slowly, her mind began to settle into a kind of — not peace, but something approaching it, an exhausted quietness of the self.

But what about Kidd's close mate, *Cooper*? Kidd must've been ordered to report back with what answers he got from me and when he doesn't, Shaheen will send someone after me — *and the man he'll send will be Brad Cooper!* With shocking, mind-blowing suddenness the realization vaporized that quietness and confronted her, stark and utterly terrifying because now she had perceived it there was no escape: from what Rob had told her of Shaheen that was the way he would react when Kidd failed to return. Cooper was Liam Kidd's close mate so, of course, that's what would happen: *Cooper* would come gunning for her and he — '

Stop it! *Stop* it! she commanded herself. Steve will find a way out of this for me — Rob and me both, he's always been there for us when the chips are down, it'll be all right now Steve's here. Carefully, Rebecca put the lid on the coffee pot, placed that on the tray she had prepared and carried it into the sitting-room.

' . . . we'll wait here till then. I'll call you again later.' Replacing the handset Steve turned as she came in, noticed she was making heavy weather of managing the tray and hurried across to take it from her and put it down on the table in front of the sofa. 'It's OK,' he said, as he did so. 'Traven's agreed. He'll set it up for that special unit I spoke of to come here — it'll be four blokes, just, and they'll take away the body.'

'But I've been thinking, Steve, and I'm scared stiff because when Kidd doesn't report back to Shaheen he'll send someone — '

'I know that — I'm still working with the

110

cadre, remember? Not on the big things like Rob and I were into, of course, but I'm still beavering away with Shaheen's lot so I know a bit about what's going on. Of course Shaheen will suspect you, but we'll cover that.'

'How?'

'One thing at a time. And don't worry about Kidd's body being found — it won't be. Not for a long, long time, if ever. Now, sit down and pour the coffee. I'll get the brandy. No! Keep quiet for the moment, and do as I say.' He slipped her a quick grin. 'I need a brandy even if you don't!'

It helped her. Swallowing the desperate words she had been on the point of speaking, she did as he asked. 'I'm sorry,' she said. 'And the brandy is a bloody good idea so go ahead.'

Neither of them spoke again until he had poured a generous tot of Courvoisier for each of them at the drinks trolley and given her glass into her hand. Then, 'Thank God for Traven,' she said. 'Here's to him and all his kind.'

Steve drank to that too, then put down his glass. 'You're still in a state of mortal terror, and I want to know why,' he said. 'Scared, horrified, got the shakes — these would all be normal, given what's happened here tonight.

But what I'm sensing in you is something way beyond that. You've beaten Kidd at his own game, and now Traven's OK'd the disposal of the body there'll be no trouble for you on that score. So — what else is there, Rebecca? What is it you're still afraid of?'

Picking up her cup, she drank the coffee straight down. Told him, then — told him the other thing, the one she had so far shied away from even thinking consciously about, or facing up to. 'I've been a fool,' she said, folding her hands in her lap and looking down at them. 'A while back, I went out with Brad Cooper a few times — oh for God's sake don't look at me like that! The guy's attractive; we knew each other a bit from when Rob was alive and . . . I was so lonely, Steve. So horribly lonely.'

'Did you sleep with him?' Cold as an Arctic wind in winter.

'You bastard! You damn *bastard*! No, I did not.'

'Was it you or him who broke it off?'

'Me.'

'Was it a friendly parting of the ways?'

'No way! Cooper was mad-dog angry — but I'd made sure to do it in a public place, so I got away in one piece.' Rebecca stood up, stared down at him. 'But he's one mean brute is Cooper, and just now I realized

— remembered, rather — that Kidd was Cooper's side-kick. So now, when Kidd seems to have disappeared, *Cooper* will come after me! Whatever Shaheen may or may not do, Cooper will come after me wanting to know what happened this evening and when I won't tell him . . . He's a wild man, Steve! Got a temper like crazy; he'll beat me up and *it's a thing he likes doing!*' Swinging away from him she flung herself down on the sofa and buried her face in her hands. 'Help me, Steve. Please, please help me!' — a desperate, half-muffled whisper of sound, an entreaty from a suppliant on her knees in desolate and stony country.

Reaching deep into Steve Remmick, her words goaded his brain to intense activity in search of a way to save Rob's wife from the dangers that would soon engulf her unless she found sanctuary. He had perceived the danger she would be in from Shaheen. But what Rebecca had just said reminded him of Kidd's special position as Brad Cooper's acknowledged liege-man, the gallow-glass he was honour-bound to protect or, if necessary, avenge; and in Cooper's case to hell with the 'honour' bit — to exact deadly vengeance for Kidd's disappearance/death would be his natural gut-reaction! So how to keep Rebecca safe?

Cooper would be a well-funded and persistent avenger: he was a skilled operator with all manner of contacts to call on. Rebecca would need a safe house of some sort. But the question was — whose house? His own flat was out of the question, to attempt to hide her away there would jeopardize the continuing success of his own position as Traven's mole inside Shaheen's cadre. And as for her friends and acquaintances — obviously they'd all be useless; Cooper could soon track them down, then run surveillance on them if Rebecca 'disappeared'. So who — ?

'Steve?' Rebecca raised her head and looked up at him, blue eyes anguished. 'What am I going to do? About Cooper?'

He shook his head. 'I don't know. But I'm working on it. Narrowing down the choices.'

Her swollen lips smiled crookedly. 'By now you must've narrowed them down to me disappearing too, I should think. Maybe I'd better just pack a few things and go to a hotel.'

'No. I thought of that, but it's too risky; they'd trace you.'

'What time is this special unit of Traven's coming?'

'He said it's best left till the small hours. They'll arrive between one and two o'clock.'

114

'A long time to wait yet, then. Would you like more coffee?'

But he had turned away, frowning, 'Christ, that'd do fine,' he murmured. 'I wonder if she would? It's a hell of a lot to ask . . . '

Watching him, Rebecca thought yeah, big deal, The Thinker racking his brains for an idea that will miraculously solve the entire problem at a stroke! And suddenly she was seized by an insane desire to giggle because the whole situation seemed so totally hopeless that you might as well give up looking for a way out and just let things go whichever way they would. All this angst so bloody useless, not getting them anywhere.

'Yes, I'll give it a try,' Steve said, and swung round to face her again. 'I've thought of a sort of safe house for you, a place where, I hope and pray, you can stay for a few days while we work out something more permanent.'

'But Cooper — the cadre, too — they know who my friends are, and yours, and Rob's. They'll have them all watched straight off if they don't find me here.'

'This is one friend of mine neither the cadre nor Cooper know anything about; someone I only met a few days ago. She's got no connection to the cadre, and no love for terrorists.'

She? Briefly, Rebecca wondered whether 'she' and Steve were lovers, then she brushed that aside: the point was, would 'she' be up for what Steve had in mind? 'But will she have me?' she asked, already hoping. 'You'll have to give her some reasons, won't you? She'll have to know I'm on the run from . . . something or other.'

'I may tell her who you're running from.'

'But you said she doesn't have any connection with the cadre, so how — '

'That's for certain highly personal reasons. I'll ring her up now and talk to her. When she understands, I think she'll take you in. She's . . . like that.'

'Like what?' Rebecca's voice was bitter, but Steve could see a longing in her eyes. 'Like a fool?'

'She's no fool. Generous in heart, I'd say.'

'To an absolute stranger, as I am?'

'When she knows what it's about, I believe she will.' And as he said it he thought — that's one of the things I love about her, I suppose. Love? Yes, love. Strange, to become aware of such a private thing, such a special thing, at a time like this.

'She's one in a million, then,' Rebecca said.

'I'd agree with that . . . If she says OK, you'll go?'

Rebecca smoothed her hair back behind her ears, straightened her sweatshirt. 'What's her name?' she asked.

'Hanna. She's five or six years younger than you.'

'Lucky Hanna. Yes, of course I'll go. And Steve — if she does this for me, I'll never forget it.'

* * *

Hanna was reading in bed when Steve called her. Putting down her book she reached for the mobile on her bedside table. 'Yes?' she said, brusquely, impatient to get back to her novel. But the moment the caller gave his name she forgot the book completely: the world Steve Remmick lived in was where she wanted to be. It's not time for him to know that yet, though, she thought as she listened to his apologies for telephoning her so late at night.

'I wasn't asleep, anyway, just reading in bed,' she said. 'We were pretty late back last night, weren't we? I was tired tonight — '

'Hanna, I have a very great favour to ask of you.'

His voice had changed. His apologies had seemed rather rushed, and now the urgency driving him came across the line to her. She responded to it at once. This was Steve, so it was easy: she would give him no less than she would expect him to give her if the chips were down — total commitment. 'Providing it's within my power, I'll do anything you ask,' she said.

Steve had no doubt he could take her words quite literally, and for a few seconds he was silent, lost in the wonder of it, her personal avowal so great a thing.

'But I can't do anything at all till you tell me what it is you want me to do, can I?' she pointed out, laughter in her voice. 'Come on, man, be brave! Get it said!'

'I have a friend who's in serious trouble — a woman, a relative by marriage, a few years older than you. She needs to lie low for a while.'

'And you want her to do that here in my house?'

'That's what I'm asking, yes.'

'How long would it be for, exactly?'

'Three days, no more. Long enough to give me time to arrange for somewhere else.'

'Beginning when?' Yet — a complete stranger, to live her in my house? It'll be . . . an *invasion*. Also dangerous, perhaps? In the light of the chosen secret life I'm presently engaged in, it could be dangerous to both me and — far more importantly — to those infinitely bigger things my secret life is in service to?

'Tonight. Now, in fact . . . Hanna? Are you still there?'

'You really mean, immediately?'

118

'Yes.' God, what a thing to ask, to spring on her like this in the middle of the night! It must seem totally mad to her, and probably brings back horrible memories of the days when that brother of hers was trying to force her into terrorism. But she's Rebecca's last hope at the moment so I have to press on. I'd better spell it out loud and clear, though — have to, in all honesty. 'It's a matter of life or death,' he added bleakly.

'Why, Steve? *Why* does she need to hide? Is it to do with the men who were my brother's confederates? Terrorists?'

'I can't tell you *why*! I don't have *the right* to tell you. Hanna, listen. I think you already know I love you. Think on that, in the light of what I'm asking you to do. Then if you find you trust me enough, say yes. But if I haven't yet earned that honour, then you'd be wiser to refuse. If you do, I'll leave you in peace.'

Leave me? No, Steve. I couldn't face that, I'd do almost anything to prevent that happening. I've never known a man like you. I want to stay in your life — if that's possible, given the life I'm committed to living until Double Talk is over. Whoever *you* want to help, *I* want to help. Yes, now we're down to bedrock choices it's that simple. 'Give me an hour, Steve,' she said. 'Then bring her here when it suits you.'

6

Contacting Steve Remmick and Brad Cooper at 10 o'clock the following morning, Shaheen, refusing to give his reasons, had ordered them to meet him in one hour's time in the safe house known to the initiated as White's, situated in a back street near Oxford Circus. Its ground-floor premises operated as a public house; the rooms on the first storey provided comfortable but aggressively secure accommodation for personnel accredited to Operation Desert Wolf.

Cooper arrived last and ten minutes late and, finding Shaheen sitting at the head of the rectangular table near the window, with Steve on his right, took his place opposite Steve. He made no apologies for being late; he simply greeted Shaheen in elaborately phrased Arabic, favoured Steve with a louche grin and a *sotto voce* 'You look played out, I hope she was worth it', then sat down.

'Liam still following up on the Remmick bitch, then?' he enquired, dark eyes direct to Shaheen's. 'I gave him a bell just before I left this morning; got no answer, though.'

'As you would have learned had you seen

fit to arrive on time, Kidd failed to report to me by the deadline I gave him.'

'*What?*' Cooper thrust head and shoulders forward across the table, sudden anger ugly in every line of his face. 'Hell! what d'you mean, *failed to report?*'

'No more and no less than the words say. Kidd's orders were to report to me by eight thirty this morning.'

'So he didn't. What've you done about it?'

'I put surveillance on his apartment soon after I awarded him the interrogation of Mrs Remmick.' Shaheen's voice measured, his eyes cold. 'At eight forty I contacted them. They informed me that he had departed from his place at seven o'clock last night, and had not so far returned to it.'

'Surveillance — *on one of our own men?* You fucking son of a bitch!'

'Watch your tongue!' The warning lashed out fast and vicious as a bull-whip. But Shaheen had his temper under control; when he went on, his voice was as dispassionate as it had been earlier. 'I work in my own way, Cooper,' he said. 'In this case, clearly most usefully, for had there been no surveillance on Kidd's apartment valuable time would have been lost. Now we will discuss what steps are to be taken.'

Steve Remmick had not spoken since

121

Cooper's arrival. Everything that had passed between the other two was grist to his mill, he was giving their words and their body language his close attention: he would report on it all to Traven, to whom the state of relations within the top echelon of the cadre working with the controllers was of vital importance. And antagonisms and disagreements between Shaheen and his lieutenants were both good news for Traven: an enemy at odds within itself was possibly more vulnerable and certainly less effective because of it. So now Steve held his peace and — careful as always not to give any impression of being suspiciously hungry for information — observed the other two men as they squared up to each other. Shaheen the leader of the cadre, the man in direct communication with the three controllers engaged in ensuring that Operation Desert Wolf was ready to roll and Cooper, his first lieutenant, with big ambitions, as his boss was well aware. Shaheen cold and steely, a dedicated fanatic for his cause; Cooper extrovert, arrogant, hot-tempered, brilliant in action but unpredictable — unpredictable, and liable to be driven by self-interest.

Cooper had sat taut under Shaheen's reprimand, but as his boss fell silent, he slammed back his chair and stood up. 'Then I say, to hell with discussion! I'm going straight round to that bitch's house and get stuck into her, find out what happened between her and Liam last night — '

'Sit down and *listen*.' Shaheen's interruption was sharp and edged with contempt. 'On receiving the report from surveillance I sent men to the woman's house with orders to seize her, by force if necessary. They have already reported back: there was no one in the house, and it was locked up. One neighbour said he had heard what he referred to as 'a bit of activity, cars coming and going and so on' outside the house some time after midnight.'

'So what now?' Cooper still standing, aggressive.

'Surely it is obvious? We track down Rebecca Remmick. We have not heard from Kidd since he went to her house, so our investigation has to start with her.' Shaheen eyed him impassively. 'You will take personal charge of that, Cooper; run checks on her friends and acquaintances, use our network and sleepers for leads regarding her movements, taxis, hotels — '

'I know the drill. If you've got nothing more to tell me I'll be on my way.'

'Not yet. There are other matters to be dealt with — '

'More important than Liam? No way! I'm

not standing for that crap! Christ, Liam might be *dead*.'

'Immeasurably more important than Kidd!' Shaheen also was on his feet now, standing ramrod straight. 'I have just received the latest reports on the target sites from Mansoor. One of them calls for searching enquiry into certain of the security measures in place: you and Remmick will undertake that investigation immediately you leave here.'

It was a direct challenge — and Cooper met it head-on. 'Nevertheless, Commander, before I do that, and whether you like it or not, I will set in place a search for leads to Liam's disappearance. I'll use my own contacts for that. It won't take me more than an hour.' Almost, then, he laughed in Shaheen's face. 'These reports from the top guns — I've seen the earlier ones, they're mostly routine admin stuff,' he said. 'Steve here can sit in with you now on this one, then he contacts me and we get together on this job you want done. Me, I'm setting up the hunt for Liam first. *Ma'salaam*,' he said, inclining his head politely, then turning away and heading for the door.

'*Fi-aman-illah*.' Shaheen gave the polite response to Cooper's polite farewell with the same irony as that had been delivered, but his eyes were daggers and the muscles around his mouth were clenched tight.

Steve had watched the clash of wills with interest. Both Shaheen and Cooper were of great importance to him in his intelligence gathering for Traven: Shaheen, as cadre leader privy to the inner councils of Mansoor; Cooper, the cadre's head of security whose friendship he had assiduously cultivated — and fully exploited — since committing himself to Traven and now, during these countdown days to the climax of Desert Wolf, hoped and expected to milk of further top-secret information. He had no doubts as to the outcome of the confrontation. Shaheen, having swiftly weighed the pros and cons, would decide that at that moment, with Desert Wolf under inspection and the controllers working in the field, his overriding consideration must be to avoid a bruising and divisive showdown with Cooper; therefore he would not push things to the wire. But he would stash the incident away in his mind and, at some time in the future, would make sure that Cooper paid the price for his defiance of orders.

As the door closed behind Cooper, Shaheen resumed his seat and opened one of the three files lying in front of him on the table. 'Cooper will have cause to regret these challenges he indulges in,' he remarked harshly. 'Once his usefulness to Desert Wolf has ended he should watch his back.'

'Speaks good Arabic, though, doesn't he?' Steve thought it wise to change the subject. 'Where did he learn it? He never talks about his time in the Middle East.'

'His accent is good, but his vocabulary is, shall we say, *limited*.'

'How come?'

'You didn't know?' Shaheen smiled that narrow, closed smile of his that seldom reached his eyes. 'That is perhaps understandable; it is a thing he would perhaps be wise not to broadcast except in certain circles. Cooper spent four years working with Hizbollah. He served first in Syria; from there he was sent to Lebanon, where he saw action in the Beka'a Valley and in the south of the country.'

'Interesting.' Extremely interesting, it was background knowledge that would help to fill in a blank period in Cooper's CV that had intrigued but baffled MI5 for some time. 'I can't see why Hizbollah should want him, though. Surely they've got plenty of their own to call on?'

'They have indeed — now. But Cooper had two assets which only a few of their own had at that time: expertise in certain weapons and, even more importantly, reliable contacts for their acquisition. These made him a welcome guest among our people.' Looking down then, Shaheen opened the file, found the page he wanted and ran his eyes over it as he went on speaking. 'This latest resumé of the controllers' reports that I've had from Mansoor indicates that arrangements for the enrolment of our agents in specialist and advanced courses in English Language at the selected colleges are all proceeding smoothly — '

'London, Brighton, Birmingham, Cardiff, Bradford.' In a congratulatory monotone Steve reeled off the names of the cities earmarked for the linguistic component of Desert Wolf. 'Good news for us.'

'The language placements were always likely to be the easiest to secure, of course. Unfortunately, the report details one other area of immediate concern.'

'Where's that?'

'Cambridge, the aviation course. At Oxford, Taunton and Guildford, the airfields nearby, admissions are proceeding normally. One of our applicants at Cambridge, however, is experiencing ... not difficulties exactly, rather say delays, *inexplicable* delays. For one thing, verification of his existing pilot's qualifications appears to be taking an unusually long time.'

'So Mansoor wants it investigated?'

'At once. He orders that two particular sleepers in the S.E. England area are to be alerted for immediate action. You and Cooper will attend to this. I will give you Mansoor's sealed orders to the sleepers before you leave here.'

'We both go down there at once?'

Shaheen nodded. 'You will follow the usual wake-up procedures, and be present when the sleepers open their orders. You are to answer any questions they put to you, provided they are relevant exclusively to the questioner's sphere of activity. On your return to London you will both report to me in person.' Shaheen pushed the file aside and sat back in his chair.

And then Steve saw a look of exultation spread across his face, the deep-set eyes brilliant as he envisioned the dream. 'I now have the exact date and the chosen site for the final meeting of our controllers,' he said. 'That occasion will see the culmination of three years' work over here. At it, each of them will make his sworn statement regarding his own field of inspection, the whole will be recorded — and those declarations will be the signal for the active phase of Desert Wolf to commence. Think of it, Remmick! Desert

Wolf will swing into action: here in Britain there will be a network of bases established at which the very best of our volunteers will acquire further skills — men sworn to use those skills in agressive service to our cause!'

Watching him, Steve perceived Shaheen the fanatic, a man enraptured by visions of imagined acts of surpassing valour under-taken to carry terror and destruction to the enemy — and he thought, thank God that for every one of your kind, Shaheen, we have a thousand who believe in a different way of doing things, a different approach to the whole business of living on planet Earth.

But now isn't the time to tell you so, is it! Damn right it isn't! 'And the supreme beauty of Desert Wolf is that once the controllers have declared it action-ready it will *go on* doing the job for us,' he said with the required amount of enthusiasm. 'Year in, year out, in varying numbers and from various countries, volunteers will gain knowledge and expertise here that will enhance their capabilities and performance.' Then, because the opportunity was there — it would follow on naturally from what Shaheen had just been saying — Steve put the vital question to him. 'So, where and when will the final meeting of the controllers take place, sir?' he asked. 'Now Mansoor has agreed to your suggestion that I should do the recordings I must make my preparations, so I need to take a look at the room I'll be working in.'

'All in good time, my friend.' Shaheen had banished the zealot in him to a less public place, he spoke now simply as the leader of one of the Desert Wolf cadres operating in Britain, no more than that. But no less, either, Steve warned himself in the secrecy of his mind, and met the enigmatic eyes with his customary, and carefully practised and maintained mixture of brother-in-arms resoluteness and loyal-disciple deference. 'Be easy in your mind, Steve. You will be informed of the venue in good time to do all that is necessary.'

Steve waited, hoping for him to elaborate, but he did not, he simply sat relaxed in his chair, that give-nothing-away smile of his masking his hawkish face. When the silence began to drag, Steve got to his feet. 'Right, I'll be on my way then,' he said. 'Have you any special . . . er, message for me to pass on to Cooper?'

'There is none.' With a slight but unmistakably contemptuous gesture of his right hand Shaheen consigned Cooper to temporary oblivion, then picked up one of the files in front of him and began studying it.

As he went downstairs and out on to the

street, Steve became aware that he was sweating slightly. Shaheen, he's a man who is somehow a little apart from the rest of us in the cadre, he thought. With him I'm never quite sure how much he knows and what he intends to do with whatever knowledge he has. And that's not a comfortable situation for a man in my position to be in, a man who's operating as one of Shaheen's trusted lieutenants — but is in truth one of *Traven's* agents. That straight-lipped, cruel smile of Shaheen's — cruel? Yes; on recalling it as it was just now I'd go along with 'cruel' to describe it. Doubtless it's open to other interpretations, which is, of course, why it's there. With Shaheen, recently, I'm never unreservedly certain he isn't simply playing cat-and-mouse with me. That in fact he's suspicious of me — to what degree God alone knows, but it can't be anything serious, or I'd be a dead man by now! — and feels I'm somehow not playing quite straight with him. But he's putting up with it for the time being because while doing so he can keep me under observation *and* be ready to cut me down fast if and when that should prove necessary. Whereas if he has me disposed of straight away, even side-lined, he'll have to use manpower, time and energy to keep up his guard against some new agent being inserted in my place. By God, I came close to discovering the time and place for the controllers' final conference just a minute or two ago, after Cooper left —

Cooper! The name jolted Steve Remmick out of introspection and into the only-too-present crisis. Now, Cooper knew that Liam Kidd was unaccountably missing since going to Rebecca's house — and he was already out there setting agents of his own to track her down so he could question her! So he, Steve, had better get in on the action. He must keep in with Cooper, monitor his progress and then, if Cooper got close to Rebecca, he must somehow defeat him — without exposing himself as Traven's mole in the process.

But hard on that realization came one which was killer to his heart. Rebecca was sheltering in Hanna's house: if Cooper tracked her to it *he would blitz Hanna also.*

★　★　★

Alone in the safe house after Steve had left, Shaheen put down the file and sat quiet for a while, considering him. Steven Remmick, brother to Robert: and both of them of proven worth to the cadre. *And yet?* With Steven, I am never entirely sure of the strength of his commitment to us since his brother's death, Shaheen thought. When Robert was alive, and the two of them worked for us together, there was never any doubt in me that Steven was one of us. But of late, there is. Nothing overt, nothing big. It's no more than a feeling. I *sense* a difference in him, that is all: a sort of wariness in my presence that was never there when Robert was alive — and should not be there now.

It's nothing stronger than *sense*, however. I have no proof of any sort, not even a whisper of evidence against him; and with his exceptional expertise in IT and electronics in general he has been and, for a while at least, will continue to be, of great value to us. So the nub of the problem is this: in the cadre's present situation, with everything we do geared to ensuring the security and success of the controllers' final conference, it is almost impossible to prove the positive of Steve Remmick's loyalty; only if some disloyalty on his part is made manifest by his proven words or deeds can I justify to myself, or anyone else, a move against him, and by then it might easily be too late! So I have to make sure, as far as it is in my power to do so, that there truly is no evidence against him.

This decision made, Shaheen acted on it, telephoning three of his sleepers resident in Greater London and nearby who had contacts in either media or counter-terrorism circles and organizations. Two of these were male; he rang them first, and ordered them to be on the alert for any suspicious rumours regarding the loyalty of Steven Remmick. The third was a woman, and her he left to last. For two reasons he placed great trust in her. One was that she had been delivered to him as a sleeper for the cadre by a true-born fanatic of the Cause, the courier who had died when Rob Remmick crashed the drug-carrying Toyota two years ago; the other was that during the last two-and-a-half years she had provided him with some very useful information. Her greatest asset as a sleeper for him was that she was in contact with Traven of MI5 and, to some extent, seemed to be trusted by him. Her *nom de guerre* was 'Tagarid'. Shaheen called her now.

'Tagarid,' he said to her, although when she answered the call she had given her real name — thereby he identified himself. 'Have you anything for me?'

'I have nothing new on, or from, Traven.'

'You have heard of Steven Remmick?'

'You know I have.'

'Yes, you would be aware of him. Robert's brother.' In the safe house, Shaheen smiled: the Remmick brothers had indeed given her good cause to feel animosity towards them, knowing as she did that on the night Traven had driven the Toyota off the hill road they had both survived the crash and run free — leaving her brother to burn to death at the scene. 'As I've told you before,' he went on, 'it is my belief that Steven Remmick is devoted to our cause. But one of the controllers has voiced doubts about his loyalty, and has demanded further checks.'

'Which one of the controllers?'

'That question is not yours to ask.' Suddenly, his voice was hostile.

'Then I withdraw it.'

'You have no choice!' Then resuming his authoritative-yet-friendly tone, he instructed her to intensify her attempts to discover more about Steven Remmick.

'But all my informants have feelers out already, I don't see what more I can do!' she protested.

'Work on Traven. You were close to him once — '

'I broke *close* contact with him. You know that.'

'Mend the break.' His voice had hardened again.

There was a slight pause. Shaheen noted it in passing but attached no importance to it.

'Traven would never be so careless,' she said, finally.

'You could . . . encourage him.'

'It was never like that between us. We were never lovers.'

'That fact is also known to me. What I meant was, you might get more from him if you were.'

'No. Traven is not a fool.'

Shaheen did not press her further. To attempt such a move when the woman was unwilling and the man as streetwise as Traven, might jeopardize Tagarid's security. Nevertheless, her refusal to co-operate angered him and he tucked the incident away in his mind as a mark against her.

7

Seated at a table for two against the wall opposite the café's street entrance, Hanna Tregorian watched Traven walk towards her. For so influential and determined a man, he was — when he so chose, as now — surprisingly accomplished at moving among his fellow men without attracting attention. Until he was within ten yards of her he kept his head down. Broad-shouldered and of average height, he was light on his feet and very polite as he made his way between the tables: just a bloke going to meet a girl for a coffee. But then, as he drew closer, he lifted his head and looked at her, looked straight into her eyes.

Three years ago I came close to loving this man, Hanna thought as she met them. But then when he spoke to me of us marrying . . . there were feelings inside me that got in the way. Loving had no part in those feelings, there was only anger and bitterness — and a degree of fear, I suppose, on my part.

I still love her, Traven thought. Over the last two years she and I have only actually met together in person — what? Half-a-dozen times or so, no more. We've done a great deal of work together, yes, but invariably it's been conducted over the phone because frequent meetings carry the possibility of being observed, while written communications carry the terrifying possibility of passing into the hands of the enemy by interception or other manoeuvrings. But now I see her again, I know I still love her. Strange. Sad. Beautiful, in a way.

'Hello,' she said to him.

There was no smile on her face, but — ? 'Good morning,' he said. 'I hope I'm not late?' Thinking as he spoke, what I see in her face now tells me that between us, from her point of view, it's the same as it was before; she cares for me, there is a deep rapport between us, but on her side it isn't love, and there's still that one thing which is an insurmountable barrier between us. Well, if I can't have the married love I'll settle for the close rapport.

'A few minutes, perhaps' — she smiled — 'which shows some improvement on past form. It's nice to see you.' There's still that same percipience and self-reliance in those steady eyes of his, she thought. Don't ever walk right out of my life, Traven, please don't do that. 'I ordered tea, it should be here in a minute.'

'Darjeeling?' It had been her favourite.

'Plain whatever-comes. I've moved on, you see.' Her broadbrowed, tanned face had returned to its usual serious cast.

She never did smile easily, Traven recalled, though when she was really happy she had that gorgeous, gamine grin that used to make my heart turn over. 'I've moved on', she'd just said — and not only in regard to the tea she preferred, he knew that for a fact; she'd had a lover a year ago but it hadn't lasted long.

Get back on track, man! he ordered himself, and asked abruptly, 'You didn't mind me giving Steven Remmick your address?'

'If I had, I'd have told you so when you phoned and asked.'

'Of course.' Stupid question, he rebuked himself, as spur-of-the-moment, escapist questions so often are.

'I can look after myself. You know that.'

'I wouldn't have suggested such a thing to you if I hadn't been sure of it.' But then the waitress brought their tea and, standing beside Hanna, set it out on the table. I tend to be over-protective of women, Traven thought, as he watched her, and perhaps that was one of my mistakes with Hanna. But it wasn't the reason she wouldn't have me, was it? That was something far more —

'Thank you,' Hanna said to the waitress, and began to pour. 'How did you ever manage to turn Steve Remmick?' she asked, keeping her eyes on what she was doing.

'Why are you interested to know?' Traven's tone was neutral.

'Just . . . I'd like to, that's all. Or is there something top secret about it, something you can't trust me with?'

'No, of course not.' He was watching her hands as they dealt with the tea. He had always liked her hands: they were large and strong, the palms broad, the fingers long and bony. 'Peasant hands', she'd called them once, grimacing and confessing to a long-time pipe-dream of suddenly discovering them transformed, almond-nailed, soft-fleshed and elegant. But he admired their strength — also their deftness; her touch always light but decisive and assured. But then she said something that stung his heart.

'Actually, I asked you that because I find I like Steve very much,' she said. 'So, naturally, I'm interested to find out how he metamorphosed from being one of the Remmick brothers, that thorn in the flesh of MI5 and MI6 — the 'quiet one' of the duo, yes, but active and important in Shaheen's cadre — into . . . well, what you've told me he is now. It can't have been easy, to do that.'

140

Traven studied her face. She did not seem to mind, meeting his gaze frankly. And then it came to Traven quite suddenly — she's in love with Steve, and it shows. What I'd like to see in her eyes for me, but never did — *it's there for him*. Breaking eye contact with her, he drank some tea. As he replaced his cup in its saucer, she spoke again.

'I want to *understand*,' she said quietly. 'Please, tell me.'

Why should I not? he thought. Time to finally let go of dreams, Traven. She stepped away from you for reasons that are still valid. 'To me,' he began thoughtfully, 'the Remmick brothers always seemed very different from each other. Robert was dynamic, extrovert, charismatic; Steve was the kid brother always living in his shadow, dazzled by his daring and splendour. Robert was born for terrorism, Steve was not: that's how I saw it. So after Robert died it occurred to me it might be possible to reason Steve out of that destructive way of life — and into one in which his insider knowledge and position would be invaluable.' Pushing aside his cup, Traven leaned his forearms on the table and went on, thinking back as he talked, warming to his subject. 'Steve first came to me two months after Robert's death,' he said, and then went on to tell her how Steve and he had

141

talked things through and, eventually, Steve had asked if he could work with him against Shaheen and the cadre and all they stood for.

'You mean he simply said to you 'I'd like to be an MI5 mole in Shaheen's cadre, will you have me?' ' An incredulous half-smile was on Hanna's face.

Traven eyed her, deadpan. 'That's it, more or less word for word. Bizarre, isn't it?'

' 'Mighty oaks do from little acorns grow',' she murmured into the silence growing between them.

'There's no denying the truth of that. Though one should perhaps add that a great many acorns either get gobbled up by squirrels or simply never sprout at all for a variety of reasons.' But then the slightly cynical expression that had spread over Traven's face faded. 'Steve is proving an extremely valuable double agent,' he said. 'He has an ability to fit in with whatever situation he finds himself in, and with the other people who are in it with him. He's a very ordinary, yet at the same time a quite remarkable young man.'

After a moment, Hanna nodded. 'I think that's right. I suppose it's one of his strengths.'

Traven's eyes sharpened. He had a well-founded respect for Hanna Tregorian's intuitive gifts — and Steve Remmick was a mole of his in a highly sensitive and vulnerable position with a vital job to carry through in a few days' time. 'Since you're getting to know him well, maybe you can help me,' he said. 'Desert Wolf, as you're aware, is approaching a defining moment in its development. Our counter-operation Double Talk is on course to strike it down at that climactic moment. That will be a complex manoeuvre, and Steve's part in it is pivotal — if he fails, Double Talk itself will fail. So I need to know all I can about him. Therefore I ask you, what are his weaknesses?'

Her eyes hardened against him. 'I met him for the first time only a few days ago, how can I possibly — ?'

'For you, it's likely that's enough. Especially as — correct me if I'm wrong — you and he are already pretty . . . close.'

She looked down. After a moment she said quietly, 'I think perhaps he trusts too easily.'

Traven pressed her for more, but he was given no more. Hanna shook her head and said with a touch of anger that if she had known he had asked her to meet him solely to cross-examine her about Steve Remmick, she would not have come.

'You'll tell me, though, if you have any

reason to suspect he's not levelling with me?' Traven asked.

'Why would I know?'

'Because — perhaps — you have fallen in love with him?'

'As you say — perhaps.' Then, smiling brilliantly into Traven's face, 'So what *did* you summon me here for, then?' she asked, using a caustic 'summon' to turn their conversation bluntly to business matters.

'To have your face-to-face assurance that the presence of Rebecca Remmick in your house isn't an unacceptable security risk to you. And — to see you again, Hanna.'

Taking her time over it, Hanna refilled her cup. Somewhat to her own surprise she had found herself rather enjoying the older woman's company. She had stayed at home the day after Rebecca's arrival, and the two of them had found an immediate ease together, the slightly self-conscious social politeness natural between two strangers thrown at short notice into close contact rapidly developing into a real and easy friendliness.

Watching her face Traven saw its somewhat severe lines soften a little, and realized all was well. When — late on the night of the Liam Kidd killing, and after the MI5 unit he had called into action had done the job he had asked of them — Steve had telephoned him again and told him he'd sent Rebecca to take refuge with Hanna Tregorian, he had been appalled. He had been careful to express no more than disapproval of Steve's action, though, and to suggest that Rebecca ought to be moved to some other secret location in a few days' time. This, because Steve Remmick was not privy to the fact that for some while now, Hanna — like Steve himself, but mostly on side issues only — had been passing information on Shaheen's cadre to Traven.

'Steve's making arrangements for Rebecca to leave the day after tomorrow,' Hanna went on, 'so the time she's with me will be too short for there to be any risk — ' She broke off, frowning. 'No, that's not really right, is it? If one's acting as a sleeper one can never say that with absolute certainty.'

'It's something sleepers have to live with. Have you talked with her, to make quite sure she isn't running with Shaheen? Like I suggested you should?'

'I have, and I'm certain she's not.'

'Isn't that perhaps too solid an assertion to make on such short acquaintance?'

Hanna leaned back, giving thought to her answer. 'It was extraordinary,' she said slowly. 'I suppose it's like they say, it's easier to talk your heart out to a stranger than to someone you've known for ages. Yesterday, Rebecca talked a lot. We cooked together; we ate and drank; we did some weeding in the garden; mowed the lawn — whatever, there was talk all the time and most of it came from her.'

'With sympathetic, but sometimes leading, questions from you.' Which is one of the things that make you such an effective informant for me, Hanna, he thought.

But she was frowning again. 'With Rebecca it wasn't like that,' she said coldly, and Traven realized she had intuited what he had been thinking and resented it.

'I shouldn't have said that. I take it back.'

'You can't. Once said, it exists — for the person it was said to, anyway.'

'So I apologize. Go on about Rebecca. Please.'

'Nett result, as far as you are concerned, two truths about her: one, she loved her husband deeply and passionately, and is still convinced that the accident he was killed in was engineered to ensure his death — although when I asked, she admitted that her conviction was purely instinctive. She paid out a lot of cash to private investigators after the accident, but none of them came up with anything.'

'And your second truth?' he asked, for she had fallen silent.

'That she hasn't ever been, is not now, and

never in the future will be party to terrorist activity of any kind.'

'Is that all? Nothing else, after a whole day together?'

Looking into Traven's face Hanna thought, thank God I didn't actually fall in love with you. I respect you, admire you, care deeply for you, but to have loved you would have destroyed me . . . Then suddenly another thing about Rebecca came into her mind, and she passed it on to Traven. 'She wanted quite desperately to have children, but Robert didn't. He laid it on the line to her, she told me: no children. He didn't want them, he said, he wanted just Rebecca and Rob. And if she persisted, he'd turn angry-quiet and take off, go drinking with his male friends. All that, it was something she couldn't handle. Didn't know how . . . Do you know the *real* reason why he wouldn't go her way?'

'Yes. I hadn't realized you did, though. Have you told anyone else?'

She shook her head. 'I see it as something which belongs to Robert Remmick alone.'

'Then we're on the same wavelength,' he said.

'We usually are . . . about most things,' she added, then smiled at him and moved away from personal matters to details that affected herself regarding Double Talk, scheduled to climax in a few days' time, dove-tailing in with the departure of the controllers from the place where they had held their final conference.

8

The following morning, Hanna, having decided to work at home for the next couple of days, went in to the office to collect the files and papers she would need. In the course of her bus-and-train journey into Central London, however, her mind was not on her job. It was on the possible implications, for herself, of what — on Steve's asking — she had done to help him, taking his sister-in-law (to give her temporary refuge, he'd said) into her own home. She wondered again, as she had the previous day following Rebecca's arrival, *why* she was on the run, and who she was running from. Since she was Robert Remmick's widow there was a chance that it was Shaheen and the cadre who were after her. And should that be so — then what if Shaheen were to discover that she, Hanna Tregorian, was providing Rebecca with a hideout? Dear God! she thought, should that come to pass, Shaheen will —

Stuff that! Don't dare so much as think it! How on earth can he find out? There's no way *anyone* can find out! Impatiently she pushed her sudden fears to the back of her mind, reassuring herself with the reminder that Traven and Steve were the prime movers in providing a hideaway for Rebecca; they'd keep the whole thing under wraps, take every precaution.

At the office she collected the papers she wanted — passing the time of day blithely but briefly with various colleagues as she did so — and then made her way home.

Letting herself in a few minutes after midday, she found Rebecca on the telephone in the hall, and went through into the sitting-room, took off her jacket, sat down on the sofa, leaned back into the cushions and closed her eyes . . .

'Hi. It's great you're back!' Rebecca came in looking relieved and excited, blue eyes alight, blonde hair tousled. 'Was it OK at the office? You got all you went in for?'

'I've survived, as you see.' Hanna sat up. 'Was that Traven you were talking to on the phone?'

'Himself. He called a few minutes before you came in. Shall I make you a cup of coffee? You look — '

'I could use a stiff gin and tonic.'

Rebecca mixed two gins at the drinks trolley. 'Like I told you before you left this morning, when Traven rang me last night he told me he's working with Steve to a find a proper hideout for me; and on the phone just now he said he's got it sorted.' She brought the drinks across, passed one to Hanna then sat down in an armchair facing her. 'He's arranged for me to go to a safe house at a place called Redbourn, it's about a dozen miles south of Luton.'

'Sounds good.' Hanna raised her glass. 'So here's to the safe house in Redbourn. I hope everything works out well for you there.'

'For me, here's to Traven.' Suddenly, Rebecca was quiet and tense. 'I drink to Traven, Steve — and Hanna Tregorian,' she said. 'To all of them I owe rather a lot.'

Hanna laughed. 'I didn't do very much, bed-and-board for a night or two is no big deal! So tell me, what exactly has Traven arranged?'

'He'll send a car for me tomorrow afternoon.' Rebecca's voice was steady, but Hanna noted with concern a sudden loss of confidence take hold of her as she faced up to the uncertain and threatful times ahead of her. 'The driver will know where to take me. I'm to live in a house — no, it's a bungalow, Traven said — called Innisfree. Once I'm there I report in to Traven every day. He'll tell me when it's safe for me to . . . to move away from there — when it's *really* safe, long-term safe, I mean. But somehow, Hanna, I don't think I'll ever go back to Wychwood.'

Hanna did not ask why. Whatever those reasons might be, they were Rebecca's business alone and best left so, she herself did not want to be more involved than she already was. 'What time will you be leaving here, did he say?' she asked — saw Rebecca flinch and rushed on, stricken with remorse for her own lack of common courtesy. 'Sorry! I didn't mean it like that, as if I couldn't wait to see you gone. It just seemed natural to ask.'

'It's me, not you. I'm so uptight — a bit scared, actually. Traven just said it would be between five and six o'clock.'

'Good. By the way, did you get things organized at your boutique in Ealing? It can't be easy for whoever you've left in charge, taking over at such short notice?'

Rebecca's face brightened. 'Oh, there's no problem there!' she said, relieved to talk about her shop. 'Jasmine — she's my manageress, she's been with me ever since I opened Roberta's, I told you, I think? — she's marvellous.' Rebecca leaned back, running a hand though her blonde hair. 'She's pretty used to taking over for me. Since Rob died I'm always going off on trips for a week or so at a time — spur-of-the-moment stuff,

152

visiting friends, a fashion show in Paris, maybe, that sort of thing. Jasmine's a treasure — not the greatest brain in the world, except fashion-wise, but she loves the job at the boutique and, to be honest, she's better at it than I am. She knows all aspects of it inside out: buying, display, accounting — and selling, of course! At selling, Jaz is an absolute natural. Customers *like* her — they trust her judgement; she's got a knack with them. I suppose she's better with them than I am because when she's dealing with someone, and they're discussing the dress or whatever, she *really is* interested in whether or not that particular garment suits that particular person — whereas me . . . Mostly, I think, I see just the dress and hope they'll buy it!'

'Sounds as if you're lucky to have her. D'you want to ring her again later, see how the day has gone at the boutique? Do, if you like.'

'Thanks, I might do that.' Rebecca sat forward, her brow furrowing, her mouth twisting in a moue of uncertainty. 'Actually, when I rang earlier she told me she'd had a sales rep in and the two of them had a bit of a barney. It seems Jaz made a complaint about goods received, the rep hit back, and the situation turned rather nasty. When I spoke to her Jaz was very worried — the woman had been quite threatening and Jaz was afraid she'd be in again so I told her to contact me if she did turn up and I'd deal with her myself. I gave Jaz this phone number to call me on.'

'You *what?*' Hanna shot bolt upright where she sat, shock and disbelief in every line of her face and body.

Rebecca had frozen, was staring at her in wide-eyed dismay. 'Oh *God!* I forgot your home number's ex-directory, and I wasn't supposed to give it to anyone! It doesn't matter, does it? I'll be gone tomorrow, anyway. But if you like I'll call Jaz straight away and tell her not to — '

'Do that! Do it *now!*'

'Of course.' Rebecca was on her feet, placating hands reaching towards Hanna, begging forgiveness. 'I'm so *sorry.*'

'Make sure she hasn't scribbled this number down anywhere — and even more important, make sure she hasn't already *given* it to anyone!'

As Rebecca hurried out into the hall, Hanna went over to the front window and stood staring out. But the sun-drenched colours of her garden were not reaching her: behind her eyes all had turned dark and menacing. Shaheen's agents were certain to be working on Liam Kidd's disappearance,

154

and they'd be fast, thorough, and — if occasion called for it — utterly ruthless. Every lead to what might have happened to him would be assiduously followed up — and obviously Rebecca would be a prime target in that exercise. Equally obviously, as soon as Shaheen's agents discovered she had also as it were dropped out of sight, they would ensure that all her known contacts were exhaustively investigated for clues as to her present whereabouts. So the staff at Roberta's would be questioned — which, almost certainly, would result in it being discovered that Rebecca had been in telephone contact with her manageress.

From there it was a more or less sure-fire bet that Shaheen's agents would home in on Jaz and try to filch from her that phone number — *Hanna's* number, from which they could and would, by devious means they were certain to be familiar with, find out her home address.

'I think it's all right, Hanna,' Rebecca said, standing at the door into the hall.

'Only *think*? You can't say for sure?'

'How d'you mean?' The question was a delaying ploy; Rebecca asked it in order to give herself time to think things through. The temptation to lie to Hanna, was almost irresistible: she had only to make a definite statement of fact, to say 'Jasmine hasn't given your number to anyone', and then all would be well again between her and Hanna. But I mustn't do that, Rebecca thought, I really *must not* lie to her about this. I don't fully understand why it matters quite so much about the phone number but obviously it's got Hanna shit-scared — so I have to tell her the truth although I don't want to. Because without what she's done for me, Shaheen — worse still, Cooper! — would have me by now. 'The trouble is,' she admitted, moving closer and looking Hanna in the eye, 'I've got a suspicion that when Jaz told me just now she hadn't passed your phone number on to anyone, she was covering up; she wasn't telling me the truth. She said she hadn't written it down for anyone, but then when I asked if she'd given it word of mouth she sort of . . . hesitated. Finally she said no, she hadn't. But — now, as I think back — I'm not sure she wasn't perhaps keeping something from me. Not *really* sure.'

'Dear God.' Hanna's mind was racing. The situation called for rapid and high-level action. Both were essential because if Rebecca was run to ground here at Hanna's house, the repercussions with regard to herself and Steve Remmick would blow Operation Double Talk clear out of the water.

She had to inform Traven at once. 'I must get on the phone,' she said. 'I'll do it from my study upstairs.'

Using the emergency calling code, she was through to him in three minutes. Succinctly, she reported to him the situation at Roberta's as just related to her by Rebecca. Twice only he interrupted her with questions; his decision came hard on the last words of her account.

'We'll have to get Rebecca out of there earlier than planned,' he said. 'The arrangements regarding her safe house can stand, but I'll reorganize time and transport.'

'You'd better not send a car to my door, Shaheen's agents might already — '

'Agreed. I'll set something up, ring you back.'

'Move fast, Traven. Please move fast.'

Traven caught the apprehension in her voice, and sought to calm it. 'I will. But remember, Shaheen's top priority at the moment is Desert Wolf: for him, that occupies the whole of the picture he's looking at; Kidd's disappearance is way off in the background. I'll have Rebecca Remmick out of your house by five o'clock this afternoon at the latest, but I'll get on to it straight away, so it might easily be considerably earlier. And, listen, Hanna, after she's left you are to go through your place and remove every trace of her stay with you — '

'I know all that. Get on with your part in this, and leave mine to me. I'm pretty good at it by this time. Good enough, I hope.'

'I'm confident of that. And Hanna . . . '

'Yes?'

'Wish Rebecca God-speed for me. And put some heart into her; she's probably going to need it.'

'I'll do that . . . for all our sakes,' she added softly as she hung up.

★ ★ ★

Traven was right about Shaheen. All the cadre's energies of thought and action were indeed focused on ensuring that Desert Wolf was on course: that the controllers' inspections were being successfully conducted in secrecy and security, and that arrangements were in place for the summit conference at the conclusion of which they were to commit to tape the declarations that would propel their operation into its positive action phase.

However, in his assessment of the reaction of individual members of the cadre to Kidd's disappearance, Traven made one serious error: he assumed that Shaheen's mindset in relation to it would be reflected in each and

158

every one of them. But that was not the case. In Brad Cooper's mind the disappearance of Liam Kidd stood paramount. Cooper, Kidd's role model hero and the man who had helped him to plan the assault on Rebecca Remmick, had sworn to himself that whatever Shaheen might say, he himself would take drastic steps to find out what had happened to his mate and then — if the worst scenario he could imagine turned out to be the true one — avenge his death. Sure, thought Cooper, he was committed to working with Shaheen until Desert Wolf was over, but that didn't mean he was simply going to put other things on hold until then. Not on your life! Not Brad Cooper, when a real mate had gone missing, no way!

Apart from the divers personnel engaged in Desert Wolf, Cooper numbered among his friends and business contacts many individuals skilled in various types of criminal activity whose professional services he bought in as needed. Men and women both, but criminals all, these people stood ready at all times to pull off a job for Cooper — he paid exceptionally well, did Brad, in cash or kind, your choice. And on storming out of Shaheen's meeting, Cooper had immediately set about calling in the services of certain of these individuals who ran agents specializing in missing persons investigations. Thus, and swiftly, he had set in motion an immediate, wide-ranging and in-depth search for Liam Kidd that was financed and directed by himself alone. Only when that was up and running did he set out for Cambridge to join Steve Remmick in sorting out — as ordered by Shaheen — the difficulties Zayani was encountering there.

One of these agents — Gilkes by name — had taken on the job of running surveillance on Roberta's and discovering anything he could about the owner's present whereabouts, her staff at the boutique, and the established lines of communication between her and them. Gilkes, in his turn, had called in a disparate — and by some standards eclectic — selection of his acquaintances to assist him. One of these was an ex-girlfriend of Cooper's, Marika Jones. Now some thirty years of age, Marika was blonde, willow-graceful, and the possessor — when she chose to use it — of considerable style. A woman who loved clothes and high living, she was chic, streetwise, sharply observant of others, and quite a good actress. In the course of her life so far Marika had put both her inborn talents and her acquired skills to largely criminal use.

A few minutes after 11.30 that day she

visited Roberta's. Finding the boutique empty of customers, as she had thought and hoped it might be at that hour, she engaged Jasmine in a conversation that at once aroused the enthusiastic interest of Rebecca's manageress.

Jasmine was on a diet, given the strength of will to stick rigidly to it by the lure of the twenty-inch waist it promised as reward. This eating-plan dictated that breakfast should consist of one glass of fresh, unsweetened orange-juice only — and by 11.15 that day, famished, she had sent her sales assistant out for lunch early, consumed an apple and a banana, and then sat down at the desk in Roberta's office and set about the ordering in of a new range of leisure wear. From where she sat she could get on with her work and, at the same time, through the archway between office and shopping-area, keep an eye on the street-door until her assistant came back from lunch.

Some ten minutes after she sat down the shop door opened and a customer entered. Looking out through the archway Jasmine saw a well-turned-out woman come in and pause just inside the door, glancing around her — a tallish woman in a beautifully cut taupe business suit. Practised in on-the-spot summing up of customer-potential Jasmine

161

thought, this one's a go-getter and she doesn't lack either style or cash — and got swiftly to her feet, advanced through the archway to meet this promising, if slightly daunting, lady. As she did so, her experienced eye took in further key details fast: the customer was thirtyish; her hair short, blonde, expertly cut; suit, raw silk, eminently covetable; handbag, Versace; legs long and shapely — shoes a surprise, though, of excellent quality, yes, but the heels medium, not the expected stiletto or wedge.

'Are you Rebecca Remmick?' Smiling and self-assured the customer held out a hand, her eyes friendly but inquisitive, too, Jasmine noted.

Somewhat taken aback — and impressed, even a little overwhelmed by her evident sophistication and aura of with-it drive and purpose — Jasmine hurriedly disclaimed being the owner of Roberta's, then introduced herself and went on to explain that Mrs Remmick would not be at the boutique for a few days. 'Perhaps I can help you, though,' she said. 'I've been working here for years.'

'Nice of you, but it's Rebecca I want to see.' The words were accompanied by another smile but this one was no more then a social gesture, and the customer was already advancing towards the desk clearly visible beyond the archway. 'We'll go into the office here,' she said, 'and sit down and have a chat. Maybe there's a way you can help, hopefully we can sort something out between us.'

Jasmine found herself meekly following in her wake, murmuring 'Of course. Do sit down. If a customer comes in, you'll have to excuse me for a moment — '

'Naturally. But I shan't keep you long; Rebecca's the only one who can say yea or nay to what I'm offering here.' Seating herself in one of the three velvet-upholstered armchairs facing the desk, she opened her handbag, took out a card-case and flicked through it. Then as Jasmine sat down behind the desk, she extracted a card and placed it in front of her. 'As you see from that, I work with a very popular women's magazine,' she went on. 'We're considering doing a piece on Roberta's in our Christmas issue.' She smiled again then, adding, 'The resulting publicity would give quite a boost to your sales, I'm sure you're well aware of that.'

Jasmine picked up the card: it was plain but elegant, cream in colour and gilt-edged, the information on it printed in chocolate brown. Studying it, Jasmine learned that the woman now facing her expectantly across the desk was Elizabeth Antorini by name and a promotions manager for *Slant*, a monthly glossy.

'So when do you expect Rebecca back?' Silky smooth now, Ms Antorini's voice.

Keeping her eyes fixed on the little piece of pasteboard in her hand, Jasmine shut the question out for a second or two, desperately wondering what on earth she should do. An article on Roberta's in *Slant*! The boutique, featured in one of the big-circulation glossies — what a break that would be! And just think what it might lead to — why, apart from the sales, it might even get on the tele! This was the chance of a lifetime, it just had to be! Miss Rebecca would never forgive her if she let it slip by.

'Jasmine! I can't sit here all day waiting for you to say something.' Ms Antorini allowed a touch of asperity to sharpen her voice. 'Is Rebecca ill, or on holiday, or what? And when will she be back?'

Looking up, Jasmine met the hard brown eyes. 'Mrs Remmick said she'd be away for at least ten days. She's feeling stressed. She just said she'd be travelling around a bit, see-ing friends.'

'But what about the boutique? She keeps in touch, I imagine?'

'Oh yes. She rings in every day, and I have

164

a number so I can call her if I'm having trouble.'

'Ten days is far too long for me. If we're to have an agreement on this I need it discussed, agreed on and signed up to within the next three days.'

'But she won't be back by then!' Panic was setting in, Jasmine's face was crumpling up in dismay at the prospect of this chance of glory being lost — and the blame for the losing of it hers, *hers alone!* 'Can't I sign things on her behalf? I'm sure she — '

'No.' Just the one word, but Jasmine wilted under the put-down and the glacial stare with which it was delivered.

Mortified, and at a loss as to what she should do, she repeated what Rebecca had told her to say. 'She's resting, just. The stress — '

'Christ, then! *Stress*, you say? So wake up, woman, get with it! If she's stressed, this is just the sort of thing to give her a boost.'

'I know that, but — '

'Hell, this isn't getting us anywhere.' *Slant*'s representative imperious, dismissive and contemptuous of 'the help'. 'I'll phone Rebecca, speak to her myself. All I need at this stage is her verbal agreement after she and I have talked things over.'

'But I'm not supposed to give out her

phone number. Won't my say-so do? I *know* she'll want in on this — '

'No, your say-so will *not* do. Don't be stupid; a deal this big has to be agreed with the owner involved, not with some employee! And I haven't got time for all this. Either you give me the number on which I can contact her *now*, or I'm walking out of here — the project's off and it'll stay off. We'll go elsewhere, there's no shortage of takers for showpieces like this.'

Jasmine recognized a crunch-point when she collided with one. She had Hanna's home number off by heart, and recited it without further prevarication. Ms Antorini picked up her elegant business card from the desk, scribbled the number on it then slipped it into her pocket.

'You won't tell Miss Rebecca you got the number from me, madam, will you?' Jasmine said, suddenly regretting what she had done, uncomfortably aware that she might have been conned. 'I was supposed not to tell — '

'Oh, don't worry!' Having got what she had come for, and already on her feet, the lady in the taupe business suit smiled brilliantly at Jasmine. 'I'll cover for you somehow; you've helped a lot,' she said, and, turning on her heel, went through the archway and out on to the street.

'Elizabeth Antorini' returned to the scarlet Mercedes Sports car she had arrived in and parked nearby, drove clear of Ealing Broadway, then parked again and used her mobile. 'Brad?' she enquired, as her call was answered. 'Marika here. Gilkes was right with all that stuff he gave me about the help at Roberta's. Mission accomplished: assistant helpfully dazzled by brilliance of my offer — so I've got what you told me to get. What next?'

'That number you got — any idea where it's at?'

'Actually, I do. It's a Chesham number — and that happens to be an area I know fairly well.'

'And since I'm at Uxbridge at the moment that means it's only about thirty minutes' drive away for me,' Cooper said. 'Right, I'll meet you there. Can you name me somewhere for us to do that? Somewhere I can easily find?'

It was quickly arranged: rendezvous at a café-bar on the main drag by the name of Ringo's.

'I can't get away from here at once,' Cooper went on then, 'so best we meet there at . . . let's say five p.m. Between then and

167

now, Marika, you track down that number to its address — you know who to contact for that — then get yourself to the house and suss it out for me. And keep your mobile switched on; if there's any change of plan I'll call you . . . You've done good so far, girl. Now work on it, I can't wait to get my hands on that Remmick bitch. See you at five.'

'How d'you mean, suss it out for you?'

'Find out who lives there, keep track on comings and goings — hell, use your brain and get on with it! See you.'

Switching off his mobile Brad Cooper stood quiet for a moment, brooding on the developing situation. *Chesham.* He was a mite familiar with the area — it was where the drugs courier had lived, the bloke who'd snuffed it the night the Remmick brothers fell into the trap Traven had laid for them and got chased through the hills, and came to grief . . . Christ, but he was a bastard, that courier. A real weirdo. Fundamentalist fanatic to the core. Streetwise too, though, I'll give him that; he was never averse to making cash on the side. I went to his house in Chesham a few times. Met that sister of his who lived there with him, maybe she's still there, who knows. Hanna Tregorian, yes . . . Quite a looker she was — if you like the serious type, which I don't. Dead against our kind she was, to begin with, but her brother *persuaded* her to co-operate with Shaheen, yeh, he was a pretty effective persuader, as I recall. Bit of a coincidence, if the Remmick bitch really is holed up around there.

⋆ ⋆ ⋆

Cooper went back to the bar and rejoined Steve Remmick at the counter, where they were having a beer-and-sandwiches lunch. 'Got her — I hope!' he muttered to himself as he slid back on to his stool, handsome face exultant, dark eyes agleam with unholy joy as he contemplated interrogating the woman who had once spurned his advances — and who surely *must* have knowledge of what had happened to Liam Kidd. 'With luck I'll get to the bitch soon now and by God I'll have it out of her then, what went on between the two of them the night Liam went to her place — '

'Who's this you're talking about?' Steve's head turned sharply as, inside his mind, Cooper's angry words spun thought-wheels that suddenly interlocked and held fast, presenting him with one perception — one only, and that inescapable and appalling.

'Who the hell d'you think? That bloody sister-in-law of yours who you dislike so much on account of her refusing to work with you and Rob, with our lot! OK, I'm on Shaheen's job now because I'm contracted to it till Desert Wolf's over but — remember? — I set my own people to work on Liam's disappearance soon as I heard about it and one of 'em's just hit pay dirt. At least, I hope she has.'

'Smart move.' Keep your cool, Remmick, keep your cool. 'What's she come up with?'

'Got me the phone number the bitch can be contacted on now she's on the run from home — '

'Where does it — ' But Steve broke off and, cramming down the fears rising inside him, turned away and picked up his glass. Watch your step! he castigated himself. Control your voice, your words, your body language — Cooper's no slouch. 'So where-abouts is she, then, that nothing of a sister-in-law of mine?' he asked. 'Not hopped off abroad like she sometimes does?'

'Nah, don't think so.' Cooper pushed away his plate. 'Hang on, Steve. It ain't all cut and dried yet,' he said quite softly, elbows planted on the counter, brows drawn together as he reasoned things out, talking the situation through to Steve as he did so. 'My agent got the phone number, and from that she recognized the area — happens both she and

170

I know it, which is a bit of luck — and she's going to track it down, get the address. Only — it doesn't follow that the bitch I'm after is actually there *at the moment*, does it? Maybe she is, maybe she isn't. But it *does* follow — bully for me! — it *does* follow that whoever lives at that address is in contact with her. So hopefully I'm in with a good chance, either way. If the bitch *is* there, I'll move straight in and get her. But if she isn't, if whoever lives there is only a *contact*, for her — well then, I'll have to work on that person, won't I? Get some gen out of him or her.'

Realizing how close Cooper was to pinpointing Hanna's house as Rebecca's present hideout, Steve risked probing further. 'So how are you going to manage all this?' he asked. 'Isn't it going to be a bit difficult, you working privately on Liam's disappearance at the same time as you're hard at it on the Desert Wolf job, which requires both of us to be available and fairly mobile if need arises? There's the controllers' summit conference — '

'Fuck that. I'll get this job tied up quick now, I reckon. Be right back on the ball for Shaheen bang on time, then.' Talking about the Kidd affair had brought Cooper's simmering rage against Shaheen to boiling point again, and he had decided to call

Marika and tell her she was to meet him at that café-bar in Chesham in half an hour's time; he was heading up there at once. 'I'm going to check on this Chesham address right away,' he said. 'D'you know that area at all?'

'I've been there. Don't know it well, though.' Christ Almighty, I must warn Traven about this fast, or Cooper'll get there before Rebecca has a chance to leave.

Cooper drained his glass, banged it down on the counter then turned to Steve again. 'You'll help me out now, won't you?' he asked, angry eyes hard. 'Liam could be alive, man, and if we get a move on we might be able to make sure he stays that way.'

'But, Shaheen — '

'Him and Operation Desert Wolf are one thing, but Liam's my mate, and as far as I'm concerned he's something else entirely — he's my priority *in all circumstances*.' Cooper gave a thin-lipped smile. 'Work in with me, Steve,' he urged. 'Could be you'll need me to do much the same for you one day; there's more to the world you and I live in than Shaheen and his like.'

High honour among thieves? Steve held the dark eyes, keeping all expression out of his own. Sure, Brad, all you say is true and I respect you for it. But your priorities and mine are running on collision courses. 'No dice, Brad, my friend,' he said evenly; and then used the opening — he hoped — to gain time for Traven, time for him to alert *and help* Hanna and Rebecca. 'But I'll make a deal with you.'

'Yeah? Shoot, then — and make it quick.'

'We've only got one more place to go to here then our assignment's done — and it shouldn't take more than a couple of hours. So here's the deal: you hold off the Chesham affair and we finish things here together, then as soon as we're done you take off, hire yourself a car and head for Chesham, chase down that shitty sister-in-law of mine. Me, I report as planned, square everything with Shaheen, make it OK.'

'It's a deal. Let's get on with it!'

Steve slid off his stool. 'You go ahead. I've got to have a slash. See you in the car in a couple of minutes.'

In the event Steve's call to Traven took a little longer than that, it was at least four minutes before he got into the passenger seat of the Rover in the pub car-park. Cooper made no comment, however; he simply slipped the car into gear and drove off.

9

'Dear God.' Replacing the handset of the telephone in the sitting-room Hanna stood with her head down, eyes tight shut as she assessed the implications of the call she had just received from Traven.

'What gives?' Curled up into one corner of the window seat, Rebecca had been watching her anxiously.

'Quiet. Wait a moment. That was Traven, and I've got to think.' But lengthy thought was unnecessary: the threat to Rebecca and herself was clear and, as Traven had just pointed out to her, so was the course of action required to meet it. A few seconds later she looked up and went on speaking. 'You've got to leave earlier than planned, Traven's transport for you will arrive here in an hour's time, that'll be around four o'clock. So we have to get weaving. First, you finish your packing — '

'It's practically all done. I didn't bring much.' Sensing Hanna's urgency Rebecca swung her jeans-clad legs off the window seat and stood up, fear and apprehension coming alive inside her.

'Good, that'll leave us plenty of time to go over every room and make sure no trace is left of your stay here. And Rebecca' — Hanna went to her and laid a hand on her arm — 'when we've done that, we have to do it all over again; we have to double-check, because the clean-up has to be faultless. The way things stand now, nothing less will keep you safe.'

As Hanna spoke those last words, it seemed to Rebecca that, for a moment, a fey and haunted look crept into the dark, lustrous eyes, and in sudden panic she wondered what ghosts lived in the secret places inside Hanna's head. But then Hanna smiled at her and all was as before, the world was a safe place to be in — almost safe, anyway, and with Steve and Traven and Hanna on one's side absolute safety would come, in time it would surely come. 'Give me five minutes to wrap up the packing,' she said, carefully and determinedly upbeat, 'then on to the clearing up.'

'We'll do it room by room and check each one twice over. And see you keep well away from all windows.'

But suddenly Rebecca shivered, sensing some new dread in Hanna, a closely *directed* one, it seemed to her, something particular within the big picture of the situation.

'Something's happened, hasn't it?' she asked bleakly. 'Why the' — she bit back 'panic' and came up with a less frightening word — 'fuss?'

Briefly, Hanna hesitated: why add to Rebecca's fears? But the answer came hard on the question, decreeing openness: when your blood-enemy gets within striking distance of you it's best for you to know he has done so. 'Brad Cooper has found out you're here,' she said. 'It's likely he'll come after you himself.'

'*Cooper!*' Sick horror laid waste Rebecca's face, drained it of life. 'That's just what I was most afraid of, as you know. Liam Kidd's close mate — and to add to that, the man I choked off so humiliatingly when he tried to make out with me within a month of Rob's death . . . So damn sure of himself Cooper was that evening. He *sickened* me — and I told him so, straight out. He left me alone after that. But I've never forgotten the look on his face then. I can see it now, in my mind's eye, and it scares me stiff. I'm so afraid of him,' she whispered. Then suppressing the welling tears and throwing out a muffled 'I'll finish my packing,' Rebecca fled. Went up to Hanna's spare room — which was to be her refuge no longer, now no more than a friendly little place that had to be cleansed, with clinical attention to detail, of every sign that a woman by the name of Rebecca Remmick had — briefly — found sanctuary there.

Left alone, Hanna weighed up the likely fallout from this recent development of which Traven had just informed her. She and Rebecca must go through the house removing — destroying, if necessary — every scrap of evidence that any person other than Hanna had recently spent time there. Because of two things she was certain: Cooper would insist on searching her house — and his search would be merciless; he'd tear the place apart if he thought that was called for.

There was also one other matter about which she must take great care if — no, *when*, she had no doubt of that — Cooper tracked Rebecca down and arrived in furious search of her. Cooper was aware that Hanna was a sometime informant for Shaheen — though not, of course, that she was in fact a double agent for Traven. Therefore her own top priority — in all circumstances, as Traven had just impressed upon her — had to be that Cooper remained ignorant of that last fact. Which might not be easy to achieve.

★   ★   ★

Cooper made it to his meeting with Marika by 4.30, slipping into the seat facing her where she was sitting at a table near the door of the café-bar, nursing a Margarita. He had bought himself a whisky at the counter, glancing around him as it was poured and spotting her at once, the well-shaped head with its smooth, gleaming cap of thick blonde hair.

'So what've you got for me?' he asked, as he sat down — but then his mind registered the frown creasing her forehead, the jittery defensiveness in her eyes. 'Christ! If that bitch has run free someone's going to pay for it,' he went on, leaning towards her, anger building in his face, his voice ugly with the reined-in violence inside him. 'Go on. Spit it out. What's happened?'

Marika kept her nerve, meeting his eyes and steeling herself to answer him with the truth. In the course of their working relationship she had lied to him once, and he'd found her out. Cooper had called his subsequent punishment of her disciplinary action, but whatever the correct term for it might be, it had had the effect he desired: from then on neither he nor Marika ever had any doubt but that she would never lie to him again. Now, however, she was too afraid of him to tell him straight out.

'I don't actually *know* whether anything's happened,' she said. 'I couldn't get anything useful from the neighbours, you've got to be careful what you ask or they can get suspicious — '

'But there's something, isn't there? Come on. Give!'

It has to be, there's no escape. 'I kept watch on the house. The owner came out into the garden a bit before three o'clock — I knew she was the owner, one of the neighbours came up with a fair description of her *and* told me her name. She's called Hanna Tregorian and — '

'*What?* Who'd you say it was?'

'Hanna Tregorian.' Marika had jerked back at Cooper's question — she knew that look on his face. I'm glad I'm not that lady, she thought briefly, but then dismissed her, well aware that to safeguard her own continued well-being she must keep her mind on herself and Cooper, and the job she was doing for him. 'But I haven't seen any sign at all of that blonde woman you're after,' she went on — only to fall silent again as she saw that Brad was not listening to her.

'Christ Almighty.' Leaning back, he said it quite quietly, eyes fixed unseeing on some point on the wall above Marika's bright head as he probed the gob-smacking fact Marika

179

had just given him for possible advantages and disadvantages there might be in it to himself in his present urgent quest. Hanna Tregorian, sister to the courier killed on that drugs-run for the cadre: was she, or was she not, of any *serious* importance to Shaheen? That was one of the questions exercising Cooper's mind since the answer to it — or the lack of one proven either way — would, perforce, influence the manner in which he conducted his next move, a thorough search of Tregorian's house. He was already determined on that: Marika had established that the Remmick bitch could be contacted at that address, so obviously Tregorian had to be involved somehow in what was going on — she must be, it was her house! But if the Remmick woman was indeed in there, then it wasn't fucking likely that if he knocked at Tregorian's door and asked for her, young Hanna was going to say oh yes, of course she's here with me, do come in and have a chat with her! So . . . ? So the best thing for me to do is force my way into the house, hold Tregorian incommunicado, and take a look around whether she likes it or not. Yeah, can do — good thing I thought to collect those two heavies of mine on the way here, got them waiting outside now in the hire car. Yeah, can do, no problem with that. Only snag is — what if, then, we don't find that bitch there *and later on Tregorian lays charges against me to Shaheen? What if —* ?

'Brad.' Marika was desperate to give her final bit of information to him before her nerve failed entirely.

'Yeah?' His eyes dropped to her face.

'There's more to tell you — '

'Maybe Tregorian had tea out in her fucking garden?' he sneered. 'You got something important like that to report?'

'Please, just listen. OK, it might not be important but I'd better tell you, just in case.'

'Get to the bloody point!'

'I'm trying to. A few minutes after she'd gone back inside, this van turned up outside the house, one of those medium-sized things, you know, a Transit or something, I think. Dark blue. I couldn't see a name or anything on its side — '

'You got its number?' Cooper was all attention now.

'Well, no. I didn't think anything of it at the time, the van was just delivering something, I thought.'

'Go on.'

'Well, there's a garage built on the side of the house, with a short drive leading to it off the road. The garage door was open when I got there, and this van' — Marika was warming up to her story now, her fear of Cooper momentarily submerged as she concentrated on recalling what she'd seen earlier that afternoon — 'the driver backed it into the drive and right up close to the open door. Then two blokes got out of the cab of the van, opened up its rear doors and — '

'*Fucking shit!*' Cooper had been visualizing the action as she was describing it, and now one possible conclusion to it exploded inside his head — and he recognized it as an only-too-likely deathblow to the plans he'd just made. But — 'How the hell could she've got from the house into the van without you seeing her, though?' he demanded.

'There must be a communicating door; remember I said the garage is built on to the house?'

'Hell, yes. Could've happened that way easy enough, from what you say.'

'*Could have* doesn't necessarily mean *did*,' Marika pointed out.

But Cooper was on his feet — take the bad luck in your stride and get on with the job as it now stands. 'You push off home now,' he ordered. 'I'm going in there, with back-up. I'll get the truth out of Tregorian.'

Can't say I'd like to be that Hanna Tregorian at this moment, thought Marika, watching him shoulder his way out past a hand-holding young couple coming in off the street.

★ ★ ★

Hanna opened her front door to them on the second ring of her bell: Brad Cooper looming tall and grim-faced, feet planted six inches short of her threshhold, and two shorter but burly men whom she did not recall seeing before standing one either side of him, close at his shoulders.

'Hanna Tregorian?' but he had recognized the young woman facing him, clad in jeans and a loose, dark-red overblouse: tall and slim, dark eyes — hostile now — in a broad-browed, high cheek-boned face. Undeniably she was beautiful.

'We've met before. You're Mr Cooper, you used to come here to see my brother,' she said coldly. 'I'm busy. What do you want?'

But her question gave him an opening. 'Not 'what' — who. I'm looking for Rob Remmick's widow, Rebecca,' he said.

'I don't know her.' *Luckily I'm quite good at lying,* Hanna thought. *It's a talent I acquired courtesy of my brother who was a brilliant practioner of that black art.* 'I've heard of the Remmick brothers, obviously. But a female Remmick? No. Sorry, I can't

183

help you there. So if you don't mind I'll go back to my ironing.' And she began to close the door.

But Cooper's two heavies had their orders and, though thickset, were both fast and experienced in forced entry of this sort. A couple of minutes later the front door of the Tregorian house stood closed and its frontage presented a picture of serenity to the outside world. Behind it, however, the atmosphere was tense, latent violence staining the air of the hall. Acutely aware of it, Hanna played a card she had intended to hold in reserve.

Facing Cooper, ignoring his hard men close at her back, 'Are you acting on Shaheen's orders?' she demanded, fairly sure that he was not.

Cooper parried the thrust. 'You still in contact with him?'

Be careful now, Hanna; give this man nothing that might lead him to suspect the true state of affairs regarding yourself, Shaheen, and Traven. 'I am,' she said. 'And my services to him in the past allow me to call on his protection against gratuitous violence.'

'More fool him. Me, I reckon you'd have shopped your brother to MI5 if you'd dared. Shaheen — '

'Shaheen is a man who pays his debts! I'm

184

under his protection.'

'Why should you need it now, if you don't even know Rebecca Remmick?'

'Why, indeed?' Hanna turned his own question against him. 'So if you want to search my house, Brad Cooper, go ahead and do it . . . And don't forget the cellar,' she added, a grin transforming her face as, suddenly, she was seized by a childish desire to needle him.

To her surprise Cooper saw it that way too and, momentarily disarmed, grinned back at her. 'We won't forget anything, Hanna Tregorian, you can be sure of that,' he said coolly. 'We're old hands at this kind of thing. And seeing you're a friend of Shaheen's we'll leave everything as we find it — always providing we don't find the Remmick woman here, or any trace of her.'

'I'll go round with you — '

'You will not. You will sit down over there' — he pointed an imperious finger towards the two chairs set one either side of the narrow table on the far side of the hall — 'until we've finished, and Murchison here will keep you company. You won't make a fuss, will you?'

'Why should I?' she countered. Then added with a flick of that mocking grin again, 'And don't *you* make a fuss when the two of you have done your thing — and got nothing from it.'

Cooper and his henchman Jacks were fast and thorough. Leaving the cellar until last they worked through it together then went back up the stone steps and into the hall: the search had taken them half an hour only.

'Well?' Hanna rose to her feet as they came in.

Cooper's face was set, his strong brows drawn together in an ugly, lowering frown but he battened down the frustration and fury seething within him. 'You win,' he said, halting in front of her. '*This* time, you win.'

'What's that supposed to mean?' The man's physical aura at that moment of confrontation seemed to her to be the personification of violence, and in instinctive reaction to it she stiffened, lifted her chin.

Cooper gave her no direct answer. 'I've got a feeling she's been here,' he said. 'Upstairs, especially. That room with the curtains with fire colours all over them — I could smell her in there, I swear I could *smell* her.'

'Why are you pursuing Robert Remmick's widow like this?' Hanna could not think of anything else to say — and she felt a need to say something because the silence grew oppressive after he stopped speaking and simply went on standing there in front of her, his eyes ranging hungrily over her face.

'I've got very good reason to believe she killed a mate of mine, Liam Kidd. And when I get to her she'll admit that — after which she'll die too, so's things are evened up ... What was that van doing here this afternoon?' His question abrupt; he hoped to take her by surprise.

'Van? Oh yes, that was a couple of hours ago.' Suddenly she smiled full into his face, a smile that went right into her eyes, ridiculing him. 'You're thinking I might have smuggled her out in that? Grow up, Mr Cooper, grow up.'

He would have liked to hit her then. They both knew it, but she kept her smile in place, and he held his hand. It cost him, though: Hanna saw that, and was glad.

'What was it here for, if not for that?' he asked, after a moment.

She relaxed, her story ready now. 'Tell me, when you were upstairs in my study did you notice an armchair over by the window, the one covered in flowery cretonne, deep-seated, very comfortable-looking?'

'Yeah, I saw it. So what?'

'It belonged to a friend of mine. I coveted it, and she sold it to me — at a knock-down price, too, I'm happy to say. She was tired of it, she said. Well, a couple of blokes she knows

187

brought it round this afternoon in their van — carried it upstairs for me, as well, nice of them, wasn't it?' Then suddenly she frowned. 'How did you know about the van?' she asked, her voice still quiet but laced with hostility once more.

Realizing he had made a mistake, Cooper moved swiftly to limit any damage already done; he certainly was not going to admit that he'd had an agent watching her house. 'Shit, forget it! I'm wasting valuable time here,' he said and, swinging away, made for the front door. But when he reached it he stopped and faced her again. His two heavies had followed him, and now ranged themselves one either side of him. 'OK, you, win, Miss Tregorian, you win — *this time*, like I said before. But there's something odd going on here, and I've got reasons not to trust you. However, Shaheen does, you say. And as he's the boss, OK, I'll go along with his view for the time being. That being so, there's no call for him to know about me coming here this afternoon, is there? After all, if you go to him about it I'll have to give him my side of the story, won't I? I'll have to inform him of my suspicions that you're involved in the Remmick woman's disappearance — I can back them up, you know. And if Shaheen gets to mistrust you, I reckon he'll withdraw his protection from you — then I'll be free to come back and question you with no holds barred, won't I? *No holds barred.*'

Hanna shrugged. 'What's just gone on here isn't that important; I see no need to inform Shaheen of it. Doubtless you were doing what you saw as your duty. Now, get out of my house.'

Cooper eyed her up and down where she stood facing him, stiff and straight in her overblouse and jeans, hair held back in a bright kerchief. You bitch! he thought, you fucking, lousy bitch! Your brother was one right-on bloke, one of our own through and through, he was. But you — Christ, years were wasted before he succeeded in persuading you to do your bit for us. God knows why Shaheen goes on protecting you. If I had my way —

Suddenly, he gave her a wide grin. 'See you again — maybe!' he said, then turned and went out, his henchmen close on his heels. He did not know quite why he'd flung that last crack at her as he left. But one thing he was sure of: Hanna Tregorian had not levelled with him; he felt in his blood and bones that she was his enemy. How or why that should be so, Cooper had no idea. But his knowledge of it both intrigued and angered him and, determined to do all he could to find out what lay behind her enmity, he detailed Murchison to maintain low-level surveillance on her house for the next twenty-four hours then report back to him.

★ ★ ★

After her front door had closed behind the three men Hanna stood quiet for a few moments, letting her anger against Cooper and all he stood for quieten down. Then she made two telephone calls. In the course of each she reported on the search visit she had just been paid by Cooper and his heavies. Her first call was to Shaheen, who reacted to his lieutenant's wildcat action in pursuit of Rebecca Remmick, and its failure, with the cold fury she had expected. And to her great relief he accepted without question the subtly reasoned but contemptuous explanations with which she rebutted Cooper's allegations against herself in the matter, blackening his name in the process.

Her second call was to Traven, who listened to her account with great interest, occasionally breaking in with pertinent questions. 'So how shall I proceed now?' she asked him finally. 'Are there any particular precautions I should take?'

'Only one. And it's not a precaution, it's an

order, Hanna: a diktat which you are to obey to the letter.'

'Go on.'

'I know you've been seeing a lot of Steve Remmick. I think you're probably in love with him, and I know he's in love with you — no, don't interrupt! Listen to me, I've nearly finished and you may speak when I have. My diktat is this: starting two days from now — on Monday, that will be — you are to have no personal contact with Steve until the completion of Double Talk and, concomitantly, of Desert Wolf.'

'Not even telephone calls?'

'Not even that. No phone calls, no meetings, no letters, no e-mails.'

Hanna argued no further — the taboo was good practice, obviously, and she had been half expecting it — but she made one last plea. 'May I at least be the one to tell him?'

'No. I will do that. And Hanna — I don't know exactly where the relationship between you and Steve stands at the moment, but if you were thinking of going public with it, even among your family only, please don't; keep it under wraps until the operations are over.' Traven listened to her silence for a second or two and then — sharply — broke it. 'I'll be on the line to you within the hour; there's news I want you to hear. Be available.'

10

The next day Steve drove out of London to Herne's Hill Farm, which lay some eight miles south of the city of Oxford and was the home of Mr and Mrs Hargest, Hanna's adoptive parents. Hanna had gone there late the previous evening. Steve had been invited for lunch, to meet the Hargests for the first time. Running clear of London as the sun was getting into its stride above the eastern horizon, he found the countryside brilliant with sunshine. Never before, he thought, as he drove through summertime middle England — *never* before have I felt so free.

Situated halfway up the slope of south-facing Herne's Hill, the Hargests' farm had stood on its own land for centuries; its paddocks and fields ran down to the river flowing along the floor of the valley below. The road he was travelling followed much the same course as the river and, as he turned into the drive up to the house, he saw it above him, old stone walls mellow in sunlight. Bill Hargest, Hanna had told him, had been born at the farm; Jocelyn had come to it on her marriage, from her home at Stoneyford village ten miles away. Having no children of his own, Bill operated in partnership with his younger brother, Harry, and Harry was father to two stalwart sons, both of whom were at agricultural college and were, by Hanna's account, 'sworn to the land, they love Herne's Hill Farm and it'll be theirs some day'.

Having heard the car coming, Hanna was at the garden gate to meet him. 'Hello, lovely to see you, glad you could make it so early,' she said, resting one hand on the car's open window as he pulled up alongside her. 'It's best you park in the courtyard round the back, I'll get in and direct you.'

But quickly he covered her hand with his own and held it tight. 'Hanna,' he said, 'Hanna I want — '

But she leaned in and kissed him on the mouth — just the one quick, light kiss then she stepped back. 'We've got all day,' she promised and, slipping round the car, got in beside him.

'You look so different,' Steve said, 'The times we've been out together you've always looked so — ' He grinned suddenly. 'Hell, what's it matter? It's just that I've never seen you in shorts, sleeves rolled up and — '

'And hair all over the place like now?' It was caught up high at the back of her head and tied with a scarlet ribbon. Laughing, she lifted her chin and swirled the lustrous mane from side to side. Steve reached out and ran his hand through it then looked into her eyes.

At once she was still. 'Drive, Steve,' she said, all laughter gone from her and the dark eyes haunted. A goose walked over my grave just then, she thought, turning away from him: as he looked at me a moment ago I knew he and I love each other, and I was afraid. Afraid of the love, him and me being what we are: double agents both in a dark and violent war, and loving each other . . . Then she dismissed the goose, telling herself that things would work out all right; as soon as Desert Wolf was destroyed, the two of them would leave Traven and his world and live together in the real one. On this thought, she smiled. 'There's roast beef for lunch, and peas picked by these very hands,' she said, 'and pudding is strawberries from the PYO down the road.'

He followed her lead. Looked at his watch and said, 'It's only eleven. Long time to lunch — ?'

'Then after we've parked the car you and I will walk over to Margaret Howarth's place on the other side of the valley to fetch the cream to go with the strawberries. But you must meet Jocelyn first.'

* * *

However they did not go to fetch the cream, for it turned out that Margaret Howarth had dropped it off at Herne's Hill on her way into Oxford. So for Steve the rest of the morning was taken up in meeting Jocelyn Hargest — Bill and his brother were out on the west slopes and would not be back until lunchtime, she explained — and having coffee in a flowers-and-sunshine sitting-room. As they sat and talked, it came out that for the last fifteen years Jocelyn had been secretary to the county antiquarian society, and from then on Steve plundered her store of knowledge while Hanna refilled cups, passed round biscuits and listened, smiling: clearly, her lover and her adoptive mother were getting on well together.

After lunch the Hargests went about their own affairs, Bill and Harry to the stables, Jocelyn to change into work-clothes and go to war on the nettles, dandelions and their like invading her kitchen garden. Hanna and Steve wandered off together, taking a grassy path that led through the gardens and on into the wood beyond, which, she told him, was known as Badgers' Spinney. They did not talk much: lunch had been an ebullient affair so now they found it good to be alone together, and quiet.

Coming to the far side of the spinney they halted, standing in sunlight now, in front of them meadowland spreading down to a brook bordered with pollarded willows. 'Good, isn't it, 'specially after London,' Hanna said. But there was an unease in her because although Steve had — just three days earlier — confessed to her that he was Traven's mole in Shaheen's cadre, a double agent for Traven and MI5, all she had given him in return was half of the truth about herself. She had confessed to working for Traven, but had presented herself as a very minor player indeed, one engaged merely in low level office chores. Steve had no idea — so far — that she, like himself, was operating as a double agent: was a trusted sleeper for Shaheen while informing on him to Traven and feeding him false or deliberately misleading information given her by Traven for that purpose. Abruptly, she dismissed those matters from her mind: she had suggested this walk through the wood for a personal, specific reason, so she'd better get on with it! Leaning back against the trunk of an ash tree, she told Steve a certain truth which, soon after they first met, she had decided she was honour-bound to reveal to him; it would be good to

196

tell him today, she had thought earlier as they were at lunch.

'There's something I want to tell you,' she said. 'It's about your brother Robert.'

'*Rob?*' Steve stood staring at her, his face wiped clean of all expression. Nevertheless she intuited the immediate grief in him, the sense of loss. And her heart went out to him — but what she had to tell him was, it seemed to her, a truth that, now Rob was dead, belonged to Steve. In all honesty it belonged to him whether he wanted it or not.

'Hanna. Go on. If there's something you think I ought to know, say it. Tell me.'

'Robert has a daughter,' she said.

'No, that can't be so. Rebecca wanted children but — '

'Not Rebecca. Long before he knew Rebecca. By a girl named Angela.'

He stood frowning at her as if she were a wayward child trying to . . . to con him into belief in the impossible. 'But what you're saying doesn't make sense,' he said reasonably. 'Rob wasn't a guy who had much time for kids; they got in his way, he used to say. Besides, he never mentioned a girl named Angela . . . When was this supposed to have happened?'

'Nineteen eighty-two. He and Angie were both eighteen.'

'But Rob . . . This girl, Rob would have married her if — '

'It wasn't that way round. Angie wouldn't marry him. She had a lot going for her, you see. She was very attractive, very clever — and extremely ambitious. She wanted a different life from the one your brother seemed to — '

'Not Rob's kind of life, you mean!' Steve's interruption harsh, and Hanna saw his face taut with — anger? No, not that, or at least not only that. Anger was there, yes, but it seemed to her to be overlaid with something more complex — regret, relief, even a sort of yearning?

'Perhaps,' she said quietly, pressing her palms against the trunk of the tree at her back, feeling its bark cool and smooth against her skin. 'But I've no way of knowing things like that about her. Neither have you.'

Steve gazed at her blankly for a few seconds, then turned away. 'This daughter of Rob's, she must be around twenty-one years old now,' he said. 'Maybe, since you seem to know quite a lot about this, you can tell me where she's living, what she's like — '

'Don't make wild assumptions! Listen, Steve. I know a bit about her, yes, but not a lot. I know that the girl named Angela bore your brother Robert a daughter in nineteen eighty-two, brought her up by herself until nineteen eighty-six, then in that year married a very wealthy man whose father was a big wheel in oil. Anything else you want to know will have to wait. I just thought it was time you became aware that a girl who was your brother's daughter existed,' she added, suddenly — and sadly — feeling separate from Steve in a way she had not experienced before, a cruel way: it hurt.

'And what made you think that now, particularly?' he turned to her again. 'Why *now?*'

'I don't know — no, wait, I *do* know! It's because of Rebecca. She's so scared, Steve, so horribly frightened — so maybe it'd help her, if you told her? It'd give her something to hold on to? Maybe? To know that a child of Robert's — '

'How did you find this out?' Steve's mind had changed tack and he stepped close to her, spoke angrily, aggressively. '*Who told you?*'

Hanna had her answer ready. It was not easy to say it to him, however — not with him like this, bitter with resentment and futile regret. Nevertheless it had to be said: if she was going to live her life with Steve she had to level with him, give him all she was, and knew. 'I learned it from my brother, the

199

courier who was killed in that car crash you were in, you and Robert,' she said. 'My brother was blackmailing Robert, about the child. I don't know how he'd found out about it, but he had — and Robert paid him to keep quiet. My brother told me that Robert loved his wife very much and was afraid that if she found out he was keeping something like that secret from her, she would leave him and — ' But she broke off there: Steve had turned his back on her, was standing with his head down, the heels of his hands pressed hard against his forehead as though trying to stifle thought itself.

He was. *I killed the courier . . . I put certain of my old skills to good (for me) use . . . fatal pressure-point manoeuvre:* the remembered words from Rob's letter to him were running riot inside his head. He could not control them, they devil-danced there howling like mad things — then, suddenly, vanished. And across a desert of silence a thought came from nowhere, severe and without pity: you have to be as honest with Hanna as she has just been with you; you have to tell her the secret Rob gave into your keeping; you have to tell her that your brother *murdered* hers.

For several seconds Steve Remmick quailed before this ruling — then he defied it. He laughed in its face — and to his intense surprise found it to be no more than a chimera; inside his head all was quiet now. Taking his hands away from his face he turned back to Hanna. He felt as if he had just been on a long journey beset by perils — but now she was standing there just as she had been before he 'left' her: young and lovely Hanna, dark eyes greeting his and she so sure inside herself. Sometimes, truths get too old to have present relevance, he thought. Anyway, what the hell, I'm not going to risk losing her.

'This girl, Rob's daughter. D'you know her name?' he asked.

'Nice to have you back.' Slowly, Hanna smiled at him. Then she pushed herself away from the treetrunk. 'Let's go down to the brook,' she said, linking her arm through his. And together they strolled on across the meadow. 'She's called Donna . . . '

11

Leaving the farm after a picnic tea out in the garden — just Jocelyn, Hanna and himself, together with an elderly and courteous retriever with a fondness for homemade chocolate cake — Steve drove back to London on auto-pilot, his mind still with Hanna. Letting himself into his flat, he showered, put on chinos and a black polo shirt, then sat wearily down on his bed and rang Traven, who had returned that afternoon from a brief trip to Bonn. As he picked out the number he noticed it was already 7.30, and recalled that he had arranged to ring at 7.00.

On answering Traven was as even-tempered as ever, cutting amiably across Steve's apologies. 'Forget it. No harm done. Let's get straight to business. You saw Shaheen yesterday evening?'

'As planned. The declarations will be made on Thursday, no change there.' Miraculously and on the instant, Steve returned to Traven's world. Straightening where he sat, he dismissed everything from his mind except the briefing he had received from the cadre leader the previous evening and the priceless nugget of top-secret information Shaheen had — at long last — given him. 'It was a hell of a long session, but I finally got told the venue for the controllers' final conference — '

'You've seen the place?'

'Not yet, but — '

'Sorry, shouldn't have interrupted you like that. Go on, Steve.'

'As I reported to you several days ago, Shaheen put forward four suitable sites, each of which he had gone over in person with an eye to security, accessibility and so on. It was up to Mansoor to make the choice. He's opted for a place called Ashburn, which, according to Shaheen, is a pretty classy private house a few miles north of Greater London belonging to a long-standing business confederate of Mansoor's by the name of Westerman. Mansoor's spun him a good story, presenting the controllers' conference as a slightly dodgy business deal in progress and calling for further discussion at a locale offering secrecy and on-site security. Mansoor will be responsible for providing both at Ashburn — '

'And will of course use Shaheen and the cadre for that.'

'Exactly. Which means that, as hoped, I'll be in the know all the way from now on.'

'Excellent news. One point, though, what about Westerman's own staff at Ashburn? Won't they — '

'No problem there. It seems Westerman himself sometimes operates close to the edge of the law — and frequently uses Ashburn for dodgy dealings of his own. Therefore, he's staffed the place with people bound to his service one way or another who are paid keep-your-mouth-shut-in-all-circumstances wages — and are well aware of the severe penalties that will follow if they fail to earn them.'

'Westerman — he's known to the police?'

'As a dubious but usefully connected and highly successful businessman against whom they've never yet been able to prove anything.'

'Hopefully we'll help them out with that, come Thursday . . . What else have you got for me?'

'Not much yet, except that the procedures covering the controllers' conference — the agenda for the meeting, the format of the individual declarations to be made by the controllers, and the taping of those declarations — have now been agreed on by them and by their boss in Paris.'

'So it's working out as we hoped. You will be in *sole* charge of getting those final declarations on tape, and then producing the copies of it?'

'I will. Then Mansoor takes the master tape, Zayani and Bakhtiary receive one copy each — '

'And the third copy, which you will have run off secretly and concealed about your person, will, in the fulness of time, be delivered to me.'

'That's the plan.'

But suddenly and for the first time that evening Steve's voice seemed to Traven to betray the slightest touch of . . . doubt? No, nothing so definite as that, it was simply less upbeat. 'Stick with it, Steve,' he said quietly. 'Only four days to go. After that — '

'After that I'll be free.' *Free in a way I never really understood about until today, with Hanna at Herne's Hill Farm.*

'If you so choose.' As Traven said this there was surprise in his voice because everything that had passed between them so far since Steve Remmick was turned — or had turned himself? — had led him to believe Remmick's greatest ambition was that, following naturally on from the successful completion of Double Talk, he would continue to work, through Traven, within the framework of MI5. *Until now, Traven thought, I've assumed — with good reason, or what has* seemed to me good reason — that Steve's desire to be involved in the fight against terrorism is so strong that it has never entered his head that his present participation is only a one-off, and after it is over he'll walk away from me and counter-terrorism. My mistake? Perhaps. On balance, though, I still think —

'How's Rebecca?' Steve asked. Since obviously it would be better for him not to contact his sister-in-law while Double Talk was so close to climax, Traven had promised to pass on to him all news of her.

'No different from when you asked the same question on Saturday.' Then regretting his faintly sarcastic tone, Traven hurried on. 'Don't worry, she'll stay safe. Only you, me, and Hanna know where she is.'

'Sure. So you said. But Cooper's hell-bent on questioning her — '

'Shaheen will be keeping him fully occupied, I imagine.'

Catching a faint impatience in Traven's voice, Steve stifled his misgivings about Rebecca — what Traven had just said was patently true, Cooper would surely have his hands full with setting up security at Ashburn. 'Right,' he said. 'So OK . . . Like before, I'll inform you of any new development as the action re the controllers and the

206

conference unfolds. No change in codes and so on, is there?'

'None. One last question, however: in your opinion, at what point between now and the final conference would it be best to put in place round-the-clock surveillance on its venue, Ashburn?'

'*Surveillance*, comprehensive and official? Christ, no! Please! The last thing we want is MI5 or MI6 blokes round there! The area's secluded and very upmarket, I'm told: a single error by a single agent could — '

'Those men don't make errors.'

'Whatever, it's best not. There's too much riding on that conference.'

Including your life, Steve Remmick, Traven thought. And in my book the man at the sharp end of the job is — up to a point — entitled to have his opinion on matters highly relevant to his survival taken into account. 'Very well, Steve,' he said. 'Up till now you've been beavering quietly away inside the enemy lines, but now as we approach the day you metamorphose into our raider — so it's your call.' Your call for the moment, Traven added in the secrecy of his mind. But I'll have to put surveillance on Ashburn soon: we'll have Special Forces going in there on Thursday, and I won't have them sent in 'blind'.

MEMO (personal): Shaheen to Mansoor

1. *Ref your orders for your body servant Mohammed RAMADAN to accompany you at all times at Ashburn, and throughout your stay there to be accorded full status and privileges as your aide and personal assistant, responsible to you alone.*
Action taken as ordered.

2. *Ref Level 5 supplementary vetting on domestic staff at Ashburn.*
Completed: All employees certified clean.

3. *Ref in-depth investigation into the pre-1998 private life of the woman known as Stacey McCain, the call-girl presently favoured by Mr Westerman.*
Exercise completed. We have no cause for concern re McCain.

12

Steve and Cooper spent the Tuesday
preceding the conference at Ashburn, each
driving there in his own car. A medium-sized
manor house fronted by landscaped gardens,
the residence lent to Mansoor for the
controllers' final meeting was set in its own
two acres of land and lay well back from a
minor road running along a narrow valley;
higher ground rose both behind it and facing
it across on the far side of the road. House
and land were girdled by a belt of woodland
circumscribed by a three-foot high greystone
wall: family and guests entered the property
through the elegant pillared gateway in the
west-facing side of the wall, domestic staff
and commercial callers through the more
utilitarianly designed entrance at the rear.
Owned by Otto Westerman, a Brazilian
businessman with assets in South America,
Germany, and Texas, but used more frequently by his friends and business associates
than by Westerman himself, the property was
run by a manager, a long-time, resident
retainer of his who was devoted to his service.
Westerman was free with his money and

contributed generously to regional causes. None of his neighbours knew a great deal about him personally, however: all of the in-house servants had been hired in London; they showed no interest in local affairs and entertainments and, without exception, headed back to the city when they had time off; while visitors — usually in threes or fours, occasionally in larger groups — came and went without creating much interest or comment round about, assumed to be either friends or business colleagues.

Arriving mid-morning as arranged, Steve was ushered by the manager — a grey-haired, hard-faced man, Baxter by name, polite but far from obsequious — into what he referred to as the morning-room, and found Cooper waiting for him there. They told Baxter they would both be back at 1.30 and would like a plate-lunch to be served them in that same room, then went their separate ways, each about his appointed duties. Cooper was responsible for all outdoor security measures, which Shaheen had ordered him to keep to the minimum possible without compromising effectiveness, so that day he planned to inspect the lie of the land surrounding Ashburn and plan out his guarding of it in readiness to brief the team he had on standby for the job. Steve's work that day was simpler: he had only to familiarize himself with the furnishings and accoustics of the room to be used for the conference, then bring in from his car, and instal, the greater part of the equipment he would need to tape the declarations to be made by the controllers, and the copies thereof.

Finishing these preparations with a good half-hour to spare before their lunch, Steve made his way to the library, which he had spotted through its open door as Baxter was escorting him to the morning-room. Going in he stood stock still, gazing around him in wonderment. 'Oh, Christ!' he murmured. 'If only . . . ' and for a moment he came near to liking Mr Westerman. Then he gave himself over to exploring the meticulously catalogued archaeology section and delving into its treasures.

'Steve! Hey, Steve!' Cooper was at the door of the library, looking impatient. 'Come on — Baxter's done us proud, and I'm starving. I've told him to leave it and push off,' he went on, as Steve joined him. 'He wanted to stay and serve us but I reckon we can just about manage without him, eh?'

Sliced ham, pork pie, four kinds of cheese, Cornish pasties, salads, rolls and butter — and tea, as asked for, off to one side of the table. The two men helped themselves and sat down to eat.

'How did your recce go?' Steve asked. 'Everything under control?'

Cooper nodded. 'No real problems,' he answered. 'Possibility of hostile chopper landing, nil. Access roads, three, all minor, one of them unsurfaced. I'll only need one man on watch-and-report at each of them. Front and rear gates, OK — two men on each. Observation points excellent, thanks to those low hills t'other side of the road from here: I'll have three men strung out along those, and I'll be stationed there myself, at the top of the hill dead opposite the front entrance.'

'What time will you and your blokes be in place?'

'All positions will be manned from seven a.m. Thursday.'

'Are all your men armed?' It's always best to check whenever you can and in as much detail as you can.

'What the hell d'you think? Handguns only, though — fuck it. Shaheen's orders. We've got no reason to expect trouble, he says, the whole op's been clean from the start according to reports from his surveillance teams and various sleepers in a position to know.'

'You don't think he's done right, then?'

Cooper shrugged. 'He's the boss, so what

212

he says, goes.' But then his face darkened, and he darted a quick, malevolent glare in Steve's direction. 'And I'll tell you something else, mate,' he said, 'when this lot's over, I'm away and gone from Shaheen and his fucking cadre!'

'Because of Liam Kidd?'

'Yeah, because of Liam . . . Now give over with the questions and let me eat in peace.'

'Sure.' Steve grinned, pushing aside his plate. 'You deserve it, you've been stomping all over hell's half-acre — '

'So how about pouring me some more tea?'

Steve refilled Cooper's cup, then sat down again. 'Me, I'd rather have had a beer,' he remarked.

Cooper stirred his tea. 'Your recording gear up in the conference room — that side of things all OK?' he asked, a touch perfunctorily.

'All done. Nothing much to it, fairly amateur stuff — '

'So how come they need an IT buff like you?'

'Use your brain! Security!'

Cooper thought for a moment, then a grin spread across his handsome face. 'Take your point. A meet like this one here on Thursday — shit, Shaheen could hardly ask the bloke from the electrics shop down the road to come along and tape what's said, could he? By the way,' he went on, frowning suddenly, 'that timetable of Shaheen's for Thursday: it seems a bit tight, to me.'

Steve turned in his chair, looked out over the garden. Privately, he thought so too, but with Cooper it was probably wiser simply to ease things along. 'Taken as a whole, the schedule seems all right,' he said. 'Mansoor and Shaheen arrive here by nine, Mansoor with his personal bodyguard Ramadan — '

'Never without that creepy, never-says-a-word bastard when he's operating outside his own territory, is he?'

'A sensible precaution on his part, I'd say.'

'Yeah? Why so?'

'You don't know? It's simple: Mansoor can be absolutely certain that Ramadan would, without question and on the instant, lay down his life in defence of him, or on his order.'

'Useful guy to have around . . . Yeah, I remember now — he saved Ramadan's life, didn't he? Way back?'

'Together with the lives of three generations of Ramadan's family.'

Cooper whistled softly. 'So OK, I'd say he owes Mansoor. What happened?'

'It goes back to the '90s, when Ramadan was in his early thirties. His father was a Hamas hardline activist, the entire family was. Israeli agents had their house lined up for a night-time mortar attack, to be followed in by hitmen who'd make sure all the males were dead. Mansoor's informers got wind of it, he warned Ramadan and then used his own cash and contacts to get the whole family out of there. They made it with only a few hours to spare, apparently.'

'So Mansoor bought himself a fall guy for the rest of his life.'

'I doubt he thinks of it like that,' Steve began, but then he got back in the groove and went straight on, 'but hell, yes, it's a good feeling to have, I guess.'

'Wouldn't mind having someone like that at my back myself, that's for sure. So, we have Mansoor and Shaheen in place here by nine. How about the other two?'

'Bakhtiary and Zayani both get here by nine thirty, each travelling by car from their separate hotels in north London — '

'And the conference starts at ten. Will you be in there with them?'

'Not at first. The three of them — just the controllers — will have an informal discussion of their inspections and the exact wording of the declarations, and they don't want either me or Shaheen there while they're doing it. When they're through with that I'm called in to the conference room, they make their declarations and I tape — '

'What, exactly, does each controller have to swear to, in his declaration?' Cooper had been following Steve's account of proceedings closely, and now leaned forward across the table.

Steve reeled it off. 'That his own particular field of investigation is all the following: one, secure in every respect; two, has all the required logistics in place; three, has all its support sleepers alerted and fully briefed; and four, has all its emergency procedures, lines of communication and lines of escape laid down, agreed, and ready for instant operation.'

'Then you make the copies, straight away, from the master tape?'

Steve nodded and went on, 'Not a one of those controllers would leave Ashburn without his copy of the declarations, you can bet your bottom dollar on that, Brad. So they push off for lunch, and I'm locked into the conference room to do the job. In due course, Shaheen comes there to collect — and I hand the master tape and the two copies over to him for delivery to Mansoor.' But in fact I will have run off *three* copies, won't I, Steve thought — and by the time Shaheen turns up I'll have the third copy hidden away, as I've prepared for.

'Weird lot, those controllers.' There was a contemptuous twist to Cooper's mouth as he spoke. 'Look at 'em! Each wanting his own fucking copy of what the others said — Christ! Where's their trust in their mates? Sure, they're tough, streetwise blokes — brainy, too, specially Bakhtiary — but they're supposed to be *mates*, ain't they? But I reckon they don't know the meaning of the fucking word. Raving egotists, the lot of 'em, seems to me. That Afghan Mansoor's the worst.'

'He's not Afghan; he's from Egypt.' Best to stem the flow, Cooper's getting mean and violent.

'Fought in Afghanistan, though, didn't he?'

'Mansoor's fought in a lot of places.' Leave it at that, Remmick, Steve told himself. It's not to the point, none of this is to the point. 'We should be on our way soon,' he said.

Cooper's mind, however, was set on its own course and was not to be deflected. 'Wherever he fought, the bastard doesn't seem to have learned to trust even his close comrades much, does he? And Steve' — he leaned across the table, a great earnestness in him — 'trust in his *mates*, it's something a man's got to have, y'know? Our kind of work especially, if you're going to work with someone you've got to be able to trust him — '

'You're dead right there but — '

' — and that's why I can't go on working with Shaheen.' Cooper talked straight across the interruption and — Steve observed with growing alarm — he was being swept along by his own thoughts as the violence grew inside him again. His eyes had a spooky sheen to them; he seemed lost in some vision of his own. 'Like I said, soon as Desert Wolf's over, I'm off. I can't *trust* Shaheen now, so he and his fucking cadre can go to hell. After the way he's handled Liam's disappearance I won't ever work with the bastard again. I'm going to find out what happened to Liam that night — do it off my own bat, use my own people. Shaheen's lost the right to Liam. Liam was *my mate*. so whoever's done bad to him is mine, *mine alone.*'

'You believe he's dead?'

That got through to Cooper. His eyes came up to meet Steve's, changed focus and saw — Steve Remmick, the closest thing he had to a mate in the cadre now Kidd was not around. 'I'd have heard from him, else,' he said.

'But you don't know for sure — you can't.'

'So I've got to find out, haven't I?' Violence paramount in the dark eyes. 'Days've gone by since Liam disappeared — and Shaheen hasn't done a thing about it! Bastard, he is! *Bastard*!'

'He'll get on to it soon as the op's done.'

'Fuck that! Yeah, sure, he'll turn his attention to Liam — when he finds time to! *Days*'ll get wasted while he ties up loose ends of the Desert Wolf stuff. Not me, mate! I'm not hanging around waiting on his say-so when it's Liam in the frame. Come Thursday I'll stand down my security blokes as ordered, after the VIP's cars have driven away from the house, then I'll take off.'

'Where to? You don't know — '

'Where the hell d'you think? After the Remmick bitch, of course, that fucking sister-in-law of yours you cut loose from straight after Rob died. Christ, you treated her rough then, Steve — blamed her for letting Rob down, didn't you? I guess you hate her near as much as I do . . . I'll get her, Steve — get her for both of us. Sure, I don't know where to find her yet, but I soon will! I've had my own men working on it since Shaheen sent us down to Cambridge that day. Not Shaheen's lot, not cadre. *Mine*, and plenty of 'em. Gangland insiders, most of 'em are; and, believe you me, that sort often turn up info the straighter guys can't get near. No dice yet, sod it. But it'll come; I'll get that hellcat in the end.' Falling silent, Cooper sat darkly intent, powerful shoulders hunched, hands balled into fists.

'Time we got moving,' Steve said.

'What?' Cooper looked up sharply.

'It's time we were on our way.'

Cooper stared at him in silence for a moment and then, with visible effort, forced his mind back to present duties. 'Yeah, you're right,' he said, getting to his feet. 'Let's go. The sooner this job's done, the sooner I'll be shot of Shaheen.' He smiled. 'Free to do my own thing, then, eh? Find that bitch and — go see her.'

'You'll have to watch your back if you suddenly pull out of the cadre.' But as he too stood up, Steve was remembering how he also had recently become aware of finding in himself a certain kind of freedom. His was tied in with Hanna; Cooper's, it seemed, was tied in with Rebecca. Freedom. Freedom? A word with many different angles to it, and, presumably, an equal number of consequences.

'You driving straight back to London now?' he asked, turning to Cooper as they walked side by side out of the house and into summer sunshine.

'Nah. First thing I'm going to do is get on my mobile and contact those snoopers I've got scouting for leads to you-know-who. With luck they've got something for me by now.'

★ ★ ★

'Wait in here, please, Mr Traven will join you almost immediately. Would you like some coffee?'

Steve declined the coffee and then, as his escorting officer withdrew, sat down in one of the chairs set two either side of the table in the middle of the room — an impersonal, severely functional cubicle of a place, and one he had never been in before. Stark overhead lighting showed three of its four walls lined with filing cabinets, the other being given over to high-tech IT equipment. In front of him on the table stood an array of recording instruments. Traven's right to want this report of mine on tape, he thought, it's likely to be the last comprehensive one he'll have from me before Thursday.

'Good morning.' Frowning and seemingly preoccupied, Traven came in, closed the door behind him and sat down facing Steve across the table. 'Nothing new has come up about your sister-in-law since your call to me last night. You've heard nothing from Cooper since the two of you left Ashburn?'

Steve shook his head. 'That's a good sign, in a way. I think he'd probably have got on the blower to me if his blokes had come up with anything on Rebecca's whereabouts.'

'You're fairly sure he would?'

'No. In fact, I'm not sure about anything

221

Cooper's doing or saying or thinking at the moment.' Steve shifted restlessly in his chair, anxiety clouding his eyes. 'Until recently I've usually been at least ninety per cent sure about Cooper, about his mindset, his strengths, his weaknesses and so on. But he's a changed man since the Liam Kidd affair . . . Because Shaheen refused any immediate investigation into that, insisting it had to wait until Desert Wolf is over, Cooper turned against him. And in the last couple of days he's become unusually self-absorbed and highly unpredictable — which could be dangerous to us.'

'Also, possibly, to Shaheen?' Traven looked away. 'Divided loyalties,' he murmured, half to himself. 'Out of which, as we all know only too well, may come either great profit or great loss to the people involved. But I digress. Let's get to work. You've brought your notes? No, I forgot, you don't need any.' Leaning forward over the table he began to shift the recording equipment on it into position between them, smiling a little as he did so. 'You know, if I were to be offered three wishes by The Devil In Person as price for my soul,' he said, 'I do believe I would accept — and my first wish would be that every agent in MI5 and MI6 immediately be gifted with the same power of total aural and visual recall as you possess, Steve.'

'Here, let me do that. This way's better, we'll get more clarity.' Steve completed the job swiftly and then sat back, concentrating his mind on the information he had so meticulously stored in his brain. 'Right. Ready now. First off I'll work straight through the schedule for proceedings at Ashburn on Thursday, covering the actions of the three controllers, Shaheen, Cooper and his external security team, and myself. I'd rather you didn't interrupt at this stage, if that's all right by you?'

'Fine. And of course you'll omit peripheral details, there's no need for them to go in.'

Steve nodded. 'Right. I'll stop at where Cooper stands down his security personnel. Then I'll take any questions you care to fire at me.'

'Sounds good.'

Fixing his eyes on the microphone in front of him Steve related to it the complete story of the conference scheduled to take place the following day at Ashburn, the pleasant little manor house briefly loaned to Khaled Mansoor by Mr Westerman — and of the declarations that would be made at the end of that meeting; declarations intended to be used to signal lift off to Operation Desert Wolf and thus bring into being in Britain a

223

built-into-the-system and continuous supply of committed men equipped to facilitate or themselves carry out acts of terrorism as, where, and when decreed by their masters.

' ... That done, Mansoor and Shaheen remain at Ashburn, while Bakhtiary and Zayani head for their respective airports. As soon as they have driven away from the house, Cooper orders the stand-down of his security personnel.' His account finished Steve relaxed, sat back. 'Now I'm open to questions,' he said, the strain of intense concentration gone from his face.

Traven leaned his forearms on the table. 'Very little to ask.'

'Shoot.'

'The conference takes place in the study on the first floor. Am I right to assume it will be guarded?'

Steve nodded. 'Two men, armed, outside the door, on the landing. They're Mansoor's own, and will arrive and depart to his orders — probably as soon as Shaheen has taken the tapes from me and delivered them to Mansoor.'

'Those two — their mode of travel is?'

'Motor bike.'

'So we'll take them, too, at the road blocks. Good ... You made no mention of Mansoor's body-servant, Ramadan. Will he be present in the conference room?'

'I don't know — and I've no way of finding out, either. There's been no reference to him being there. But Mansoor's a law unto himself: if he wants Ramadan in, he'll be there; if he doesn't, he won't.'

'Understood. Who'll chair the meeting?'

'Mansoor . . . and I've just remembered something interesting, not important enough for the main statement but worth knowing, perhaps. I think — from something Shaheen said to me way back — that he, Shaheen, hoped and expected to be allowed to be present at the conference, and hear the declarations. Clearly, though, Mansoor wasn't having any.'

'Will his exclusion rile him?'

'It certainly will. He'll be furious — he'll feel humiliated, and to him that's gall in the mouth.'

Traven grimaced wryly. 'Hopefully he'll soon have more serious matters to worry him. So when the controllers go off for lunch, leaving you in the conference room to run off the copies — you'll be alone? There's no check on you while you're doing that?'

'Unless there's some change in the planning, there won't be.'

'They're very trusting.'

'I've been with them for a long, long time,

never given them any reason to doubt or distrust me. Besides, Mansoor trusts Shaheen's judgement, and Shaheen trusts me.' Steve gave a tightlipped smile. 'And Christ, I've worked hard for that trust! Believe me, Traven, I've been working for it from the moment you signed me on. Luckily I had firm ground to work up from, because of the way Rob and I always did his bidding, Shaheen's always seen me as a born follower, a dogsbody unquestioningly faithful to his leader — so it's never actually occurred to him *not* to trust me . . . Yes, I'll be left on my own while I'm making the copies of the master tape of the declarations. So Shaheen will lose out because he trusted me: that will be a grievous blow to his overweening hubris.' At the thought, he smiled again.

Traven saw the smile ugly on his face and felt a stab of self-accusation for his turning of Steve Remmick, for the new hatred he had reasoned into him. But then swiftly, and from long practice, he assimilated the guilt, subsuming it into the belief that the greater good invariably demanded sacrifices. Of one sort or another. 'And while you're making the copies, those two guards remain at the door?' he asked.

'Outside the door, yes. After I've finished I stay in the conference room until Shaheen turns up. When he does, I hand the two copies and the master tape over to him.'

'And he delivers them to Mansoor for distribution — but doesn't receive one himself.' Traven frowned. 'Odd. I'd have expected him to want one.'

'He wanted one, all right. He asked for it; he told me so himself. But apparently Mansoor turned his request down flat.'

'Why, I wonder? Surely he's absolutely trusted?'

'Myself, I put their refusal down to iron-hard hierarchical arrogance: their ranking is higher than Shaheen's, and by refusing him a copy they're drawing a line between him and themselves, making clear his lower status.'

'Is that how Shaheen sees it?'

'I think so.'

'So he resents it, but at the same time he accepts if for the simple reason that if he were in their place, he would do exactly the same thing and for exactly the same reason.' An expression of distaste — contempt, almost — passed across Traven's face, then he pushed back his chair and got to his feet, stood frowning down at the table top. 'No wonder we never get anywhere,' he murmured.

Who does he mean by 'we'? Steve

wondered. Anti-terrorists like us, Arabs, straight Brits — or even the whole of mankind, maybe? To hell with it! As far as I'm concerned it's them and us, so lets's get on with the job. 'Bakhtiary and Zayani are scheduled to leave Ashburn as soon as they've received their tapes, which should be around twelve thirty,' he said. 'Each will be travelling in his own car, with armed driver-cum-bodyguard. Bakhtiary will be bound for Heathrow, Zayani for Manchester.'

'That hasn't changed since your earlier report: it's in hand, both will be arrested at their airports. Go back to Ashburn now. Confirm for me the timings for Mansoor, Shaheen, Cooper and yourself after those other two have left.'

'Mansoor and Shaheen stay put in the house until at least six o'clock. They're the anchor-men, the others contact them if they run into trouble — which is why you have to co-ordinate all the arrests damn tightly. And don't forget Ramadan. He'll almost certainly be wherever Mansoor is, or nearby.'

Traven nodded, and began pacing to and fro across the grey, heavy-duty carpeting of the small room. 'The plans for the assault on those who remain at Ashburn have already been roughed in,' he said. 'I can firm them up now, get them relayed to all units involved.

How about Cooper, Steve? Any alterations to his security arrangements as you detailed them to me after you got back from Ashburn?'

'None. And unless Mansoor himself orders changes, there won't be any from now on.'

'We'll be going in hard on all fronts. Have to deal with the fallout later. Criticism's bound to come from some quarters.'

'You've got all Desert Wolf's designated action-sites covered? Any cock-up there — '

'That's not your pigeon.' Traven's smile was sardonic as he halted and turned to Steve Remmick. 'You know as well as I do that *total* success in this particular mission of ours could never be promised by any man — any honest man, that is. You'd need Godlike powers to promise that . . . I use the adjective literally,' he added, sitting down again, 'and as I neither have nor make any claims to have such powers, we will move on.'

'I was out of line there. Sorry.' Steve's eyes were hooded, introspective. 'With an op as complex as Double Talk, and over such a long period of time, we've been fantastically lucky to've made it this far without some slip-up or other busting the whole thing wide open.'

'Hopefully that luck will stay with us over the next forty-eight hours . . . Now, back to Cooper. He'll stand down his men between one thirty and one forty-five. They take off — and will be arrested at the road blocks positioned along the two surfaced roads affording access to Ashburn.'

'But the people in the house — '

'Won't have time to do anything. The Special Forces' covert penetration of the building follows within minutes of the departure of Cooper's men. You know that.'

Steve nodded. 'How about the road blocks, though? Cooper's blokes will be travelling in separate cars — what if one of them sees the car ahead of him pulled off and gets suspicious, uses his carphone?'

'He'll have no reason to be suspicious. The Specials at the blocks won't be visible to passers-by, they'll be in their incident vans off to the side. Ordinary traffic police control each block, they tell drivers it's a drugs bust, there's a dealer on the run in a stolen vehicle carrying cocaine.'

'Sounds OK. But what about Cooper? Shaheen left him to please himself what time he takes off — like he did me.'

'Is he likely to stay around after he's dismissed his men?'

'No way! He'll want out of there fast.'

'Then we'll take him at the road-blocks, like the others . . . So that's it, Steve. Providing all goes according to plan, by three o'clock tomorrow afternoon we'll have the men who comprise the nerve centre of Desert Wolf in custody.'

'Whereupon you'll radio out the go-ahead for the arrests of the army of sleepers, collaborators, and plain subversives scattered across England and working to Mansoor's orders.'

'God willing . . . No, wait a minute.' Traven put out a restraining hand as Steve stood up to leave. 'There's one more thing.'

'I thought we'd covered everything.' Steve remained standing, and now Traven also was on his feet.

'Not quite. It's this: what if Shaheen searches you after you've handed over the master tape and the two copies? Might it not occur to him that you've actually done exactly what you are in fact going to do — made an extra copy and hidden it on you with the intention of taking it out? Surely that's on the cards?'

'Sure it's on the cards. But . . . Shaheen won't search me.'

'So you've maintained, right from the start. But how can you be sure?'

'I can't.' Steve grinned. 'That's the gamble.'

'Take that damn grin off your face!'

Traven was angry in a way Steve had never

seen before: there raged inside him a deep-down, complicated passion, an anger threaded through with bitterness and — of all things, in a man like Traven! — guilt and grief. Guilt? Grief? — in *Traven?* Cut it out, man! Steve thought. *You* weren't the prime mover in turning me, recruiting me to go up against Shaheen and Desert Wolf! I came into Double Talk *of my own accord, on my own initiative*. Nevertheless, for a moment, Steve Remmick felt oddly moved by such — vulnerability? Human frailty? — in Traven. Then he pushed the incident to one side, grimaced and relaxed. 'Take it easy,' he said. 'It *is* a gamble. I know that. But I also know Shaheen, and I'm betting on him not searching me.'

'Bully for you, as they say — but what happens if he makes a move to do exactly that?'

'Then I'll josh him out of it somehow.' Smiling again now, Steve.

'And what if you find you can't do that? If he's not to be joshed?'

'Ach, hell! Leave it alone, can't you! Let me — '

'*Answer me!*'

His smile gone, Steve stepped close to Traven, eyed him coldly. 'If that happens, I'll do what we both know I have to do to get the hell out of there with my copy of the tape and deliver it to you,' he said.

'Good. You do that.' Traven broke eye contact, looked down. When he looked up again a few seconds later he was — Steve observed with relief — his usual composed, reserved self. 'You'll be armed, of course?'

'Of course. I'm a member of Shaheen's cadre; we'll all be armed I imagine. Me not so bullishly as some — Cooper, for one, he carries a raft of lethal stuff in the back of his car when he's on a touchy job. Me, I'll have a handgun, it's small but packs considerable punch. If I do have to use it, it'll do the necessary.'

'Good. I'll be at the command post from tonight on — or available on the number you've got for it. Call me as soon as you have the tape and are well clear of Ashburn — and remember you are to deliver it in person and to me only.'

'As if I didn't know.' Steve nodded, swung round and started for the door — only to stop again and turn to Traven with the question that had shouldered its way past all the priorities of Double Talk to the forefront of his mind. 'Hanna Tregorian — can't you tell me now when it'll be OK for me to contact her again?' he asked.

For the first time since he had entered the

room, Traven smiled. 'Once you have delivered that tape into my hands, Steve, you're free to contact whoever you like — no, wait!' His face clouded. 'Your sister-in-law, Rebecca. Don't go near *her* for a few days yet — no contact at all, please, until I've made certain checks on Cooper, what he's done about Liam Kidd's disappearance.'

'Understood. Till tomorrow, then. See you soon after three o'clock. Hopefully.'

Traven watched him turn and go out: a tall, athletic young man. *Young* man, he thought the word again. Thirty-odd to my fifty-three. By Christ, Steve Remmick, if you ever cause Hanna Tregorian grief or harm, I'll kill you. I will *kill* you.

★ ★ ★

Innisfree, Rebecca's hideout. The bungalow, lying some twenty miles south-west of Ashburn, stood in its own half-acre of land off a quiet road called Heath Way. A three-bedroomed property, it had a long, paved path leading from the road to its front door; its name was prettily announced on the decorative plaque affixed to its wooden gate. This path was overlooked by the windows either side of the front door which opened into a fair-sized hall wall-to-wall carpeted in dark red.

The bungalow was home to Mrs Arden. She and her husband had moved in there in 1980, a quiet-living couple, both active in local affairs without being pushy, and proven good neighbours always ready with a helping hand if needed. Widowed twelve years later, Laetitia Arden could easily have afforded to move into a comfortable flat nearer to her preferred shopping centre. Nevertheless she stayed on at Innisfree. She liked the bungalow, she said, she revelled in the garden, and she couldn't ask for better friends and neighbours: only an idiot, she said, would walk away from such blessings unless she absolutely had to!

But — although naturally she made no mention of the fact to those same friends and neighbours — Laetitia had another reason for staying on at her home, and it was actually the paramount one. This was that, when her husband died, Traven asked her to do so. For the Ardens had been long-serving sleepers in MI5's employ; they were two of Traven's own. When they moved into the bungalow they had done so on his specific orders. He had recruited them following a covert and exhaustive search of them reaching back into their student days and covering all personal, social and political aspects of their respective backgrounds. And after she had been widowed, Traven had told Laetitia that the work she and her husband had done for him over the years had been invaluable. Then he had pointed out to her that although certain aspects of it would perforce have to be transferred to other sleepers, there remained many she could continue to do alone — the codes, the contacts, the internet analyses and so on — and he would greatly appreciate it if she stayed where she was. Laetitia had agreed immediately.

Wednesday afternoon, and inside Innisfree Rebecca was prowling restlessly around the sitting-room. She was nervy, unhappy, and prey to sudden bouts of fear about Brad Cooper — and on top of it all, was feeling guilty. Not much of this last was on account of the death of Liam Kidd, for she saw that as a matter of non-culpable, last-ditch self-defence, and knew both Steve and Traven had accepted that. The guilt in her was for the trouble she was causing those two men — Steve, especially — and Hanna Tregorian. It's bizarre, how things sometimes work out, she thought. If Kidd hadn't come to my house that night, I'd never have met Hanna, whom I already think of as a friend. I'm glad she knows where I am now, and Traven's given me permission to call her once a day. Steve knows where I am, too, but he's *not* allowed to call me for the time being, nor me him. I like Hanna enormously. She's *different*. She seems a finer person, somehow, than most of the women I've met so far, she's more . . . oh, I dunno. Forget it.

Halting in front of Laetitia's upright piano she ran her eyes over the family photographs arranged on its polished top, then picked up one that caught her attention. A colour enlargement, it was silver framed — and obviously an amateur snap, the woman shown in close-up, caught halfway up a ladder, picking apples. It looked, thought Rebecca, as though whoever was taking the picture had called something out to her and she'd turned to him, laughing, her long pale hair all over the place. She's got a lovely smile, Rebecca thought, knowing the woman was Laetitia Arden, the absent owner of this bungalow Traven had decreed she should live in 'for a few days'.

Replacing the photograph, Rebecca went into the kitchen to make herself a cup of tea. While doing so she thought about Mrs Arden. I haven't met her, never will meet her — yet quite probably she'll have saved my life, I guess. I wonder *why* she agreed, at the drop of a hat as she must have done, to move out and let me be here? Traven told me quite a bit about her, of course, dinned it into me because *I need to know!* Gave me names of places and people, their ages, life styles — as much as he could cram in, in the time we had. Enough — hopefully! — to make my cover story for being here hold up when local people ask questions. No one has, so far, not much; easy to deal with, nothing I couldn't handle. All I've had are polite enquiries for news of Mrs Arden, advice about local shops etcetera, offers of help if needed, invites to morning coffee and — one only, hard luck me! — to a drinks do. My neighbours are far too well-mannered to pry, I think. The cover story Traven gave me seems to be playing OK with them. It's ordinary enough to make sense and I've got it off pat, with the bits and pieces of inside family stuff to help it pass muster. It goes like this: Mrs Arden's sister lives with her husband in Devon, and she's been taken ill — no, nothing life-threatening, thank God! — so Mrs A. has gone down there to help out with the teenage kids, two boys and a girl. I'm a friend of hers from London who happens to have time to spare at the moment to move in and look after house and garden until she gets back which, hopefully, should be within a week to ten days. Laetitia's garden's absolutely *gorgeous!* Scares me stiff, actually, I daren't do much bar pull out things that are obviously weeds, mow the lawn and dead-head her roses . . .

Pouring herself a mug of tea, Rebecca carried it back into the sitting-room, crossed over to the front window and stood gazing out over the garden, hands clasped round the mug, seeing the path from roadside gate up to front door bordered with lavender, sunshine everywhere.

Cooper! Suddenly the fear couched down inside her came alive again and clawed its way into her mind, into her blood: Brad Cooper will find me, I know he will. He won't give up — not on his mate Liam Kidd. He'll hunt me down and when he gets me *he'll make me tell!* He'll hurt me till I tell — and then he'll *kill* me! Blood for blood, but he won't do it clean and easy like Liam Kidd had it, *he'll make it last.*

Wave after wave of sheer terror surged through Rebecca and she shook where she stood, seeing nothing of the sunlit garden now, the whole of her being possessed by fear of the man who was hunting her. *Cooper.*

Rebecca mastered her fear: somehow, whipped it back into its cave in the darkest recesses of her mind. When she had it caged there, for the moment, she carried her mug of tea back into the kitchen and sat down at the table, setting the mug down with the utmost care on its cream Formica top. A few minutes later she picked it up to drink, and saw that where it had stood there was a brown ring of spilt tea staining the Formica; at once she got up, fetched a cloth from the sink and wiped the table clean.

As she sat down again she thought, God but I'm scared! I wish Traven had allowed me to have a handgun like I asked, but — yes, I see his point. He couldn't trust me with one, could he? Not after what happened with Liam Kidd.

13

At 09.00 on Thursday morning, Mansoor was in the study on the first floor at Ashburn — a light and airy room, sumptuously carpeted, its two long windows overlooking lawns and flowerbeds — where in an hour's time he and the other two controllers were to hold their final conference. He was standing at the head of the fine oak table in the centre of the room, surveying the recording equipment set out on it in readiness for the three of them to commit to tape the declarations that would in effect activate Desert Wolf.

'So, at last, we come to the time of fruition,' he said, speaking in Arabic. 'Desert Wolf has been years in the making — '

'But the terror that will arise and spread among our enemies once the operation moves into its active phase will be our just reward.' Standing stiffly erect, just inside the door, Mansoor's body-servant, Ramadan, interrupted without fear or embarrassment, as always empathizing swiftly and effortlessly with the man to whom, many years earlier, he had sworn fealty to the death. Ramadan was Mansoor's bounden henchman, yes. But

241

during his years of service to him, he had become infinitely more than that: by right of his proven, steadfast adherence to his oath and its deep obligations, he had become, as it were, a member of Mansoor's blood family. 'Many unbelievers will perish as a result of what will come to pass here today,' he went on, his sombre, lined face intent. 'And the many facets of Desert Wolf, being well hidden from enemy eyes and embedded into the very fabric of the infidel society here in England, will not easily be discovered. In the course of time some of its component parts may be traced and destroyed, but long before that happens our network will have bred many martyrs to feed our cause with the blood of the enemy.'

'You speak truth.' And indeed that is so, Mansoor thought, his eyes lingering on the tall, sparely built figure of this personal retainer of his. The Arabic phraseology gives that truth barbaric overtones, but nevertheless it is in accordance with fact, for not long after the declarations have been made those things Ramadan spoke of will come to pass. And at the prospect of such success at last within his grasp, Mansoor smiled grimly and went down to his war room on the ground floor, where his lieutenants were awaiting him. Ramadan followed, closing the study door behind him.

As soon as both had gone downstairs the two armed guards — Mansoor's own men, Cooper's writ for security ran only outside the house — moved to stand on watch, one in front of the study door, the other at a spot further on along the landing from which he had a clear line of fire to the two staircases — one to his left, the other well off to his right — giving access to the first-floor.

* * *

Mansoor's improvised war room was small, but well suited to his purpose. Normally used as an all purpose house-staff utility room, it opened off the entrance hall and was amply furnished with chairs, tables and office equipment. When he entered he found his four senior aides for the conference already present. Steve Remmick, standing gazing out of the window, turned and greeted him; Cooper, sprawled in an armchair beside him, straightened up but stayed where he was; while the other two, both of whom were at ease in upright chairs at the table in the middle of the room, sprang to their feet with a sharp 'Sir!' then stood attentive to their commander.

These last two were Mansoor's own, not cadre, and were responsible to him alone for security inside the residence. With a quick 'I'll be with you in a minute' to Remmick and Cooper, Mansoor sat down with them at the table — on which were spread out annotated ground plans of the entire property and its environs — and ran through the security arrangements each man had put in place.

Casting a quizzical eye on this procedure, Cooper murmured to Steve out of one corner of his mouth, 'Double check,' then added with a grin, 'Fucking well needed, if you ask me, some of these in-house blokes are — '

'Shut up.' Steve turned away and concentrated everything in him, every last ounce of mind and brain, on what he, Steve Remmick, had to do that day, up in the conference room at Ashburn. He had to be convincingly the controllers' liegeman — while at the same time committing acts that (hopefully!) would later destroy them. True, none of them had any reason so far to suspect him of duplicity, but at a time of such vital importance to them they were all likely to be hypersensitive to any wrong word or deed on his part. Also, the matey relationship he had cultivated with Cooper was proving hard to sustain as Traven's Double Talk operation closed in for the kill — a kill which depended for one vital aspect of its success on hard, inside-enemy-lines action from him alone, Steve Remmick.

Yet maintain his act with Cooper he must. So keep your head down, Steve, he warned himself, and watch every word you say. Meanwhile, follow the plan — the plans, rather, those opposed ones of Shaheen's and Traven's being linked together through yourself, who has been working for both but is sworn to one only.

Mansoor, his double-check completed, dismissed his two security men and turned to Cooper. 'You reported all your agents in position, so go ahead,' he began, but broke off as the door was opened and Ramadan came in. 'They are both here?' he asked him in Arabic, already on his feet and striding towards the door.

'Bakhtiary is in the hall, sir.' Ramadan stood aside to let him pass. 'Zayani's car passed in through the front gate two minutes ago.'

In the main hall Mansoor greeted with due politeness first Bakhtiary, and, a few minutes later, Zayani. Each of them had his driver-bodyguard in attendance: Zayani's a desert tribesman, lean, gaunt-faced, his suspicious eyes raking the new environment for possible dangers; Bakhtiary's, a man of quieter mien yet his menace — evident in the coiled-spring strength of his body and the deadly stare of his grey eyes — equally apparent.

'Your bodyguards will wait here in the hall while the conference is in progress,' Mansoor stated when the greetings were over.

'As will Ramadan, I assume?' Zayani's question sharp; he suspected he was being demeaned, and resented it.

'Ramadan will go wherever I go.' Mansoor turned with his answer, his eyes direct to Zayani's, cold, calm — and challenging. Then he smiled. 'Here in this house you have no need of your bodyguard, Zayani, my friend,' he said. 'Or do you have reason to doubt either the expertise or the fidelity of Shaheen and his cadre?' he added, a suggestion of steel beneath the velvet of his manner and voice.

Curbing his rancour, Zayani produced a narrow smile. 'Indeed all of us here are brothers in the service of Allah the Merciful,' he murmured.

'Then we will proceed to the lounge, where coffee will be served. At ten o'clock we will go up to the conference room, the study on the first floor.'

'Where does the recording technician, the European Steven Remmick, wait during our discussion prior to the declarations?' Zayani asked, as he followed Mansoor out of the hall.

'There is a small anteroom opening off the study. He will wait there until we require his services.'

'He will be there alone?'

'No. Shaheen will be with him. But — as I have assured you before, my friend — you have no need to be suspicious of Steven Remmick. When his brother was alive the two of them served us well, and since his brother died Steven has continued to prove himself a loyal and extremely valuable tool to our hand.'

'In the light of your trust in him, I accept these things. I merely yearn for the day when we no longer need to employ such . . . outsiders.'

Mansoor smiled at him, but Zayani knew the smile to be no more than a politeness. 'That day will soon be here,' he said.

★ ★ ★

A few minutes after Mansoor left the war room to greet the other two controllers, Steve and Cooper repaired to the games-room in the west wing, which had been assigned to them as their personal rest-room. In addition to being equipped for table tennis, billiards, backgammon and chess, this offered television and a library of videos — also a refrigerator well stocked with sandwiches and a variety of soft drinks and lagers.

'Not long now before the conference kicks off,' Cooper observed as they went in.

'Reckon I'll grab me a quick beer before I go outside and take up position. Join me?'

Declining the offer, Steve yanked a straight-backed chair to him, swung it round and sat astride its seat, watching Cooper help himself from the fridge. 'Your blokes all set?' he enquired — Cooper always liked a chat.

Flipping open his can, the security boss reeled off the disposition of his forces. Then he took a long pull of beer, walked across to Steve. 'I still reckon Mansoor's running it pretty fine on his time schedule,' he said.

'It should go OK provided the prelim discussion doesn't overrun.'

'*Discussion* — oh yeah? Prelim *arguments*, more like, I reckon. Bound to be, given those three big guns all thinking they're *top* gun. Blood on the carpet, I'd think, Zayani and Bakhtiary aren't what you'd call buddies, are they? Even I'm aware of that.'

'Zayani's not a man who has buddies. Mansoor's in the chair, though; he'll run proceedings on a tight rein.'

'Yeah, he won't want the timing to slip, will he? If they run late it'll bugger up those flights out of the UK — and if that happens there'll be hell to pay.' Cooper sipped his beer again then moved away and changed the subject, 'What time did you say you expect to get off?' he asked.

Steve pushed himself up off the chair. I'll make tracks out of this place quick as I can, he was thinking, get that cassette to Traven.

'Should be on my way soon after one,' he said. 'Once I've handed the cassettes over to Shaheen, I'm done here. The IT equipment stays where it is, apparently Westerman wants it.'

'You lucky bastard. Can't see myself leaving till around two fifteen.'

'You'll be heading back to London?' Idly, Steve picked up a table-tennis bat, reached across the table for a ball.

'Maybe, maybe not,' Cooper's voice had changed. Now the talk had turned to his own personal plans and affairs his mind had veered to Rebecca Remmick, and he spoke with concentrated malevolence. 'Hopefully my private sleuths will have some news for me and I'll be on my way elsewhere.'

Steve put down bat and ball as the implication of what Cooper had said drove into his brain. 'What sort of news?' he asked, his manner casual, terror for Rebecca in his heart.

'Shit, man!' Cooper slammed his beer can down on a nearby stool and faced Steve. 'Ain't you been listening to what I've been telling you lately? I want news about Liam's disappearance — with special reference to

249

that fucking sister-in-law of yours, the bitch he went calling on the night he vanished — '

'I've got no more time for her than you have, Brad, and you know it! Calm down. So you've had no luck in that direction yet, then?'

'No, I haven't. Won't be long now, though. I'll get to her — and when I do, she'll talk, you bet she'll talk! I'll find out about Liam. By Christ, will I put the bitch through it! She knows, she knows all right and I'll have it out of her — '

'Cool it, Cooper! You're on a job for Shaheen, remember?'

'Not for much longer, though, am I?' Nevertheless, Cooper cooled it. 'You know what, Steve?' he said after a moment and more quietly. 'I've got a hunch that someone I've had dealings with recently knows more about where Rebecca Remmick is than she's let on about. So if my blokes haven't come up with anything by the time I've finished here, I'll be paying that cagey lady a visit, put a bit of pressure on *her* and find out — ' Cooper broke off as his mobile bleeped. He answered it, listened, snapped out 'OK, I'm on my way; be with you pronto,' then sheathed the phone and with a brusque 'That was Watson, I gotta go. See you,' to Steve, made for the door.

Alone in the games-room, Steve stood

tense, cursing his ill luck; for given even a few more minutes he would have had time to get from Cooper the answer to the question that had been burning inside his head since Cooper had broken off to take his phone call. 'I'll be paying that cagey lady a visit, put pressure on her and find out — ' Cooper had said, only to stop there and be called away. 'So who is this cagey lady, Cooper?' Steve had wanted to ask. 'Who is the cagey lady you've got a hunch knows something about where Rebecca is hiding, and intend to 'put pressure on' to make her tell what she knows? *Who is she?*'

His head down, Steve Remmick fought to a standstill the dread consuming him as his brain — working in the light of his insider's knowledge of the situation — quickly provided him with the most likely answer to his own question: *Hanna Tregorian.* Yet — he couldn't be sure of that, could he? He did indeed know a great deal about the Rebecca-Kidd-Hanna affair, but it would be madness for him to assume he knew *everything* about it — and then actually *act* on the assumption! Apart from which, he had a mission to accomplish that day: a bounden duty to Traven which must take precedence over everything else. *Everything* else.

But so has Cooper, to Mansoor, he

thought. Like me, he's tied here at Ashburn for the present; and if things go according to plan he'll be tied here later than I shall. Not a lot later, but — through Traven, who I'll put in the picture as soon as possible — it will surely be long enough to get some sort of security around Hanna in case it really is her Cooper has in mind, his 'cagey lady'.

Hard on the thought, Steve took his chance. Cooper was gone, Shaheen and the controllers were all fully engaged, and he, Steve Remmick, was alone in this secluded room: what better chance could he hope for! He used the emergency number. It got him through to Traven in three minutes.

★ ★ ★

Steve glanced at his watch: 10.25. I should be called in to do the recordings any minute now, he thought, prowling aimlessly around the small room he and Shaheen were confined in while the discussion phase of the conference was in progress next door. A small anteroom to the study, where the conference had been in progress for the last twenty-five minutes, it was simply furnished with armchairs, two coffee tables, and a good-sized table to one side of the connecting door (firmly closed now) into the study. At one end of this table sat Shaheen, morose, outwardly composed — and very aware of Steve Remmick: *hostilely* aware, though he was taking care neither his face nor his body language betrayed his animosity.

This hostility had been born in him the previous day. A swift and cataclysmic birth, it had followed fast on Mansoor's decree that he, Shaheen, was not to be present either during the discussion period of the conference or — even more devastating, to his way of thinking! — when the declarations were being made. Exclusion from the discussion, yes, he could accept that, it was a matter of minor importance. But to be denied a place at the making by the controllers of the empowering declarations, despite the fact that Steve Remmick, his inferior in status within the cadre, *would* be present at the glorious culmination of the preparatory stage of operation Desert Wolf — that was an insult, a direct insult to him, Shaheen, who had liaised so closely with Mansoor throughout the mission. Shaheen had quickly realized jealousy lay at the root of his newborn hostility to Remmick; but realization had not brought acceptance. Previously perceiving their IT expert as no more than a trusted and extremely useful tool to his hand during the groundwork of Desert Wolf — by virtue of his being experienced in illegal activities here in Britain, highly skilled in IT technology and, above all, totally biddable — Shaheen had suddenly found the man elevated above himself by Mansoor! He had slept on this perceived injustice — this *personally humiliating* injustice — and by morning his anger, now grown huge within him, had centred on Remmick alone.

Watching his new enemy now, Shaheen saw him halt beside a PC and run his fingers lightly over its keys. You, Steve Remmick! You are not of my kind in blood and heart, he thought; from now on you are expendable.

'Half-past exactly: time I was called in, if they're on schedule.' Steve swung round to Shaheen, tense, frowning. 'Hope there hasn't been some sort of cock-up — ' He broke off, and both men looked towards the connecting door into the study as it was opened from within and Ramadan entered. Ignoring Shaheen he strode straight up to Steve, stared him in the eye and addressed him in Arabic — he spoke English reasonably well but never used it if he could avoid doing so.

'They are ready for you. You will go in now,' he said, then turned on his heel and without even a glance at Shaheen went back into the conference room. Steve followed him, closed the door and went forward to the table in the middle of the room, seeing Mansoor seated at its head with Ramadan now standing behind his chair and Zayani and Bakhtiary on his right and left respectively.

★ ★ ★

As Steve took up his appointed position beside the recording equipment assembled on the table, the eyes of the controllers were on him. Mansoor's were cool and observant, certain of his own authority but in no way arrogant. Those of Zayani, fierce and suspicious, betrayed a desire to tear him apart. Soon now we shall not need unbelievers like you, Remmick, he was thinking, you'll have served your purpose and therefore will be got rid of one way or another; personally I'd cast my vote for immediate death to make sure you stayed silent about us for ever. Bakhtiary, as was his way, had stripped his face clean of any expression which might reveal the drift or substance of his thinking.

'We will proceed with the declarations,' Mansoor said, watching Steve make a minor adjustment to the positioning of one of the microphones. 'Tell me when you are ready to commence, Remmick.'

'One moment, sir.' Thank Christ Shaheen isn't in here with us, Steve thought. Suddenly, just this morning, I find his presence unnerving — he's different towards me, somehow, seriously different. I can't think why — don't like it, though . . . 'Ready now, sir.'

Mansoor first, then Zayani, then Bakhtiary: in turn, each made his declaration along the lines they had finally agreed on. Logistics, lines of communication, support sleepers, security, emergency procedures: keeping to that order, each reported his inspection of his own specific section of the Desert Wolf network completed, and swore on oath that it was ready to move into operational mode. Standing watchful over his machines, making slight swift adjustments as required, Steve listened to the statements with growing but suppressed elation: they were so detailed regarding names and places, so precise in logistical information — MI5 and MI6 would have a field day! Once they got the rogue tape and subjected it to in-depth analysis — Hey, hold on a bit Steve, he cautioned himself. We aren't there yet, keep your mind on the here and now *and watch your body language*, you're among the enemy.

Bakhtiary came to the end of his declaration. Then Mansoor concluded proceedings with a brief restatement of certain pertinent facts relating to the timing of the declarations and the names and status of those who had made them (no details were given, Steve noted, of the location of the conference), then Mansoor gestured to Steve to cease recording. Steve obeyed the order. And for a moment then a tense silence ruled the room; each man present very still inside himself, absorbing the fact that a momentous event had just taken place, and that he himself, in his own particular way, had played an integral part in bringing it about. Feeling the tension, Steve steeled himself against it. It's me against them, my will against theirs, he thought, and schooled his face and body language to fit his image among the enemy as 'Shaheen's devoted and trusted running dog'.

'We have completed our business in good time. Thank you, gentlemen.' Mansoor stood up, the smile on his face masking the relief in him that the making and taping had been completed without trouble of any kind. 'We will retire to the dining-room and take a light lunch before you leave for your flights to Europe. While we are doing so our technician here' — he made a gesture towards Steve — 'will make two copies of the tape — '

'What becomes of the master tape?' Already on his feet Zayani put his question quietly and with none of his usual truculence, for he was in a state of controlled exaltation: soon now the fight would be taken to the enemy with renewed ferocity, the supply of highly trained terrorists to work at the killing end of operations both ensured and *increased*.

'The master tape stays in my keeping, as you well know. This was agreed long ago, and the fact was included in the information file you were given following the final session of the 2000 forum in Paris.' Mansoor turned to Ramadan. 'Soheil Shaheen will have lunch with us,' he said to him. 'Inform him of this change of plan and then escort him at once to the dining-room.'

'A wise decision.' Bakhtiary came up alongside Mansoor on his way out. 'Shaheen resented his exclusion. This will placate him somewhat.'

'Such was not my specific purpose. I simply have further instructions to give him.' Then talking quietly together the controllers went on their way.

Waiting beside his recording equipment Steve heard them go downstairs. Ramadan had gone into the anteroom to summon Shaheen to the dining-room. Steve heard a brief exchange in Arabic pass between them, then they came out together and went out on to the landing, passing by him without a word. Ramadan closed the door behind them, then locked it.

Outside on the landing, the two guards moved back into position, one in front of the door, the other further away, his duty to cover all approaches to the study. Listening intently, Steve heard one of them mutter a few words *sotto voce*, but he could make no sense of them. Then giving thanks that with Shaheen now invited to the lunch there was no danger of him coming back to the study before the scheduled time, he set about running off copies of the tape he had just made. He had no time to waste: the third, clandestine tape had to be completed and securly secreted about his person before Shaheen came to collect the master tape and the two copies destined for Zayani and Bakhtiary.

★ ★ ★

Established in his observation post across the road from the front entrance gate of the Ashburn property, Cooper took another look at it through his binoculars. What he saw satisfied him: from his position in cover at the outer edge of the copse capping the hill facing the house, he had a clear view, so he would have no difficulty in keeping tabs on all comings and goings through it. Relaxing, he sat down on a fallen treetrunk. He had a bit of time to spare. There were still ten minutes to go to midday, and the VIPs were not due to leave until around 12.30; his security men were all in position and none of them had had anything of importance to report — he had just finished the latest of his regular soundings of them, contacting each in turn on his mobile. In a few minutes' time, if none of them had called him, he would make his next check on them; meanwhile, he let his mind run free.

It homed straight in on the Remmick bitch, and his hunt for her. Some ten minutes earlier he had called each of the six agents he had hired to organize and maintain this hunt, but he had got no joy from any of them. The bitch, the fucking *bitch!* he thought now. It had been too long, so many days gone by and no word from Liam, no news about him in spite of all the enquiries made — and all the time the one woman who knew what had happened to him was alive and well, living her life. I'm not having that, Cooper thought. I'll find her, and I'll find her p.d.q. There's a person I know who quite possibly knows where the hellcat is hidden up; when I challenged her at her place over in Chesham the other day she said she didn't even know Rebecca Remmick, but I've got a hunch she was lying then. Hanna Tregorian: she's the one. The Remmick bint was at her house, I'm fucking sure of it. So she's got questions to answer, has Tregorian. OK, she's still under Shaheen's protection, but the way things are now Shaheen's nothing to me once this op's done. Soon as I've stood down my blokes here, his writ no longer runs over me, I'm my own boss. So you watch out, Tregorian! I'll be coming to your place and — you better believe this — I'll get answers to my questions from you. If it turns out I'm wrong, and you really don't know where Rebecca Remmick is — well, hard luck on you, girl. Tough shit, 'cos I've got to *make sure* you don't know, haven't I? You'll get over it. Maybe.

* * *

It was midday, and at his command post in north London, Traven was conning over in his mind the salient points of the long arranged but frequentiy revised — still being revised as fresh information came in — master plan for the arrest of all personnel engaged in Desert Wolf; an exercise which would be the culmination of operation Double Talk and as such would bring about the collapse of the controllers' established network in Britain. This plan stood thus:

1. *Road-block* on road out of Ashburn to be taken by *Zayani* and *Bakhtiary*.
   11.30. Vehicles and personnel will be in tight cover inside the wood thirty yards back from the road. One officer in place, in cover, keeping road under surveillance.
   1.35 (approx). Vehicles of Zayani and Bakhtiary pass along road on way to airport. Lookout man reports this and the road block is set up immediately.

2. *Ashburn residence*.
   12 noon. All attack units to be established in their allocated positions and ready to go into action on the locally given signal. On receiving this Units A and B will attack through the two rear doors and make house arrests. Unit C will hold secure all other entrances to the house, also car-park at side of house. All domestic staff will be detained and held incommunicado.
   Mansoor, Shaheen, and body-servant Ramadan will be arrested and transported immediately to their designated locations

262

for interrogation.
Est. time of attack: 2.55 to 3.00.

3. *Ashburn (environs)*.
Road blocks on all approach roads, ostensibly manned by traffic police but with Special Forces in support and maintaining low profile until action required.
All road blocks are more than one mile distant from the house and strategically placed. As security personnel (Cooper's) leave the site they will be pulled off the road (given reason, blanket hunt in progress for on-the-run, armed drugs baron with cargo). All persons in each vehicle will be taken into incident control van parked off to side — 'Just a routine check, sir, once we've OK'd your ID and so on, you'll be on your way' — and once inside will be arrested if on list of suspects.
Expected haul: Cooper, plus ten men. Up to six possible others.

Between 12.30 and 12.45 Zayani and Bakhtiary depart residence for their respective airports, each travelling in his own car, with chauffeur-bodyguard.
NB. Strict orders to all officers at road blocks: ensure that no suspect uses carphone or mobile on being stopped or thereafter.

4. *Steve Remmick*. His car is known and will be waved through.

5. *Cooper*. Est. time of dep. 2.15. Will be arrested at roadblock. Gets fast-track travel under double escort straight through to McGovern.

6. By 2.30 all rogue visitors have left Ashburn. Apart from domestic staff, Mansoor, Shaheen, and Ramadan are now alone there.

7. *Approx 2.45* Arrest of Zayani and Bakhtiary at their respective airports.

8. *3.00 p.m.* All assault units at Ashburn — Go! Go! Go! Shut-down interference on all mobiles/communication equipment inside Ashburn.
Arrest of Mansoor, Shaheen and Ramadan inside the house.

'Poised on a knife-edge, some of the timings we've got.' Quiet-voiced, the MI6 officer got to his feet as he spoke and walked across to stand facing Traven as he sat behind the desk. 'Huge risk, allowing things to go to the wire like this — '

'If you don't take big risks, you'll never

make big hauls.' Brusquely, Traven interrupted; he had heard it all before, the arguments for and against the way Double Talk was being run — thought all of it before, also, in the sleepless small hours of many a night. 'The decision's been made so stick with it, Jack, and keep your eye on the ball.'

'What else?' the MI6 man murmured and, turning away, resumed his seat at the table on the far side of the room and set about checking over — again — the 'disposition of forces' sites marked on his maps. Traven's right, he thought. We're into the action now so get on with the job in hand — God knows it's big enough and complex enough to merit a heartfelt prayer.

14

Steve set to work on making the copies of the master tape. The small, hardcover case containing the two blank cassettes he would use for them lay open on the table, its key in the lock, as he had left it for all to see. The third blank was secreted inside the custom-tailored kid pouch fitted snugly inside the waistband of his trousers, above his left thigh. Playing safe lest some change of plan by Mansoor led to a messenger arriving at the study door with some new instruction to him, Steve ran off the two authorized copies first. Only then did he make the rogue one destined for Traven.

But the precaution proved unnecessary: no interruption came. The recordings proceeded smoothly, and by a few minutes after midday all three copies had been made. Steve packed two of them into the case and left it open on the table. Then he settled the rogue copy into the kid pouch at his waist and closed the zip fastener over it. With five minutes to kill before Shaheen arrived, he sat down in the chair from which Mansoor had controlled the conference, and concentrated his mind on a swift mental recap of the overall plan for himself and the main players in the imminent collision between Desert Wolf and its counter-operation Double Talk.

Shaheen arrived on time: at 12.15 Steve heard the guard outside the door step aside and snap to attention again. Then the key was turned in the lock and Shaheen came in, his eyes going at once to the case on the table. Crossing to it, he hand-checked the master tape and each of the two copies; when satisfied that all was as it should be, he closed and locked the case, picked it up off the table and turned to Steve.

'You will report to Number nine safe house tomorrow,' he ordered. 'Evening, six thirty. Until then you are free to do what you wish.'

Steve had risen to his feet. Warned by the hostility in the cadre leader's eyes, he took his orders meekly. 'I'll be there,' he said, thinking, it's probably a good thing that, here with me now, and Traven's tape hidden at my waist, Shaheen's so full of anger. For anger often rides a man once it's in him; it claims his full attention and thereby — possibly — leaves him less observant of other things than he might have been were the whole of him devoted to the job he's actually doing. 'Things here have gone well, you will be commended,' he added, filling the growing silence with words because he did not like the look on Shaheen's face, mistrust and antagonism showed there as he stared at his IT specialist.

Abruptly, Shaheen withdrew his hostile regard. 'We shall see,' he said harshly, then swung round and went out.

Swiftly, Steve shut down his equipment — it was to be left for Westerman to deal with as he wished — then followed him out of the room. All I have to do now is drive away from this place and deliver my copy of the tape to *my* boss, he was thinking and, as he went down the stairs to the ground floor, he slid his right hand under his open jacket and pressed it lightly, briefly against the flat, solid shape cached snugly there, in against his body. Going out to his car parked at the side of the house he drove away from Ashburn, heading for Chandler's Cross, some ten miles north of Uxbridge: Traven would be there, he and the MI5 and MI6 teams monitoring and recording developments as Double Talk came out of cover and — hopefully! — smashed each and every one of the many component cells comprising the Desert Wolf operation in Britain.

★   ★   ★

From his vantage point atop the hill across the road from Ashburn, Cooper saw Steve Remmick come out of the front door, walk round to his car and drive away. Lucky bastard, he thought. A half hour or more yet before my turn comes. Once Zayani and Bakhtiary have cleared off I'll give my blokes the signal to pull out and go home — then I'm out of here but *fast*, got my own business to attend to.

There was a flurry of activity over at Ashburn's front door. Using his binoculars Cooper saw two immaculate black autos glide from their nearby parking places — Zayani's Range Rover first, followed by Bakhtiary's slick Mercedes Sports job — and pull up at the foot of the steps leading to the front door. As they did so, a group of five or six men emerged from the house and came down the steps — two of these moved forward and got into the cars, then both vehicles sped away and the remaining men turned and went back inside.

According to plan, Cooper allowed ten minutes for the two cars to get clear of Ashburn's immediate environs; then he swung into action, impatient to be shot of Shaheen's affairs and go seriously and in person about his own. Contacting each of his security personnel in turn on their mobiles, he gave them the order to pull out. 'Op completed,' he said to them. 'On your way as of now. Report in as usual on Saturday a.m. — meanwhile, have yourselves a good time, boys.'

Right, now for Hanna Tregorian! he thought when that was done, and quickly made his way down to his own car, a dark-green Mondeo which he had parked beside a farm gate in a side track at the bottom of the hill. Getting in behind the wheel, he switched on, but as he reached for the handbrake his eye fell on a small, dark object lying on the floor in front of the passenger seat. He picked it up, stared down at it as it lay in the palm of his hand. A *wallet!* Fucking hell, the thing was a brown leather, well-used wallet! Whose, though? It certainly wasn't his. Opening it, he saw the owner's name at the top left-hand corner, lettered gold on the brown leather: John S. Watson. Then as realization dawned, Cooper swore aloud: Watson was one of the security men he had just dismissed from duty here at Ashburn; he'd summoned him to the Mondeo earlier on, before he went on stake-out, to explain to him an alteration to the siting of his observation position.

Cooper's first thought was, leave the fucking idiot to stew in his own shitty juice!

But then he recalled the man — and grinned and relented. Watson was — Johnny Watson, who'd been on his payroll for near on ten years; who'd proved himself to be brave, fast on the draw, cruel if so ordered, loyal even under duress — and who'd got sodding great burn scars on his body in proof of it. Recalling those dreadjul scars Cooper thought — shit, the joker can't have gone far yet, I've only got to give him a bell and he can pull off the road, get the thing from me when I catch up with him. So thinking up suitably cutting witticisms with which to torment Watson when he answered, Cooper called him on his mobile.

But Watson did not answer, his mobile was switched off. Cooper swore again, thought to give up but changed his mind and called Watson's oppo Blake, who was travelling in his own car. However this second call raised no response either, and then as he sat mobile in hand behind the wheel of the Mondeo, Cooper's mind went cold and sharply focused. One phone switched off — OK, people do switch off their mobiles. But — two? A bit of a coincidence, surely? Maybe — but then again, maybe *not*? This could be serious so he had better check and make sure, he decided; and in turn he called the numbers of four more of his Ashburn squad, all of whom had left the area at the same time as Watson. Every call he made encountered a dead line.

Trouble! It had to mean trouble of some sort; it could not possibly all be put down to coincidence. Somewhere along the line, something had gone wrong for those engaged in the security op covering outside security for Mansoor's conference. Maybe it was nothing big, but — ? Putting away his mobile, Cooper thought the situation through to its — from his strictly self-orientated point of view — only logical conclusion. His assignment to Ashburn had been completed ten to fifteen minutes ago with the standing down of all his on-duty agents there: therefore, as of now, he had no further responsibilities towards any of the Desert Wolf personnel. His own unit of command, it seemed, was beyond his immediate help. Mansoor and Shaheen were still inside Ashburn, what about them? Cooper dismissed them without compunction: Mansoor was too remote to bother him, while Shaheen had forfeited his claim to any personal loyalty from Cooper on the day he'd favoured Mansoor's interests above those of Liam Kidd and, in doing so, quite possibly doomed him to death. So now I'll pay you back in your own coin for that betrayal, Shaheen! Cooper vowed. I'm not going back into the house to warn you, nor am I going to contact you on the house phone. I'm going to get out of here while the going's good and follow up my hunch about Tregorian knowing something about where the Remmick bitch is hiding out. Yep, that's it, Cooper: get to Tregorian. So — *move!* Get off this road in short order — something's gone wrong here, it ain't safe.

Shoving Watson's wallet into his back pocket, Cooper took his survey map of the Ashburn area out of the glove compartment and stuffed it into the pocket of his anorak, felt out the shape of the Larsen .32 holstered under his left arm to make sure he'd have fast access to it. Even as he did so, a new slant on his situation suddenly occurred to him: the gun can get you out of some kinds of trouble, mate, he thought, but there's certain other kinds where only something with a lot more clout'll fit the bill, and you've got a couple of that sort right here in the back of the car. On this thought he got out and opened up the hatch of the Mondeo, took his keyring out of the pocket of his chinos and used one of the keys to unlock the red heavy-duty plastic attaché case labelled First Aid he had stowed in the car. Packed securely inside the case were two grenades and two small, square, black-metal boxes which were in fact pocket-sized, high-tech time bombs. With a quick grin, Cooper lifted out one of these last then relocked the First Aid case, closed the hatch and got back behind the wheel. Delivers more of a punch than you'd expect, does this baby, he thought, slipping the little time bomb also into the pocket of his anorak, I've found her kind useful before and you never can tell . . .

Then he drove off. As soon as he was out of sight of the house he parked the Mondeo on the verge, locked her up, darted into cover on the far side of the road and set off across country. It was easy going on the whole and he was familiar with the topography of the area — he had recce'd it himself in advance of the conference — and he had the survey map with him to refer to if necessary. Given these advantages, he felt confident he would be able to carry out the plan he had made — was actually checking over and perfecting as he worked his way across pastureland towards the nearest small town — and get to Tregorian before the hunt for him was up and running.

★   ★   ★

On Traven's suggestion, Hanna had arranged her work schedule for Thursday so that she had no need to go into the office then. 'Stay home,' he had counselled her — ordered her, more like, she had thought, listening to his voice over the phone, hearing the authority hard in his tone, but also intuiting the solicitude behind it, the deep concern for her personal safety on this climactic day in the long-lasting, undercover war between Double Talk and Desert Wolf (with the personnel of the latter unaware that any such war had actually been in progress!).

After a sandwich lunch, she went out into the garden and planted two rose bushes she had bought the previous day. As she finished putting her tools away in the garage, she heard the telephone ringing in the hall and rushed to answer it, apprehension boiling up within her — for while it might be Traven or some friend or other, it was equally possible it was Shaheen, and God knew what that might portend.

'Hello, Hanna! Jocelyn here. Hope I haven't interrupted you in anything vital to the well-being of the world — hoovering the hall, say?'

Jocelyn! Jocelyn, jokey as she occasionally was: the known and healingly welcome voice washed over Hanna, memoried as it was with the lovely safety of life at Herne's Hill Farm. Making a suitably flippant response, she perched herself comfortably on the edge of the hall table and settled down to chat, asking after affairs at the farm and giving a heavily censored account of her own.

The call over, she went into the kitchen and poured herself a glass of orange juice. Jocelyn's call had made her feel good. But now it was over, and she was alone again. Glancing at her watch she saw it was a few minutes after three o'clock. By now Double Talk and Desert Wolf are well into the endgame, she thought, sitting down at the kitchen table. Traven is at his command centre monitoring Double Talk nationwide as it unfolds; he's hearing reports, charting positions on his maps and sketch plans — dear God, I wish I was in touch with it all! I must obey orders though — they were explicit enough, God knows, especially re communications. Do not use your phone after 3.30, Hanna, Traven had said. Mobile or other, *do not use it.* Leave your answerphone switched on, and listen to it every ten minutes or so in case I've called you. My point is, *you are not to speak to any caller.* And this interdict runs until 8 p.m. unless I have instructed you otherwise, in person, via the answerphone.

Now, the focus of her thought changed. *Traven,* she thought. Traven, who'd wanted her to be his wife but she'd come into his life too late, he was already wedded to his job and he knew he was ... He loved me, though. Still loves? Maybe. I don't know. Perhaps he doesn't know, either. 'A many-splendoured thing' — yes the lady was right. But by God it must be hard to have love in your heart when all you are given in return is high regard, close friendship and an affection you know is as strong as sisterly love but *stops there*. I wish —

But Hanna broke off that line of thinking. Because to wish that part of Traven's life to come right for him, she would have to *unwish* the love which existed between herself and Steve Remmick.

★ ★ ★

The small town of Dunham lay below him. Approaching it across the higher ground lying north of it, Cooper stopped for a breather on the crest of a low hill rising a mile or so from its outskirts. He had picked out Dunham on his survey map as being well suited to his purpose — he planned to make his way to the town centre and hire a car there. A risky move, car hire, given present circumstances. He knew that — but he needed wheels, and a straight theft could easily backfire on him — also it took time, which he was likely to be short of, he reckoned, Traven and Co. weren't blokes to pussy around once they realized he, Cooper, had slipped through whatever trap had been laid at Ashburn for the Desert Wolf operatives there.

Studying Dunham through his binoculars, Cooper found its layout fairly ordinary: there was a sizeable, shop-lined square sited a bit off-centre, and radiating away from it a network of roads and side-streets fanned out into garden suburbs. Deciding to go for it, he focused the glasses on the land between himself and the town and plotted his way in.

No problem, by the look of it, he thought. Easy going all the way. I'll take that narrowish unsurfaced road at the foot of this hill I'm on — it's not much more than a track by the look of it, good thing, means it'll be quiet. It broadens out as it approaches the suburbs and after a bit there's a turn-off into the square. Yep, looks promising. I'll go down to the unsurfaced road and head into town, get me some wheels.

However, in the event, things did not work out quite like that — they worked out even better. At first everything went according to plan. He made his way down to the road and set off along it towards Dunham, walking mostly on the grassed verge, a broad band of coppiced woodland on his left. But then on turning a sharp corner he stopped abruptly — and quickly dived into the tree cover on his left and peered cautiously out at what he had seen some sixty yards further on along the road.

A car was parked there. A black hatch-back — Honda, he thought — its nearside wheels on the verge. The hatch was up and a man was standing by it, his back towards Cooper as he fiddled about with something in the interior of the car. Cooper could not see what the man was doing, but on sight of the vehicle a mind-blowingly brilliant idea had flowered almost complete inside his head. Thus: I need a car; one is standing right there in front of me; I'm carrying a gun; it's still loaded — and I'll bet my bottom dollar the bloke up ahead of me ain't armed. So, provided he hasn't got company — and from here I can't make out any sign of anyone else either in or around the car — I'm up for this. This is one way-out slice of luck, a chance not to be missed. I'll do me a quick recce, suss out him and the Honda, make sure he's alone — and if he is, by Christ, *you'll have wheels*, Cooper! You're made! 'Course, if it turns out he's got company in there — tough shit, man, but that's the way the cards've been dealt, so walk on by, Cooper. Walk on by.

Although a big man, he could move fast and light-footed when he chose to. And now, slipping deeper in among the trees, he homed in on his quarry, keeping parallel with the road as he worked his way towards the parked car. Halting a good thirty yards short of it, he leaned a shoulder against a treetrunk and studied it through his binoculars. He liked what he saw then. In the back of the Honda the service shelf was in place; on it stood a Thermos flask, a plastic cup, and an open packet of sandwiches — and the man standing beside it looked to be no threat at all, for although youngish he was slightly built and of less than average height. Casually dressed in navy-blue sweatshirt over grey trousers, dark hair untidy, he was eating a sandwich, strolling around as he did so, easing his shoulders, gazing about him at the sunlit wood and the blue, blue sky.

So far, so good, thought Cooper — but now for the crunch, the real decider. And turning the glasses on the interior of the Honda, he searched it for any sign of passengers. When he lowered the binoculars he was grinning: the man was travelling alone. So he's easy meat, is this one, thought Cooper, and made his way back to the corner, fine-tuning his plans to allow for possible unexpected developments as he went.

Some four minutes later he went round the corner for the second time, sauntering along the unsurfaced road, whistling quietly, a man without a care in the world and out for a walk in the afternoon sunshine. As he drew near to the Honda its driver, hearing him approaching, put his half-eaten sandwich down on the service shelf and turned to greet him, smiling.

'Hi! Nice day, isn't it?' he said.

'Great. Couldn't ask for a better,' Cooper offered, stepping up on to the verge and coming to a halt half-a-dozen paces short of the car. Fiercely aware that he had to be ready to change his plan of action on the instant should traffic or other people come into sight, he was keeping himself mentally and physically hyped-up, but outwardly relaxed.

'Nice country round here.' Pushing his hands into his trouser pockets the driver of the car also stepped up on to the verge (which was exactly where Cooper wanted him to be). 'You like a lift into Dunham? I'll be passing through when I go on.'

'Nah, mate, I'm just out for a walk. Thanks for the offer, though . . . You going far?'

'Little place called Brinkhall, a few miles north of Ferndown.'

Cooper had heard of Ferndown, knew where it was. 'You're taking your time, I see,' he said.

'Why not? I'm not a great fan of motorways, useful though they are. A day like this, it makes sense to go the long way round and enjoy a bit of country.' The stranger smiled. 'I'm in no hurry, just off on a visit to family, my brother Ben and his wife. Two kids they've got — boys aged nine and six, and are they a handful! Great fun, though, it's a lovely, come-and-go-as-you-please sort of family. I told them I'd be arriving around six o'clock this evening but they've probably forgotten what time I said anyway . . . You live around here?'

'Sure. Work in Dunham, but I'm off sick. Where are you from yourself?'

'Balham way . . . Would you like some coffee? I've got plenty with me.'

Now's the time, Cooper — *now!* 'No, thanks,' he said sliding his right hand inside his anorak as he spoke — then aiming the drawn Larsen fast and true at the stranger's forehead he shot him once between the eyes. The impact of the bullet drove the man backwards — then as death took him for its own, he fell to the ground and lay sprawled face up on the grassy verge, his arms outflung.

OK so far, thought Cooper. Great. Road's empty both ways so get on with things, now. Heaving the body over to lie on its front he put a second shot into the nape of the man's neck, then pushed his gun back into its shoulder holster. Another quick glance showed the road still deserted so he darted round to the front of the Honda and opened the driver's door — noting as he did so that, as he'd hoped, the key was still in the ignition. Then he took off his anorak, slipped off gun and harness, flung them down on the passenger seat and covered all with the anorak. Checked the road again then: still clear. Back on the verge he gripped the body under the armpits and hauled it into the wood, working his way a good ten yards into the cover of the trees before letting it slump to the ground. Thank Christ the bastard's not a heavyweight, he thought as he straightened up. He stood quiet for a moment, sweating, his chest heaving as he got his breath back.

Then — always with an eye on the road, but finding his luck holding, nothing coming into view — he went back to the Honda, cleared away the stranger's picnic, closed the hatch, locked the car and went back into the wood. Once I've got the bastard across this belt of woodland it's downhill going and I'll soon be shot of him, he was thinking. Given that what I saw on my map is actually there, all I have to do is dump him and then the Honda's mine for the taking! And where I'm going to dump him, he won't be found for God knows how long, and before police alerts are out for his car I'll have got what I want from Tregorian and be on my way to deal with the Remmick bitch.

As expected, he found the next step in disposing of the body relatively easy. Slinging the dead man over his shoulder in a fireman's lift he cut straight across the wood, weaving his way through trees and undergrowth, often stumbling over the uneven ground but never falling. As he drew near to the far edge of the wood he saw before him, through the trees, first a stretch of downward-sloping sunlit grass and then, as he came out into the open and stood still, looking down the slope, the readymade 'grave' he had remembered from his survey map as he was planning his murder of the driver. For in front of him, just as he had seen it on the map, the sun-bright turf sloped down gently to enclose a fair-sized pond. There was a band of reeds growing on its far fringes but the side nearest him was clear of them, only sandy mud and shallow water showed there — and in the middle, the surface of the water was covered with green plant growth of some kind. As he looked down at it Cooper grinned, hardly able to credit his luck. Jesus, that pond's made for it! he thought. The weedy stuff in the middle, it's like a great fucking blanket — get the body in under that and even if it floats it'll hardly show, won't be spotted easily. Besides, the bloke's unlikely to be reported missing for hours yet; and even when he is it'll take the police some time to make the connection between him and me — time I'll put to good use, get me the Remmick bitch!

Quickly now, Cooper let the body slide to the ground and searched the man's pockets. He chuckled as he came up with first, a wallet with plenty of cash in it and, second, a driving licence — it named the dead man as Paul Stewart — and pocketed both. Then he straightened up and swept his binoculars over the surrounding countryside: cows and sheep in the felds, but no people visible and the few roads mostly shut away behind hedges, the farms behind wind-break stands of trees. Was it safe to go ahead with what he planned to do? Yep, sure it is — safe as it'll get, he thought. So — move, chum, get on with it!

He rolled up his chinos, shouldered the body once more then worked his way down the slope to the edge of the pond. As he had thought, the water was shallow there. Wading in, he advanced towards the middle of the pond, edging forward cautiously, feeling the water cool against the skin of his calves. '*Shit!*' he swore once, as his foot slid off a stone and he floundered, almost fell, wrenched a back muscle as he fought to stay upright. At the edge of the mass of pond weed he stopped, the water just above his knees. Carefully he shifted his feet level with each other, then worked them down to a firm hold in the mud and pebbles below.

Now the clincher! Smoothly co-ordinating every movement, Cooper eased the body off his shoulder, set his hips and back ready to take the strain of the coming throw — then lifted the dark shape of the dead man high and hurled it as far as he could out over the water. He almost lost his balance as he let go of it but he steadied himself — and his eyes did not leave the body for a split second because there had come in him a sudden panic fear that the water might not be deep enough out there! It might be too shallow to cover the body when it settled on the bottom — ?

But his luck held, so far as he was able to judge at that time. The body hit the surface of the water — smashed apart its water-weed skin — then sank out of sight, the water closing over it, swirling angrily at first above the death hidden within it but then

286

. . . quietening. Slowly, the pondweed drifted back into place, sealing the door of the tomb.

Cooper waited where he was until it had done so. Then he turned and waded back to dry land, laving his hands in the water as he went, then rubbing them over his sweaty face and blood-stained forearms. Christ, what a fucking wonder of a break! he was thinking. Nothing left to do but get inside that Honda — 'Paul Stewart' I'll be for a while, must remember that — and go on my way. Hope she's well tanked up — no sweat if she ain't, though, thanks to Watson and now that guy Stewart I'm not short of the readies, am I?

Regaining the cover of the wood he halted and, working fast, tidied himself up. When he went out on to the road there was little about him to excite curiosity should he pull in for petrol. True, there were areas of dampness on his chinos but with them being dark in colour it didn't show much. Same with the blood-stains on his sweatshirt — besides, when he got back to the car he would put on his anorak and that would cover the worst of it; short of close inspection, he would pass muster all right.

When he stepped out on to the road again he found it as quiet and empty as it had been since he had first turned the corner and seen the parked car ahead of him. Unlocking the driver's door he put on his gun harness and anorak again then got in behind the wheel, switched on and drove off. His plan was going well, he thought. That little caper with 'Paul Stewart' must have saved him a lot of time, let alone the risk involved in stealing a car off the street, or hiring one.

When he was well clear of Dunham, he pulled into a lay-by and, studying his map, worked out the route to Chesham, where Hanna Tregorian lived. I should make it within an hour, he thought. Sure, could be I shan't find her at home. But things are going well so I'm going to ride my luck, bank on finding her in — and alone!

As Cooper pulled out into traffic again and drove on to Chesham, his face was grim. For quite suddenly, he had lost his hope and belief that, quite possibly, Liam Kidd was still alive. He had no idea why he had lost faith: it had simply happened. He had not con-sciously been thinking about Liam at the time — he'd been on duty atop the hill opposite Ashburn — but all at once the thought was there inside his head: *Liam is dead*. And Cooper had felt it to be an absolute truth. So the only thing left to him was revenge.

Which now I'm bloody well going to take, he vowed. Whatever the risks to me may be — loss of liberty, even of life itself — I'm going to get to Remmick, and she's going to die. She *knows* what happened to him. I'll have it out of her, then kill her . . . Have to find the bitch first, though, don't I? And for that, I've a hunch Tregorian's my best bet. Reckon I should make it to her place around 5 to 5.30.

15

Ashburn: Thursday afternoon

In addition to the four officers of Unit C detailed to watch, and if necessary prevent escape from, the parking area at the side of the residence, Traven had two Special Forces units, each comprised of four officers, positioned on the high ground rising behind the house; armed and in combat gear, they were scheduled to launch their individual attacks simultaneously. The building had two entrance doors at the rear, a good ten yards between them. Attack Unit A was holed up in tree and bush cover opposite the left-hand door, through which they would gain access to the residential rooms. Mansoor, Shaheen and Ramadan were their nominated quarry; once inside they would fan out through the house in 'aggressive covert search' mode and arrest the three men as they encountered them. Attack Unit B was concealed opposite the door on the right. They would effect entrance through it and secure the service area, detaining domestic staff and preventing them from warning Mansoor and the others of the raid. All personnel in both units were — thanks to information gathered by Steve Remmick and certain other undercover agents — fully familiar with the layout of the entire building.

Bill Grover was leader of A Unit, a compactly built, red-haired man. Hunkered down in the lee of a massive, moss-covered boulder, he glanced at his watch: 2.57, and he'd had his orders. 'Check and make ready,' he said quietly, rising to his feet.

'Sir.' Allason, a clean-cut, personable young man, left Grover's side and padded swiftly across a few yards of patchy grass to his mates nearby. 'Check and make ready.' He passed on the order but it was not needed, Jack Wilshire and Liz Summers could tell the time too.

'Go-go-go!' Grover's voice low and sharp and Unit A, moving swiftly and stealthily out of cover, closed in on Ashburn, advancing in spaced formation, making for the left-hand door. A few minutes later, the three men were crouched behind the three foot high wall at the back of the house, then as Summers joined them, Grover gave the hand signal to advance and all four rose to their feet, swarmed over the wall and hared for the door. Getting there first Allason found it ajar, pushed it wider and slipped inside. The others followed him, then all four pressed on through their section of the house, entering and searching each room as they came to it. They progressed in arrowhead formation, Grover in the lead, Wilshire close beind him and Allason and Summers following, guarding their rear and casting off to left or right to investigate laterally as called for by the layout of the building.

Finding all the rooms on the ground floor unoccupied, they went up the stairs to the first floor and began working their way along the landing there, Grover ordering Allason and Summers to take over lead positions while he and Wilshire followed on.

The first room Allason checked yielded nothing. Moving on to the next door, with Summers guarding his back, he found it slightly open. Putting his ear against it he listened intently for a couple of seconds. Heard no sound from within so pushed it wider and, weapon at the ready, stepped across the threshhold — then at once snapped into firing stance, gun trained on the back of the dark-haired woman standing with her back to him on the far side of the room, looking up at a picture hung on the wall there.

'Armed police! Freeze!' he ordered, but as he spoke she turned to face him. He saw her flinch as shock hit her but then she lifted her chin and gave him stare for stare. Allason noted that her eyes were large and dark, she was thirtyish, attractive, and gifted with a gorgeous figure.

'Who are you?' she demanded. But she also was observant, and it was quite clear to her that although the intruder was armed with an assault rifle and gave every impression of being ready to use it at the drop of a hat, he was not one of 'them'.

'Police. Your name?' Allason maintained eye contact and held the gun steady: there was no woman on the list of 'wanted' his unit had been given, but — you never knew!

'Liliane Batouli. Lebanese citizen.'

'What's your job here?' As Allason spoke, Liz Summers advanced to stand at his left shoulder.

'I am librarian for Mr Westerman. I come here once a year to catalogue new books. I have worked here ever since he purchased this residence — '

'We're not concerned with him. Mansoor, Shaheen, Ramadan — d'you know where any of them are at this moment?'

'They are in the house — '

'We're aware of that. Can you tell us exactly where?'

'Why do you want them?'

'Answer my question. You surely know why we want them, what they are.'

'I know nothing about them. To me they are simply Mr Westerman's guests.'

'They're terrorists. Penalty for aiding and abetting same, imprisonment.'

But Liliane Batouli had made up her mind. 'It is not necessary to make threats against me,' she interrupted, smiling at Allason. 'I grew up in Lebanon. I know quite a lot about terrorists and my dearest wish is to see this sweet world wiped clean of their kind. The men Mansoor, Shaheen, and Ramadan are together in the small study on the second floor; you will find the stairs to it — '

'I know where I'll find them.' Keeping his eyes on Liliane Batouli, Allason turned his head slightly towards Summers. 'What do we do about her, d'you reckon?' he asked her.

'Trust her.'

'You sure?'

'Absolutely. I can tell.'

Liliane Batouli had heard this exchange, whispered though it was. 'Only a person of her own gender is able to intuit whether what a woman is saying is the truth of her heart and intention,' she said.

'Mansoor and friends — can you tell us if they're armed?' Summers asked sharply.

'Ramadan sometimes carries a gun. Shaheen is quite likely to have a knife and has the reputation of being fast and accurate with it.' The Lebanese woman's eyes had not left Allason's. 'As for Mansoor, I do not know. Unlikely, I think, now that his VIPs have left.' A half smile touched her lips then, as she realized what was worrying the man who was holding her at gunpoint. 'I have a suggestion to make,' she said to him. 'There is, as you can see, no telephone in this room, I do not have a mobile on my person or in here — and there is a key on the inside of the door behind you. So to be sure I do not warn those men, you simply need to lock me in.'

For a second Allason searched her eyes; then he grinned. 'Damn right,' he said. 'I'll do that.' Turning, he gave Summers a meaningful nod then led the way out, locked the door behind them, put the key in his pocket and sped on along the landing towards the stairs giving access to the floor above. And in the room they had just left, Liliane Batouli whispered, 'May God guide your hand!' as she heard the key turn in the lock.

Summers knew what Allason's nod to her meant. Pausing by the door she contacted Grover on her mobile, reported to him the location of the three men they were after — and was instructed that on reaching the second floor she and Allason were to wait at the top of the stairs until Grover and Wilshire joined them there.

A few minutes later Unit A stood ready to rush the study and arrest anyone they found inside it. Grover in front of the door, his left shoulder pressed against it and his right hand on the knob, Wilshire beside him to his right, the other two close at Grover's left. '*Go!*' he whispered, turned the knob and burst in shouting 'Police! Armed police! Freeze or we fire! Stay where you are!', raking the room with eyes and gun then bringing his weapon to bear on Mansoor who, caught standing facing him on the far side of the study, made one lunging step towards him but then froze at the stabbing menace of the gun. Storming in behind him, his squad fanned out, training their weapons on the enemy, Summers targeting Shaheen, Wilshire singling out Ramadan, Allason as back-up man keeping tabs on the situation from behind them and ready to crack down on any crisis that might erupt, his eyes darting from one to the other of the enemy as he summed up their disposition, noting that Ramadan, ramrod-straight by the left-hand wall beside a bookcase, was no more than half-a-dozen paces to Mansoor's right and only a little further from Shaheen who was standing in the middle of the room.

'Start arrest sequence!' Grover ordered and, weapon ready for instant use, advanced on Mansoor. Doing it by the book, Summers and Wilshire held their respective targets at gunpoint while behind them Allason stood guard, his eyes ever alert, scanning the raised hands, the faces and the body language of the prisoners for the slightest sign of intention to move, to attack.

But other eyes were also active: Shaheen and Ramadan each maintained a steely impassivity but each was in fact sizing up his personal, immediate enemy — assessing his armament and his physical potential, searching desperately for some weakness to exploit.

Mansoor offered no resistance: he could see no hope whatsoever of it being either effective or in any way useful to the others. On Grover's orders he put his hands behind his back, then turned and allowed them to be handcuffed together there ... Christ Almighty, Grover thought as he snapped the cuffs on, the bastard's lost his bottle, he's funked it! But then looking into the lost dark eyes staring into his, he perceived the totality of the man's mental and emotional agony at his own surrender, and rebuked himself: it's been too long since this bloke saw action, although his world is falling apart before his eyes he *cannot* do a thing about it, and the fact that he can't has broken him — but maybe only for the moment so don't let your guard down, Grover, don't let it down for the blink of an eye! And pushing Mansoor up against the wall behind him, he gave Summers the nod to get on and secure Shaheen.

At once she advanced on the cadre leader. He watched her approach, holding himself erect, his eyes brilliant with the violence coiled up inside him awaiting his order to strike — then as she halted a couple of feet in front of him he crouched low and sprang, at her, bringing one arm up from under to sweep her gun aside, both hands grabbing for her hips. He was fast but not quite fast enough — Summers squeezed off one shot but the bullet ripped through the flesh of his left forearm and then he cannoned into her and the impetus of his charge carried her backwards, the gun falling from her hand as the two of them crashed to the floor in a heap. Allason was beside them in a flash, looked for but couldn't find a line of fire to put a bullet into Shaheen — then saw him knee Summers in the guts and, as she curled up in agony, *reach out a clawing hand for the gun!* But that movement exposed his back to Allason — and as Shaheen's fingertips touched the weapon Allason's bullet took him high up in the right shoulder, he arched over backwards, twisted, and collapsed on his side.

The gun lay on the carpet, there for the taking: as Shaheen fell away from her Summers rolled clear of him, grabbed her weapon, scrambled to her feet and trained it on the Arab. 'Keep still or I fire!' she shouted, seeing his face contorted with pain but his slitted eyes glaring up at her, rabid, fighting mad — then he began inching towards her snakelike and she caught the glint of a knife in his left hand. 'Drop the knife!' she ordered. Smooth and swift, Shaheen slid his hand over the blade and lay still. But his eyes did not leave hers: I'll roll over to my right then throw the knife left-handed, he was thinking, feeling the steel against his skin, lost to all things but the imperative to destroy this woman who thought she had him beaten.

'Get your hand away from the knife or I'll shoot it off!' But even as she spoke Summers saw the brown sinewy hand slide down along the blade to curl around its tip so she shifted aim and fired . . .

As A Unit burst in, Ramadan had reached for the pistol holstered under his jacket, but Wilshire had him at gunpoint before he could touch it so he raised his hands in surrender — play for time and with Allah's help he would live to take out the enemy later. Wilshire relieved him of his weapon, but then heard Summers' first shot so abandoned the agreed sequence of arrests and secured Ramadan at once. Jabbing his gun into the man's chest 'Turn round, put both hands behind your back,' he commanded, then snapped on the handcuffs.

Grover had stayed put near Mansoor, trusting his officers to prevail but ready to intervene if necessary. He also caught the sly movement of Shaheen's hand as he slid it down the blade of his knife. Shifting his gun, Grover aimed it at the bony brown hand — but before he could fire saw it disintegrate into a mess of blood, flesh and bone and heard the report of Summers' gun. Casting a quick glance to his right, he saw that Wilshire had handcuffed Ramadan so he lowered his own weapon and used his mobile, calling in one of the two ambulances on stand-by a half mile back from the nearest road block. 'One man injured, gunshots to shoulder and hand, not life-threatening but he's losing blood pretty fast. We'll apply makeshift tourniquet.' That done, he contacted his opposite number in B Unit, in action over in the service wing of the house.

'Everything under control in your neck of the woods?' he asked.

'No sweat. Serious resistance nil. Eight domestic staff, five male, three female. All immobilized.'

As Grover lowered his mobile, Allason called across to him. 'Sir!'

'Trouble?' Grover went across to him.

'No, sir. This bastard's as well as can be expected; it's up to the medics now — '

'They'll be here any moment. So?'

'The woman, sir, the one who put us on to where we'd find these buggers. Do we arrest her?'

Grover's smile was narrow and wintry. 'Have to. You volunteering?'

'Ready for anything, sir.' Jeez! the boss actually smiled! Once in a lifetime, that is, Allason thought. 'She helped us, though — she's not like this lot we've got here, is she? Treat her gently, can I, sir? You'll put in a good word for her, won't you?'

'You may. And I will.'

* * *

Soon after 3 p.m. Traven, at work in Double Talk's support centre at Chandler's Cross, some minutes' drive north of Uxbridge — seven officers in there with him, busy at separate tables — was informed by radio that Zayani and Bakhtiary had been arrested at

301

their respective airports.

'Their chauffeur-bodyguards — success-fully taken also?' he asked, and was assured that they too were in custody.

Ten minutes later, Steve Remmick reported to him and handed over the taped copy of the controllers' declarations. Traven took it and stood staring down at it, turned it over once in his hands. He looked up and smiled. 'Congratulations, Steve,' he said quietly. 'Never thought I'd live to see the day.' Then he went over to the safe on the far side of the room and locked the tape away inside it.

'The controllers — any news in yet?' Steve asked as Traven turned back to him.

'All three taken — ' but there he broke off, gestured towards his working staff officers. 'What these chaps are engaged in needs a bit of quiet, we'll use the rest-room downstairs,' he said, and headed for the door.

The rest-room was comfortably furnished, and fitted out with a mini-bar and tea- and coffee-making equipment. Waving Steve to an armchair, Traven sat down facing him and brought him up to date on Double Talk's assault on the Desert Wolf network. ' . . . The controllers are being transferred under guard to their allocated interrogation centres,' he ended, 'and arrests are in progress at all Desert Wolf's designated sites of instruction.'

'Where's Cooper been taken?' Steve asked.

'What?' Traven looked up from a note he had started making on a scratch pad he had brought with him.

'Brad Cooper. Which interrogation centre was he scheduled to be taken to?'

Traven frowned, already impatient to get back upstairs, 'He should be in with the Ashburn security's group. They're being processed over at Uxbridge; McCarthy's in charge there. Why d'you want to know?'

In the face of Traven's brusqueness, Steve shrugged and turned away. 'Just interested.' I'll give it half an hour, then try again, he thought.

Traven got to his feet. 'I'm going back to the ops room now,' he said. 'Like to come? Follow things through as we get reports in?'

Steve jumped at the chance, and he grew so absorbed in all that was happening throughout Britain as Double Talk took Operation Desert Wolf apart that it was not until nearly six o'clock that he pressed Traven about Cooper again. He found himself in luck: Traven had time to spare to take the matter up.

'I'll contact Jarvis first,' he said, 'and check when Cooper was sent to the Uxbridge interrogation centre.'

'Who's Jarvis?'

'The MI5 officer who was in overall control at the road blocks on the approach roads to Ashburn. He'll have it all on record.'

It transpired that Jarvis had indeed recorded all of the arrests made at the road blocks, and of the centres to which the detainees had been sent for interrogation. But what he now told Traven took him on the blind side: Cooper had *not* been intercepted at any of the road blocks — and Jarvis, on noting the fact, had simply assumed that since the man was Shaheen's security boss he had remained in Ashburn with him and, consequently, would be arrested when the house was raided by Units A and B.

'God Almighty!' On his feet now, Traven looked across at Steve, his face tight with anger and disbelief as he interrupted Jarvis.

'What? What's up?'

'Cooper's not accounted for!' Traven snapped it out then spoke to Jarvis again. 'Get your men on to this fast,' he ordered. 'Find Cooper's car, search Ashburn again, check with Units A and B then report back to me. And move it!'

'*Not accounted for?*' Steve slammed the question at Traven as he cut the call. 'What the hell d'you mean?'

'It means Cooper has escaped our net. He's on the run, and we've no leads at all as

304

to where he's gone or is heading for — '

'Only one place he'll make for, to my mind.'

'Rebecca? That's a non-starter — he doesn't know where she is.'

'You can't say so for sure! He's been free since a bit after two o'clock — and I know for a cert that for days now he's had a wolf pack of his own agents trying to track her down. I last spoke to him around midday, and he said nothing had come in from them so far. But that was hours ago; he might've found out where she is any time since then. We have *to do* something!'

'I agree. Difficult to see exactly what, though.' Traven stood quiet, his head down. It was imperative that Cooper be caught, and he was considering an idea which had come into his mind as to how that might be achieved — only *might* be, true, but as things stood at the moment they had no other lead to follow. So I'll float this idea with Steve and see where it gets me, he decided, and looked up.

'I can't spare the men to guard Rebecca, it would take at least four of them to be effective,' he said. 'But it could be there's profit for us here, Steve. I think I see a way to that — nothing lost if I've guessed wrong, but huge gain if I've guessed right . . . Listen now. I'll rough out my idea, then you tell me what you think.'

'Shoot.'

'If you're right, and the one thing Cooper's bent on is revenge on Rebecca, then there is one other source of information as to her present whereabouts that might occur to him.'

'Who, for God's sake?'

'Hanna Tregorian. I know we got Rebecca out of Hanna's house in time, when that assistant at Roberta's gave the address away, but it's quite likely Cooper suspected — '

'Why the hell should he?'

'There are reasons for it that you don't know, and I certainly don't have time to spell them out to you at the moment. Just take my word for it so we can get on.' Traven stared him in the eye.

Steve nodded, looked down. 'OK. Good enough. Go on. What's this idea of yours?'

'Myself, I don't agree with you that — as things stand now — Cooper's so obsessed about Rebecca and her part in Liam Kidd's death; to my mind he's more likely to be concentrating on getting out of the UK as fast as he can. But at the same time I realize you could be right. And if you are' — Traven paused, and Steve saw a flicker of unholy joy glint in his eyes for a second — 'if you are, *we can use first Hanna, then Rebecca, to trap him.*'

Steve frowned. 'I don't get it,' he said slowly.

'Suppose Cooper really does believe Hanna's likely to know where Rebecca is, then surely he'll go to Hanna and try to get the address out of her. So what we do now is contact her and instruct her that, if Cooper turns up there asking about Rebecca, she simply gives him the Innisfree address straight away — '

'No! It's too risky, too dangerous for Hanna!'

'Not so. Hear me through, Steve. As you say yourself, it's *Rebecca* Cooper wants to get his hands on. In which case Hanna will be no more to him than a means to an end: all he wants from her is the address of the hideout; the minute he's got it he will push off and head there.'

'Hang on. Mightn't Cooper be suspicious — Hanna giving him it straight off, just for the asking?'

'I've thought of something to cover the possibility — '

'It'd better be good; Cooper's a mean, suspicious bloke. What'll she say?'

'We don't have time for that now. I'll tell you later.' If I ever tell you, Traven added in the secrecy of his own mind — it will be up to Hanna herself whether you ever know the reasons why she can make her cover story jell with Cooper. 'So, Cooper gets the Innisfree address — and we will have laid a trap for him there, take him if he turns up . . . What do you say? Does it set your mind at rest about both Hanna and Rebecca?'

Steve stood silent. Inside his head he was hearing Cooper's savage words as, only a few hours earlier, he spoke of what he would do to Rebecca when he caught up with her — 'I'll get her, and when I do, by Christ, will I put the bitch through it!'

'I'm with you.' He looked up at Traven. 'We'd better get a move on. We can be damn sure Cooper will.'

'We shall. This is how it will go: Hanna gives him Rebecca's address. When — *if*, of course — he arrives there, she lets him in. But we will have our men at her hideout before him. By the time he knocks on the door those men will have recce'ed the bungalow and be positioned ready to take him the moment — '

'Should work OK.' Steve was convinced, seeing before him a future with Cooper jailed for years and Rebecca safe. 'The whole ploy is something of a gamble, obviously. Seems one worth taking, though; like you said, nothing lost if he doesn't show, but big gains if he does. But — manpower? You said — '

'Pared down to two men at the bungalow it would be effective, given the element of surprise on Cooper's side. I can detach one officer from other duties, but — '

'Hell, surely — ' But then Steve read the message crystal clear in Traven's expression, and a sober elation spread over his face. 'Of course! Makes sense, doesn't it? Rebecca knows me, trusts me.'

'In fact you're just the bloke for the job. So let's get moving. I'll provide you with a car and give you one back-up officer with his own vehicle. You will have command of the strategy to be employed at the house.' Traven reached for the telex phone on a nearby table. 'I'll — '

'Wait on.' Steve spoke urgently, moved closer to him. 'The part about Hanna — you're sure *she'll* be OK? Cooper is one rough bastard and he'll be rabid now.'

'Rest easy.' Traven's hand dropped to his side. 'Her story will be good. Besides, I'll send men to her place to check on developments — ordinary coppers, but armed. One other point, Steve: stick with the communication edict re you and Hanna for a bit longer, please. Don't contact her until I give the word. All right?'

'But why? I was counting on calling her soon now.'

'Security precaution. I've told her not to answer her phone, but to leave the answer-phone on — so there'd be just a chance that if Cooper does go there he might happen to switch it on and hear your voice.'

'Pretty slim chance. OK, though . . . But how come you'll be able to call her with the story she's to produce for Cooper?'

'I'll put through a coded instruction on her answerphone for her to call me at once on my special number giving a certain name; when she does, I simply give her the story and ring off.'

Satisfied, Steve nodded. 'You'll make sure she's OK, though?'

'Like I said, I'll send a couple of officers in an unmarked police car. I won't be able to get them on the road for a while but they'll get there, Steve. Just in case.'

Steve accepted it. Went, then. God knows where Cooper is right now, he thought as he found his car and set off for Rebecca's hiding place. The bastard has been on the run for hours. What's in his mind? Is he using every trick in the book to get out and away from the UK? Or is he working his way to Rebecca? Has he had info on her whereabouts from one of his spies, and is already on his way to her?

Leave it, Steve, he told himself then: drive, and get to her.

16

Cooper made good time on his journey to Hanna Tregorian's house. On reaching the Chesham area he parked in a side street, consulted his AA map and worked out his best route to it; then pinpointed a road close to it wherein he could park, and drove there.

Good vehicle, this Honda, it's done me proud, he thought, as he parked again, got out and locked up. Many thanks Mr Paul Stewart . . . Standing on the pavement, he glanced down at the legs of his chinos and saw with satisfaction that although a bit creased they were more or less dry. Anyway it wouldn't matter either way to Tregorian, with her being one of Shaheen's sleepers she — But at that moment his mobile rang and he answered it.

The call was from one of his recently hired agents. He had news to give Cooper, but it did not concern Rebecca Remmick. 'Sawyer here,' he said. 'I reckoned you'd want to hear this although it isn't to do with the woman we're after. Mick was on the blower to me a couple of minutes ago, said he'd latched on to an interesting whisper and wanted to know if

311

I thought he should drop the Remmick search temporarily and follow up this new bit of dirt or — '

'What's the dirt?'

'Hanna Tregorian. The word is she's playing double, has been for a while now. She works in with the MI5 bunch same time as she acts as a sleeper for Shaheen.'

This hit Cooper like a mule kick in the guts but he forced himself to absorb the shock of it and keep his mind focused on the one thing he was burning to achieve *now*: revenge for Liam Kidd. 'Is it fair dinkum, or just a floater?' he demanded. 'And I want a straight answer, no mucking about to guard your own back or your pal's.'

Cooper's voice betrayed the violence riding him and Sawyer thought, thank Christ I'm not Tregorian when, if ever, he gets to her. Then he made swift assessment of (a) his oppo Mick's actual words and their given source, and (b), Mick's streetwise nous and credit-worthiness — and made cautious answer. 'Reckon we can count on there being something in it. So what'll I tell Mick?'

'Keep on the job you were given, both of you! And now get off the fucking line!' Shoving away his mobile, Cooper stood glaring into the middle distance, seeing nothing. There was burning inside him a fury he could barely contain — against Hanna Tregorian. What Sawyer had just told him might be only rumour, but in Cooper's experience rumour invariably had at least a grain of truth at its core. So it looked as if the woman had made fools of them all! Himself, Shaheen, Steve, the whole bloody cadre — she'd run rings round the lot of them! And Christ alone knew how long she'd been playing them for suckers, outmanoeuvring them, able to outwit them because she knew *both* sides of things that were happening. And how big a part had she played in whatever had just gone wrong at Ashburn? That had targeted the controllers presumably — and they were the power-house of the Desert Wolf op, of its entire UK network. If they went down, the whole fucking thing would go down — quite likely fallen victim to a trap set by Traven with the help of Tregorian's insider knowledge from her ties with Shaheen.

Get focused, man! Quite suddenly, a stark image of Liam Kidd had projected itself on to the eye of Cooper's mind — and at once his thought centred on his reason for being where he was now. He was there to get the present address of the Remmick bitch so he could drive there and beat the hell out of her until she came up with what had happened to Liam that evening he'd gone calling on her.

And when she'd done so, he'd kill her: Liam dead, she too, in payment for it.

Keep your mind on that, Cooper told himself. But first, there's Tregorian — and things are different now, aren't they? About her. Sure, she's not *proven* to be doubling, but it's likely to be true — fits in with what happened earlier, too; the information Marisa got for me, the telephone number which was the Remmick bitch's contact just after Liam disappeared. Yes, I've got good reason to get stuck into Tregorian!

Forcing the anger inside him to die down to a slow burn Cooper conned rapidly the methods he'd planned to use to force her to give him Rebecca's address, searching for some way they might be 'improved' — not that *she*'d see it that way, natch! — and thus punish her for her treachery. He discovered such an 'improvement' quite quickly, recalling the pocket-sized, high-tech time-bomb he had brought with him from the Mondeo outside Ashburn and stashed in the Honda. Yeah, he thought, use the little beauty right and I can make Tregorian sweat and suffer . . . Opening up the Honda again, he took out the small black box, slid it carefully into the pocket of his anorak then locked up again and went on his way to Tregorian's house.

By chance, Hanna saw Cooper come up to her front door. So what Traven referred to as a possibility when he phoned me a while ago becomes true fact, she thought, watching from behind curtaining, seeing Cooper's tall, burly figure striding up her path and recalling what Traven had said on the answerphone, 'Don't think this will necessarily happen, Hanna, but it might, and here's what I want you to do if it does.' Well, it was occurring: Cooper was about to knock on her front door. So get your act together, Hanna Tregorian, she told herself. And it had better be good; you have to spin your story — Traven's story — to him as though it is a truth in your heart and mind.

Settling her navy sweatshirt to rights over her jeans and smoothing into place the scarlet kerchief she had tied over her hair, she went through into the hall and opened her door to him.

'Mr Cooper! What have you — ' But Hanna's ability to speak ended there for the moment. Cooper bulled straight in — came at her with his right fist flashing out to clout her on cheek and mouth and his left following up with a punch that drove hard into her stomach. She staggered backwards under the weight of his assault, then, as his second blow struck home she bent double in agony, her arms hugging the pain of it, her head down as she fought for breath. Dimly hearing him close the door, she straightened up — but then he was on her again. Grabbing her jaw with one hand he jerked her head up and belted her across the face with the other, then backed her up hard against the wall behind her and — expertly, comprehensively — beat her up. During the first minute of it she cried out to him in protest, but Cooper only laughed, so she shut her mouth and buried her face in her arms and from then on he heard nothing but muffled gasps of pain coming from behind the shielding bone and flesh.

By the time he stopped her entire body was hurting but she was still conscious because he wanted her that way. She was half lying on the floor of the hall. Roughly Cooper picked her up bodily, carried her to an upright chair against the wall and dumped her down on it. Then he stood back and smiled at her.

'Where's the Remmick woman?' he asked, quite quietly.

Hanna did not answer at once. For one thing there was blood in her mouth and her lip was split so it hurt to make words, but secondly and more importantly, she wanted time to think. Chin on her chest, she forced herself to sit upright, moving each part of her aching body as she needed it, cracking down hard on a physical compulsion to gasp, moan or whatever at the pain, and gathering her mental forces to stand fast against Cooper's physical dominance of her. Finally, sliding her hands along the wooden arms of the chair she gripped them tightly, raised her head and looked him in the eye, ready for him now.

'You are a fool, Mr Cooper,' she said — heard her voice come out as no more than a miserable croak so cleared her throat and tried again. 'What you've just done was stupid. I already know why you're here, Shaheen told — ' But excruciating pain stabbed into her chest and she broke off, hunched over, her mouth closed against the scream inside her.

'I reckon you're the fool.' Cooper eyed her contemptuously, then stepped closer and lashed out at her with his foot, kicking her on the shin, watching her shudder as the new pain hit her. 'Come on, then!' he jeered. 'If you know what I want, get on and give it me, woman!'

Again she straightened up. Tell it clear and hard now, Hanna, she willed herself: tell him the story Traven gave you and *make it convincing*. Cooper has got to believe it. So, dredging up her will power she faced him and taunted him, the way he would probably expect her to do if her story were true.

'I tell you again, you are a fool,' she said quite firmly. 'You're wasting time here, Cooper. Shaheen contacted me yesterday — like I began to tell you, but you cut me off. He gave me the address Rebecca Remmick is hiding at, and ordered me to call you this evening at seven o'clock and give you that address — the place is north of here, about an hour's drive, he said — together with his personal authorization to take whatever action you deem suitable against the woman. *Whatever action you deem suitable.*' She repeated the bait-words, seeing him frowning as he weighed things up, torn between belief and disbelief.

Cooper stepped closer to her again. And this time he laid no hand upon her; he only leaned down to her, stared into her eyes as if he would like to claw the truth out of them, and attacked her with rapid-fire questions

'What's the address?'

'It's a bungalow called Innisfree, in a road called Heath Way.'

'She got guards? Minders?'

'I don't know.'

'Didn't Shaheen say?'

'No he — '

'What time did he ring you?'

'Afternoon.'

'What *hour*?'

'I can't remember.'

'Who set up the hideout? Traven?'

'I believe so.'

'This place Remmick's at — she living by herself there, or what?'

'The owner's away visiting family, Shaheen said. Mrs Remmick's alone there.'

'You said you *believed* Traven set the thing up. Why d'you believe that?'

God help me I can't keep this up much longer. 'From what Shaheen said it seemed — '

'Forget it; doesn't matter.' Cooper changed tack again. 'Shaheen, the cadre — we're bust.' he said. 'Did you know?'

'I heard a rumour of it less than an hour ago — '

'Who from?'

Think, woman! Must come up with someone he can't know much about but is credible. 'John Wakeford.'

'Who's he?' Suspicion darted in Cooper's dark, intent regard.

'One of Westerman's PAs.'

Searching her eyes, her face, Cooper could pinpoint nothing to suggest she was lying — but nothing, either, that convinced him she was telling him the truth. And this bloke

319

Wakeford? He had heard Shaheen mention the name, but he did not know the man and certainly hadn't got the time to chase him up and check her story. He'd got the Remmick bitch's address, hadn't he? That was the important thing. On the thought he grinned and stepped back a few paces. 'Give me her address again,' he said.

Hanna repeated it, then leaned her head back against the chair and closed her eyes.

'*Look at me!*' Cooper's order was a snarl of sudden rage. 'Don't you fucking well turn away from me till I give you permission . . . Now, say it over again.' When she had done so, he nodded. 'Got it. So I'll take off now, go see the Remmick bitch. Got one special thing to do first, though. I don't trust you, Tregorian, so I'll have to truss you up — and take certain precautions. You got some cord around?'

'Shaheen will — '

'Shaheen's history as far as I'm concerned. This is between you and me, here and now. Where's the cord?'

It's safe to give in now, surely? Yes. If I try to go on I'll probably mess things up, I'm too . . . tired. Too used up to think straight. 'You'll find some in the garage. You can reach that through the house, there's no need to go outside.'

'We'll go get it together.' Cooper pulled aside his anorak to show her the holstered gun. 'Do I need this?'

Hanna shook her head. 'If I wasn't on your side, would I have given you the address?'

'That remains to be seen, doesn't it?' Cooper smiled at her, thin-lipped, his eyes brilliant with malice. 'Could be it isn't the right address, could be — ' But seeing she was barely listening — she was concentrating on struggling to her feet — he grinned again and watched her. 'Good girl,' he said, when she was standing. 'Let's go. You lead the way, I'll follow. Try any tricks and you'll be sorry.'

Ten minutes later, Hanna was back in the same chair, tied to its legs and arms with nylon rope at her wrists and ankles, the upper part of her body held tightly against its wooden back by three strands of the cord passed round them both. Having tied the last knot, Cooper picked up her scarlet kerchief from the floor to gag her — changed his mind, stood back and surveyed her with satisfaction.

'That'll keep you in your place and quiet, I reckon,' he said. 'And if you're playing fair and square with me you'll come out of this OK — alive and kicking, as they say. But like I said, I don't trust you, Tregorian — and right now I ain't got the time to check up on the story you spun me about Shaheen and the bitch's address. So' — he paused, reaching into his pocket and bringing out the small explosive device he had brought with him from Ashburn — 'here's what I'm going to do . . . You ever heard the acronym M.A.D.?'

But staring dully up at him, afraid to look away, she shook her head; exhausted and in great pain she was past caring now, wishing only that Cooper would go, would leave her alone.

'M.A.D. was big-time stuff,' he went on. 'Set up between Russia and the US of A during the Cold War, it was. Worked like this: equal amount of nuclear weapons held by both sides, so if you nuke me, brother — will I nuke you back! See? Mutually Assured Destruction. Neat, eh? Well, what I'm going to set up here for you and me works on the same principle.' He placed the small black box on the palm of his hand and held it out towards her. 'See this?' he asked — and on the instant saw her eyes go wild with terror because she knew the thing in his hand for what it was. He chuckled. 'Yep, you're right, Tregorian. This here's a bomb — not a big one, sure, but I reckon from close up you'll find it's big enough to do the job OK. It's on a timer, so I'll set that now.' He turned his back on her to do so, then faced her once more. 'Right, it's set now. I'll put it on your lap so you can keep an eye on it.'

Frozen with horror and despair, Hanna could not look away. Her bruised and swollen eyes were riveted on the time-bomb and when Cooper took his hand away she went on looking at it: a little black beast squatting there on her lap, so close, so *close*.

'Can you hear it ticking?' Cooper asked, savouring the death fear on her.

Cocking her head sideways, she listened with dreadful intensity. 'No. I can't hear anything,' she whispered — then suddenly gasped as hope surged inside her just as he had meant it to. 'So you haven't — '

'Not a chance,' he said, grinning, and saw her chin sink down on her chest. 'Join the real world, Tregorian. That baby on your lap, she's quality stuff, doesn't make a sound — punches well above her weight, though, believe you me . . . Look up at me!' he ordered harshly. 'I've got more to say to you so come on, look up! I want to see your face!'

Summoning the last reserves of her will power Hanna raised her head and fixed her eyes on his face, seeing him fuzzily, hoping against hope.

'I'm playing fair with you, Tregorian,' he said. 'I'm pushing off now, going after the Remmick bitch. But what I've set up here

— like I said, it's an M.A.D., scenario.' Cooper's voice was hard as he went on and his eyes, hot and dark, bored into hers. 'Outside I got a bloke watching your front door, which I'll leave unlocked. If all goes well for me and I find Remmick where you told me she is, then I call my bloke on mobile and tell him to come in and switch off the timer on our friend here, because you'll have played fair with me. But if I haven't called him by eight o'clock — which is ten minutes before she's set to blow — it'll mean either Remmick isn't where you told me she is, or I've been caught by Traven's lot. Either of those'll mean you've played me for a sucker, so M.A.D. will swing into action — my bloke will simply take off and ten minutes later . . . Well, that smart little fellow cosying up to you there can tell time too. See? M.A.D. rules! If you've levelled with me, I'll come out of this OK and so will you. But if you've cheated on me — it probably won't be good for me, but you'll be one dead lady.'

'But Shaheen — '

'Like I said, to me he's history.' Then Cooper turned on his heel and went out through her front door. Leaving Hanna Tregorian alone in her house — except for the monstrosity he had left on her lap.

Jarvis was back on the radio to Traven within fifteen minutes of his first call. 'Found the car, sir. Mondeo, dark green. No keys, no one inside.'

'Was it hidden?'

'No, sir. Cooper'd left it on the verge, out of sight of Ashburn but not far from it.'

'The house itself — any luck there?'

'Negative. Personnel from Units A and B hadn't eyeballed him.'

'You've searched the Mondeo?'

'Prelim. search only. In the boot we found two grenades and a time bomb — '

'*Jesus!*'

' — inside a custom-built case marked First Aid. There were two bomb compartments in it and one of them was empty.'

'Right. Noted.' Noted indeed, Traven thought, but what I do about it, if anything, I've no idea. 'Clothing? Personal effects?'

'Negative.'

'Papers?'

'Nothing relevant to present enquiries.'

'Then get the search for him started, taking his Mondeo as your axial point. I'll send reinforcements, local officers should be with you in ten minutes, Special Forces in thirty.'

'Do I call in support search? Choppers?'

'I'll handle that. Right? And — Jarvis!

— you take great care. The guy you're after could be crazy enough — '

'Sir.' Jarvis got down to the job then and he gave it all there was in him to give, he ran himself and his men ragged: he had a reputation to win back.

★ ★ ★

'What time was it you said you expect Paul to get here?' Jenni Stewart deposited her trug of just-gathered lettuces and tomatoes on the kitchen table, then swept back her mane of blonde hair with both hands and looked across at her husband as he came in from the garage at the side of their house.

'Never did say, actually — knowing my brother, I don't suppose he told me.' Ben Stewart put his briefcase down inside the door and went across to his wife. 'You know Paul — should do, by now!' And pulling an unresisting Jenni into his arms he kissed her, glad to be home and with her. Then she broke free from the embrace and, humming to herself, set about making a pot of tea, while her husband took off his jacket and slung it over the back of a chair, chatting as he did so, a half smile on his face at the prospect of his brother's visit. 'A lovely day like this, Paul'll take his time. He's not that fond of driving, and serious traffic scares the pants off him. If I know him he'll find a nice quiet spot of country on the way, pull off the road and stroll around a bit.'

'Judging by past form, more like he'll find a nice quiet country pub on the way and pull in for a leisurely pint! God knows what time he'll get here.'

Ben Stewart chuckled, wandered over to the kitchen window. 'You could be right, at that,' he said, gazing out over the sweet green countryside spreading beyond his own half-acre of land. 'One thing we can be sure of, though, darling: knowing you'll have your famous roast duck ready for him this evening he'll damn sure make certain to get here by eight o'clock.'

'And as always — ah, hell! — Harry and David will claim kids' rights to stay up late because it's the first night of Uncle Paul's visit.' But there was a smile on Jenni's tanned, smooth-skinned face: brother-in-law Paul was fun to have around, she was looking forward to his stay with them as much as Ben and the boys were.

★ ★ ★

The unmarked police car *en route* to check up on Hanna Tregorian was making good time: a dark-blue Volvo, it looked ordinary enough, but it packed an awesome punch under its bonnet. The two Specials in her were both armed.

'If traffic stays this quiet we should be there in fifteen minutes.' At the wheel, Venner — a dark-haired man in his late thirties known among his peers as a hard-nosed bastard but straight as a die and good to have at your back in a tight corner — was concentrating on his driving. They were travelling along a dual-carriageway, populated country on their left but the houses all set well back from the road; the grassed verges were fenced off against fields and woodland. The car radio was on with the sound turned down low, but he was not listening to it. That was Carson's job.

'Yeah. We've had an easy run so far, hope it lasts.' Younger by a good ten years, Carson answered automatically, half listening to the flow of police chat on the radio, a slight frown on his narrow, sharp-boned face. Carson was regarded (not only by himself) as a high-flier, and he saw every job he was on in the light of what it might offer him in the way of personal kudos to be won in the successful doing of it. 'If Traven was right we — ' But he broke off and sat forward, tension mounting in him as he listened to the police flash coming over the radio.

'What gives?' Venner asked.

Carson gestured for quiet but did not turn up the sound. The young bastard always plays things as close to his chest as he can, thought Venner. And with a sour grin he got on with the driving.

Half a minute later, 'There's a cop chase in progress fairly close behind us on this road,' Carson said. 'It's a drugs bust. The vehicle they're tailing slipped their net: a stolen Transit van, white, cargo heroin, two suspects aboard — hang on!' He listened to the radio again, then went on with renewed urgency. 'There's two police vehicles after the Transit. As of now the chase is five miles back from us and the cop plan is to drop a stinger mat in front of the target — '

'So we'd best get off the road quick, give them a clear run,' Venner said, then as they rounded a left-bearing corner he spotted a lay-by 500 yards ahead, it looked big enough for three cars but at the moment was empty so he pulled the Volvo in at the near end, leaving room ahead of him for the pursuit cars behind to do likewise if they so chose.

Beside him, Carson swore. Of all the cheesy rotten luck! Why the hell did the cop chase have to happen *here* and *now*? He and Venner stood to lose a quarter of an hour or more, stuck in this shitty little lay-by while the anti-narcotics boys did their stuff. Traven would *not* be pleased. 'Should we call in and report the delay?' he asked, turning to Venner.

'Nah. Later, if we need to. See what happens, first.'

Venner was the senior officer, the decision was his. Mouth tight, Carson shrugged. 'Reckon I'll get out, stretch my legs,' he said. 'They'll be coming round that corner any minute now.'

★　★　★

Five miles behind them but travelling fast the two police pursuit vehicles were working in tandem to their prearranged plan: Ajax — a Rover saloon carrying two officers — was sitting on the Transit's tail; Hector — a black Escort van with two officers in front and a two-man stinger crew in the back — was travelling a short distance behind it ready to overtake their target on cue then drop the stinger in its path, puncture its tyres and thus force it to stop.

'You ready to jump target?' Ajax driver said to Hector on sight of a longish, straight and traffic-free stretch of road in front of him with a sharpish-looking left turn in the distance. It looked promising, he judged, and they ought to make a move before they hit traffic again.

'Yeah, all set to go. We'll drop the stinger on the far side of that corner then pull off the road and be ready for him. Go!-Go!-Go!'

Holding his position on the road, the Ajax driver saw Hector pull out — accelerate and challenge the Transit — gain on it — draw level with it — hold level — then with a sudden burst of speed shoot ahead, speed on to the corner then vanish round it to drop the stinger that would cripple the Transit.

★   ★   ★

In the cab of the Transit, the driver hunched himself closer over the wheel and kept his foot down on the accelerator. The two cop cars had been tailing him ever since he'd worked his way clear of town traffic and was on the highway, and he could see no real hope now of shaking them off — but he wasn't going to fucking well *give in*, was he? OK, they'd got him pinned down, and they'd make radio contact with their own kind, likely call out air surveillance but —

'Cool it, Bill, for Christ's sake!' From the passenger seat Spinner McCoy's high-pitched, whining voice advanced its plea for the second time in as many minutes. 'We're never going to make it now, we've had it, might as well pull — '

'Shut it!' Bill shouted, then spat on the floor and got on with his job. It was obvious McCoy was shit-scared, him sitting there crouched up against his door like a fucking monkey, staring pop-eyed at what he was seeing in his side-mirror — poor sod, he was a quitter, was Spinner, no spunk in him these days; when he hasn't got his heavies with him he just folds. 'Tell you one thing, Spinner,' Bill said. 'If it does look like we've had it I'm going to bloody well make a fight of it — and make damn sure one or two of them go down with me!'

'We should've ditched the Transit and made a run for it like I said.'

'Stop whingeing — ' But Bill broke off because in his rear-view mirror he had seen the picture on the road behind him start to change, the lead cop car was still keeping station some twenty yards back but the one behind, the Escort van, was pulling out — was accelerating — had passed its mate and was coming up fast!

'Shit! Oh Shit! Oh God Almighty! Give up, Bill! *Give up!*' Spinner McCoy's voice was a wail of pure terror. 'He'll get ahead of us then put down a stinger!'

'Think I don't know it?' But Bill's response was automatic, he was concentrating on being ready to take on the cops. He saw/sensed the

Escort drawing level with him and increased his speed — the Escort matched the increase — they were running parallel — but then the Escort was gaining on him! Slowly but surely it pulled ahead — it was clear of him, it sped on and vanished round the corner.

'*Give in*, Bill! It's no good, we're done for!' Handfast to whatever he could grab hold of, McCoy was yelling, his face livid, eyes starting out of his head. 'Stop, man! *Give in!*'

But Bill didn't even hear him because the Transit also had rounded the corner now and he'd seen the stinger mat across the road in front of him — seen too that, not far beyond it, there was a lay-by with a Volvo stationary at the near end of it and the Escort parked just ahead of it, it's crew still inside. He was too close to the stinger to run clear of it — that bloody Escort crew had beaten him! And Bill had only ever had one response to losing — fight fair or fight foul, but fight to your last breath and make bloody sure to take at least one of the enemy with you if you go down. So now, as his left rear wheel passed over the stinger there was murder in his heart and head. He felt the wound take hold on the tyre, begin to shred it. 'Bastards!' he swore. 'Sodding bastards!' But I'll get you yet. Not going to *give in*, am I? Not bloody likely. Never have, never will. I'll show 'em. The van's the only weapon I've got so I'll bloody well use it. I'll keep her on the road somehow, drive her straight at that Escort — then at the last moment swing the wheel hard over *and send the darling's rear end smashing straight into those cops!* Sure, their back-up blokes will take me then — but, by Christ, some of their own will've caught a packet!

But things did not work out that way. With the one rear wheel deflating fast Bill found the van harder to control than he'd reckoned. Sweat pouring down his face, he struggled to keep mastery of her. I gotta hit the Escort, there's cops inside it, gotta get even with the bastards. Come *on*, you darling, do what I'm asking of you — give me that Escort! I gotta miss that civvy saloon then swing in and sideswipe the Escort so stay with me, darling — stay with me — *go where I'm telling you to go, for God's sake! Shit! I'm not going to make it! Too close to the saloon — too bloody close to it —*

★   ★   ★

As pursuit vehicle Ajax rounded the corner its driver was hit by a full-on picture of what was happening in the lay-by ahead — and slammed on his brakes, skidded to a halt. He saw the white van slewing crabwise off the carriageway towards the parked Volvo, strips of flayed rubber flying off its rear wheel — saw it recover — but then almost immediately lose road-hold again, the back end of its chassis swinging wildly from side to side and then — ah, *Jesus!* — it caught the Volvo a swingeing side-on swipe that sent it careering across the verge to end up canted drunkenly against the fencing there. The Transit shuddered at the impact, gained the road again, lurched on for a few yards but then stopped dead.

'*God Almighty!*' breathed Ajax's driver, sitting shocked, staring. But his mate was already out of the car and sprinting towards the wrecked Volvo.

17

Steve made reasonable time on his journey to Innisfree, Rebecca's hideout. Although he had not been to it before he was familiar with the layout of the bungalow: straight after her moving in there they had talked together several times on the phone and she, delighting in the pleasantness of her temporary home, had described it to him in considerable detail. Now as he drove, he recalled its ground-plan and — being near certain in his own mind that Traven's scheme would work, Cooper would get Rebecca's address from Hanna and go there gunning for her — thought out a plan for effecting Cooper's arrest when he arrived.

Finding Heath Way without much difficulty he parked his Clio in a road branching off from it and, using his mobile, instructed Giles Andrews, the officer Traven had detailed as his back-up and who was travelling behind him in his own car, to park in a side road a few minutes' drive away from Innisfree and wait until Steve contacted him again — almost certainly to summon him to

336

the bungalow and assist in the arrest of Brad Cooper.

That done, Steve got out of the Clio and walked quickly to Innisfree. He found the bungalow looked exactly as Rebecca had described it to him, right down to the scarlet and green curlicues adorning the name-plate affixed to its gate . . . Wish you were still alive, Rob, he thought suddenly; Rebecca needs you, she needs you badly — like you needed her, murdering Shaheen's courier that night to keep her shining, polished image of you untarnished. Then he banished his brother from his mind, opened the gate, went down the flower-bordered path and rang the bell beside the door.

Rebecca let him in at once, slid free the security chain, turned the key and opened the door narrowly — closed it behind him quickly as soon as he had stepped into the square, red-carpeted hall. She turned to him then and he saw with shock that her face was ashen, and the blue eyes had a hunted, hag-ridden glaze to them.

'Oh Steve, I've been watching for you through the window over there,' she said, her voice light and fast, her hands never still, smoothing nervously over her hair, her green blouse and black trousers as she spoke. 'I can't tell you how glad I am to see you.

Thank God you're here! I'm so scared, so damn *scared*. Traven said Cooper might come here and I was afraid you might not — '

'I'm here now, love.' It was years since he had called her 'love'. It was a word which belonged back in the early days when she and Rob had been together, during the time when she had learned too much, too suddenly, about Rob's real way of life and been terrified *of* it and *for* him. She had run to Steve for comfort and understanding then because she feared that if she confessed her panic to Rob, his love for her might be gutted of its wild and wonderful élan. The little close word had worked then, it had helped her; it did so now.

' 'Love'.' A sudden quietness in her, Rebecca repeated his word softly. 'It's been a long time since you called me that.'

'It says what I mean.'

'Because I was Rob's wife — '

'That's how it started; it was because of what the two of you were together. But it's you at the heart of it now, not him.'

Rebecca looked at him in silence for a moment; then she smiled faintly. 'Thanks,' she said. 'You've made me feel a lot better.' And Steve saw the fear gripping her loosen its hold — she was unable to drive it right out of her, but at least she didn't seem so humbled before it. He capitalized on this little victory at once, turning her mind away from present fears and on to ways to combat and defeat them.

'We must work out what we're going to do right now,' he said. 'There's no telling when Cooper will turn up — '

'So it's certain he'll come here, then? From what Traven said — ' 'There's no certainty either way,' he interrupted, seeing the fear back in her and cursing himself for being so blunt. Watch your tongue, you cretin! he upbraided himself; she's only just managing to hold herself together, if you get it wrong she'll fall apart. 'But it's no good pretending he *won't* come, so let's plan exactly what we're going to do if he does. You and me together — beat anyone, won't we?'

'Rob used to say that to me.'

'I pinched most of my best sayings from your Rob, I guess.' Steve gave her a quick grin, then moved forward into the hall, looking around him, sizing up his battle-ground. 'This is where we'll take him, Rebecca,' he went on, noting with relief that it was just as she had described it to him. Ten to twelve yards square, wall-to-wall carpeted in deep red, the hall had one window either side of the front door, opposite which stood another one, half open. 'The door over there leads into the sitting-room, doesn't it?' he asked, turning to her.

'Yes, like I told you on the phone.' Hope was growing in Rebecca: Steve's here with me now, she thought, so I'll be safe, Steve's a match for anyone. Even for Cooper? Yes, even for him.

'I know Cooper's carrying a gun, and I know his methods on a job pretty well by now,' he went on. 'He'll almost certainly come to the door and ring the bell like any ordinary above-board caller. With other houses either side of the bungalow he'd be stupid to bank on no one spotting him if he comes snooping around the back of the place. And Cooper is not stupid.'

'To come straight up to the front door — is that what you'd do if you were in his place?'

'In a situation like this — and if I was as full of anger as Cooper is right now — sure I would. I'd walk up the path and ring at the door. I'd have my gun ready in my hand, then the minute you opened it, I'd crowd in on you fast, barge inside with you, shut the door behind us and get on with whatever I'd come to do.'

He saw Rebecca wilt again as the brutal reality of it hit her. But an alteration to the plan to neutralize Cooper he had thought up earlier was taking shape in his mind — and for it to succeed he would need Rebecca's active help, not simply the passive acquiescence called for by his previous intentions. So I have to give it to her straight because Cooper may turn up here soon now and if he does I've got to take him at once, before he has a chance to use his gun.

'But if he comes in like you say — barges in hard, with a gun — what'll you do?' Stricken eyes wide to his, she whispered it without hope.

'Not me alone. You and me together.'

'*Me?* Oh no, I can't, not against Cooper; I just couldn't do it, Steve. I *couldn't!*'

'Yes you can. You've got to. Me opening the door to him wouldn't work, he'd likely use the gun straight off and either kill or incapacitate me — then you'd be on your own against him.'

Rebecca buried her face in her hands. 'I can't face him. I just can't!' she whispered, tears trickling through her fingers. Then she brushed away the tears and looked up at him. 'Look, Steve — can't I simply . . . go next door?' she begged. 'Leave you to deal with this? You said you've got a gun, so it'd work out; you could take him by surprise and arrest him. Sheila's next door, we get on well together — I'll think up some story and go across, stay with her till this is over? *Please*, Steve! You . . . you're used to this sort of thing.'

There was shame in her eyes as she spoke. Seeing it, Steve felt first a terrible anger against her — but then, only grief. Rebecca — I know she's better than this really, I know it. 'Come into the sitting-room,' he said, but she stood staring at him so he took her hand and led her in, halted beside an armchair in there. 'Sit down, love,' he said.

She sat, then raised a tear-stained face to him. 'Sheila would — '

'Forget Sheila,' he said. 'Listen to me. I need your help to pull this off. All you have to do is open the door to Cooper when he knocks or rings the bell — you open it wide then pull it right back to the wall, and as you're doing so you dash in behind it and hide there. I'll be standing over by the door into this room, I'll be only four or five yards away from him as you open the door — and I'll have my gun aimed straight at him, I'll have him cold. I simply yell 'Freeze!' — and he won't have time to direct his weapon anywhere at all, let alone at you where you're hidden behind the door. And — we're there, love. Cooper drops his weapon; he's got no choice but. I use my mobile, call in my Special Forces bloke who's waiting round the corner, and he and I arrest Cooper.' He smiled at Rebecca. 'You can come out from behind the door then,' he said.

'But what if Cooper's too quick for you?' Doubt was still on her face. 'Like you said he'd rush me, he might — '

'Then he gets a couple of slugs in the right shoulder, which will stop him dead and put him out of action.'

'But I'm *too scared* to do what you're asking, Steve! I just couldn't *do* it!'

Steve swung away from her, stood racking his brains for a way to motivate her. Surely what she needed was something outside herself, yet of vital importance to her — something to focus on, to live for, to *fight* for? Then suddenly, an idea stood clear in his mind. He thought it through carefully, found it good — and decided it would be *right* to tell her now; she was Rob's *wife*, for God's sake, so it was only proper she should know; Rob ought to have told her it himself, years ago. Turning to her again he laid a hand on her arm.

'I've something important to tell you,' he said. 'It's about Rob.'

'About *Rob*? What the hell! It's *Cooper* we have — '

'No — well, yes, because this'll make you look at things differently, but what I have to tell you — it's actually about Rob.'

'Go on, then. Tell me.' Her voice and her face were hard and cold.

Get it said, man. Just — get the words out, plain. 'Rob had a daughter,' he said.

Rebecca was stone still. After a moment said dully, 'I don't understand.'

'Before he met you he had an affair, and the woman had a baby. That baby is now around twenty years old.'

She stood up then, and for a full minute said nothing at all. Steve was forgotten; Cooper was forgotten: her mind was reeling about, lost, blind, groping wildly around its hostile surrounding dark. Steve intuited from her eyes that she had as such left him. She was with Rob, it seemed to him: and he, Steve, was no more to her than a blank PC screen which, when she pressed its controlling keys, would present her with the information she requested of it.

'I don't believe you.' she said. 'Why should I?'

'Have I ever lied to you?'

'No, never.'

'What I just told you is true, Rebecca.'

'When was it?' she asked — and now he sensed the beginning of anger in her.

'Nineteen eighty-three. Rob was very young. So was the girl.'

Rebecca nodded — and went on pressing keys. 'Who was she?'

'Angela Langley. Our families were neighbours; we grew up together.'

344

'What's the . . . daughter's name?'

'Donna.' Don't give her too much: the point of this is to make her *want* to know more; that way she'll see something ahead to live for, to strive for and —

'This Langley person — did she and Rob stay together long, after the baby?'

'No. She had other ideas.' It's time to stop this now, Steve thought, we must move on. 'We'll leave it there for the moment,' he said firmly. 'We've got Cooper to deal with.'

For a second she stared at him in silence, reasoning her way to the obvious conclusion. Then, 'You bastard!' she hissed. '*You're blackmailing me!*'

'That's exactly what I'm doing, so let's get on with the deal. You want what I'm offering, don't you?'

'Yes. But why didn't you tell me before? Why *now*?'

'Forget about yourself and for one second flat think about what's at stake here — then you'll bloody well realize *why!*'

But she did not need the full second: his flare of anger caught her on the raw and she blinked, shook her head. 'I'm sorry,' she said quietly. Smiled at him then and, a new determination in her face and body language, went towards the door. 'I'm not really so feeble. Thanks for telling me what you did, and yes, I do want — I want very much — to know more about Rob's daughter. So let's go back into the hall and you explain to me — *show* me — exactly what you want me to do when Cooper comes.'

'If he does. We can't be absolutely sure.'

'I think we can. That's why Traven sent you, isn't it?'

'He didn't *send* me.'

'Nice, hearing you say that.' But she hurried on into the hall without a backward glance.

Ten minutes later, with their preparations for Steve to confront and arrest Cooper complete, Rebecca went into the kitchen to make some coffee, for although she accepted that Cooper might arrive at any minute she realized it was equally possible he might not turn up for hours yet. There had been no communication from Traven, so they assumed Cooper had not so far been traced — that in spite of the search Traven had mounted, where he was and what he was doing had not yet been discovered.

The moment Rebecca had left, Steve went back into the sitting-room, cast himself down in an armchair and thought about Cooper, recalling the kind of man he was, and trying to work out how he'd behave in the long term. He'd come to know the security man well over the last eighteen months, the two of them often working closely together as, under Shaheen's direction, the cadre had assisted Mansoor in the Desert Wolf operation. Now, as he worked his way towards a reasoned judgement as to Cooper's likely course of action in regard to Rebecca *after* his arrest, and, hopefully, his subsequent trial and imprisonment, a terrible dread was born inside him. From what I've learned about Cooper, his reasoning ran, I've no doubt that, irrespective of whether he sees Rebecca as the actual killer of Liam Kidd or no more than an involved observer, he intends to kill her. He feels honour bound to kill her because *someone* has to pay for Kidd's death and she, being at the very least compliant in it, is therefore fair game. And *Cooper will never give up on that*. So, if I effect his arrest here today and he's convicted and jailed, one of two things will result. First possibility: from jail he'll simply hire a hitman on the outside and have Rebecca murdered; second possibility: he may be convicted of no worse crime than 'involvement in the logistics of a terrorist operation' as it's quite possible that's all they'll be able to pin on him, and therefore he'll serve no more than five or six years, bide his time, then when he's free again he'll hunt her down and kill her himself. I *know*

Cooper. His mind works that way. While he's alive, she'll never be safe from him, he won't give up —

Hang on! What were those words that came into my mind a moment ago? 'While he's alive she'll never be safe from him.' *While he's alive.* So there is a way I can keep her safe from him, isn't there? And I'll have a chance to take that way here, today. If Cooper *does* turn up — and I believe he will — I'll have a chance to make sure Rebecca's safe from him, won't I? Safe not just for today but for the rest of her life. Because I'll have Cooper at gunpoint, and there'll be no witnesses bar me and her.

'I made us sandwiches as well while I was about it. I'm quite hungry.' Rebecca came back into the sitting-room carrying a loaded tray. Steve got to his feet and took it from her and, as he did so, he saw her a prey to fear again, her eyes terror-ridden. Saw Rob's wife in mortal fear of the man who was hunting her — and who would go on hunting her *while he was alive.* No witnesses bar me and Rebecca . . .

★ ★ ★

'*If you've played me false — then M.A.D. rules and you'll be one dead lady.*' Cooper's

348

words went on repeating themselves over and over inside Hanna's head. At first their voice was quiet, half drowned beneath the rip tide of physical pain surging through her body, leaching from her both the desire and the ability to think coherently. But as the minutes and then the hours crept by, the potency of the pain decreased — and controlled, directed thought became possible once more. But then almost immediately she wished it had not. Because as her mind searched out and fully comprehended the realities of her present situation she perceived the full horror implicit in it, built into it by what Cooper — suspicious as ever, vindictive as ever — had done to her, binding her fast and placing his time bomb in her lap. And she *had* played double with him: as planned, Cooper would be taken by Traven's men when he went to Rebecca's hideout, and consequently when the time came M.A.D. would swing into action — whereupon Hanna Tregorian, bound fast to a chair in her own house, would be blown to pieces by Cooper's bomb. At the full realization of it she panicked for a moment — freaked out, her body jerking uncontrollably as she struggled wildly to free herself, rope lacerating flesh, drawing blood at wrists and ankles and all the time her eyes fixed on the little black box at the centre of her life, eyes bereft

349

of reason, dilated in terror before the imagined but at the same time *unimaginable* horror of the total disintegration of oneself, mind, body, *me*, all gone for ever.

Is there a limit to fear? Hanna Tregorian discovered one inside herself that day. By sheer force of will she set a barrier in place against the wildfire terror raging through her as she envisioned her own death. Staring her fear in the eye she shouted it down — Enough! Be still now! *What will be will be!* — and then as she heard the cliché repeat itself inside her head a frail, self-mocking smile came on her bruised and bloody lips . . . Come on, Hanna, get with it! she chided herself. Such an unlived-in, hackneyed bromide? You're better than that — should be, *must* be. You can and will stick this out. Think *Steve*. Think *Traven*. One or other of them — both, with luck! — will be sure to do something long before . . . it happens. You'll be OK. They love you so they'll make sure you're OK — and anyway, apart from the love it's their duty, isn't it? Traven's sending a couple of officers here to check all's well, but like he said they'll have to play the situation with care, allow time for Cooper to have been told Rebecca's address and gone on his way before they show their hand . . . Think *Steve*. Think *Traven*. They'll make sure you're all right . . .

* ★ ★

'Emergency call from Carson, sir.' The Special Forces officer turned to look up at Traven who was standing beside her studying the information showing on her PC. 'He and Venner have hit trouble.'

'I'll take it . . . Traven here. Speak.'

'Carson, *en route* to Tregorian in Chesham.' He gave the map reference of the lay-by the Volvo was in. 'We've been caught up in an incident.'

'Venner's senior officer. Where's he?'

'Injured — severe but not life-threatening. Ambulance on way, due in ten minutes.'

'You?'

'OK bar bruises. Venner took the brunt of it; we were parked in this lay-by, just round a corner — '

'What's the state of your vehicle now? Volvo, isn't it?'

'Yes, sir. She's wrecked. Got hit here in the lay-by.'

'Not operational, then?'

'Not a chance. There's a couple of police vehicles here with us, though.'

'Tell me what happened. Keep it short.'

'Venner pulled the Volvo into this lay-by because there was a cop chase on the road behind us, drugs bust. Two police vehicles

351

involved. The Escort van put a slinger across the road then pulled in here, parked ahead of the Volvo. Suspect van tried to get past the stinger, couldn't make it and punctured its rear wheel.' Carson paused briefly; when he went on his voice was quite different, Traven noted, it was no longer dispassionate, it was grim and angry. 'Then the bastard rammed us mid-chassis — '

'*Rammed* you?' A deliberate act, you mean?'

'That's exactly what I mean, sir, except — it wasn't the Volvo he was aiming for!'

'Explain.' Although impatient to get on with what action should be taken Traven's rational mind could not let Carson's seemingly bizarre statements pass unchallenged.

'The bastard was after the Escort, sir. The car that dropped the stinger. He was aiming to trash it and the blokes inside it — '

'Hold it, Carson. That's a monstrous accusation, but not one for us to deal with now. You're on a job. Let's get it done.'

'Sir . . . The two cop cars — a saloon and the adapted Escort van — are still here in the lay-by, both fully operational. On your say-so I could proceed to Chesham in the saloon immediately.'

'How many anti-narcotics crew?'

'The Escort, four officers, the saloon two. All uninjured.'

'Armed?'

'Only the saloon crew.'

'And your assessment of the situation is?'

'Our priority is Tregorian. The anti-narcotics squad's business is right here in this lay-by and recovery vehicles and so on are all on way. So I suggest they loan us the saloon and one officer, and he and I proceed with the Tregorian job.'

'But if you get into a confrontation scenario with Cooper — '

'I'm armed, so is the driver of the saloon — and I know him, sir, we worked together on a job last year, he's good.'

'Right. Let me speak to him. I'll co-opt him, and the two of you get on with the Chesham mission — suss out the situation there then act as agreed before. Keep me closely informed re Cooper. Now, first, put me on to the senior officer of that anti-narcotics squad.'

*   *   *

It was nearly five o'clock that evening when Hope Ridley finally got her strange story told to the local police. Miss Ridley was in her late forties, and a lady of independent means. A gifted artist, she painted exquisite, beautifully detailed studies of the birds and flowers native to the countryside she lived in. Nowadays her work commanded high prices, but she continued to live in Hawthorn Cottage, on the outskirts of Tansley village, a few miles from Dunham town. Farmland surrounded her half-acre of garden, and on most fine afternoons she went walking its fields and woods, a pair of binoculars slung round her neck for scanning trees and hillsides for birds, a small pencil-in-the-spine notebook in her pocket for the recording of her observations by word or sketch.

On the afternoon when Paul Stewart parked his black Honda in an unsurfaced, narrow side road a couple of miles outside Tansley in order to have a break from driving and enjoy the countryside, Miss Ridley — sensibly but expensively clad in brown moleskin trousers and safari-style jacket, a jungle-green bushhat on her trim, light brown hair — was strolling nearby in the belt of woodland bordering the road. As always, she was taking care to move slowly and quietly so as not to disturb the wild things whose home it was. And on this occasion she had decided to work the inner edge of the wood so that she could keep a close eye, through her binoculars, on the pond at the bottom of the slope to her left, for she had a special purpose in mind that afternoon: a local farmer had told her that he had noticed a pair of wading birds active along the reedy side of the pond, and, although he'd had no idea what species they might be, his description of them had aroused her interest. So she had come to see for herself: she was hoping the birds would be there that afternoon and she would be able to identify them, even sketch them in their habitat if she was lucky.

Catching sight of the pond some 100 yards ahead of her, she halted beside a full-grown oak tree and focused her binoculars on it. A sweep-search of the reedy area on the far side of the water afforded no sign of any bird life there; nor did her next move, a painstaking foot-by-foot examination of the entire site. 'Shit,' she murmured, without malice. Then, being accustomed to similar disappointments, she sat down with her back against the trunk of the oak tree and composed herself to wait. It was a pleasant afternoon. The air was warm and such clouds as drifted across the sky moved lazily content, the white, puffball sails of summertime. But Miss Ridley stayed wide awake, observant of her pond; and as quietness re-established itself in the wood behind and ahead of her she heard more distinctly the sounds of the small creatures living their lives amongst undergrowth, moss and —

Cr-rack! Hard, sharp and shockingly alien in that place, the sound smacked into her ears and she sat bolt upright and, head cocked to one side, listened . . . *Listened.* But heard only . . . ? Silence . . . What I heard just then sounded like a gunshot, she thought. But — a gunshot, here? Don't be an idiot! At this time of year, what is there hereabouts for anyone to shoot at? The bang seemed to come from the other side of the wood and almost level from where I'm sitting, I think. It must have been a car backfiring, over on the road there. I haven't heard a car, though. I can't hear one now, either. Puzzled and vaguely uneasy, Miss Ridley forced herself to relax, smiled a little after a few moments, put her binoculars up to her eyes again —

Cr-rack! It came again — and this time she knew for sure that what she had heard both times was someone firing a gun. And suddenly uncomfortably aware of being alone in a very lonely place she scrambled to her feet and stood close in against the trunk of the oak tree. Again, she'd heard no sound of a car, so what on earth had happened on the other side of the wood? And — what was happening there *now?* Was the shooting finished? Would there be more? How many

356

people were there over on the road? . . . Questions streamed across her mind but no answers came — then suddenly all were silenced and one stood alone there, black and terrifying. Who had shot what — *or shot whom?*

'Oh God.' Closing her eyes, Miss Ridley pressed her body against the treetrunk, one cheek to its rough bark, her fingers clawing into its living wood, and fought the fear in her to a standstill. It's my duty to go through the wood and find out what has happened there, she thought then. I have to do it because someone might be lying there hurt or even . . . dead? I *must* go and see.

But even as that thought came, she froze because she heard . . . *other* noises, different and ominous sounds. They were coming from the same direction as the gunshots had: the crack of twigs snapped underfoot, the swishing and loud rustling of . . . of a person pushing through or past bushes? Yes, someone was coming towards her through the wood! He (she had no doubt it was a man) must be making for the open country beyond, but if he kept to his present course he'd be no more than twenty to thirty yards away from her when he reached the edge of the wood. So what if he should see her? Was he the man who'd fired the shots? Had he . . . had he *shot* someone? For if he had, and he saw her now, realized she'd seen him, he might —

Crouching down close to the ground, Miss Ridley made herself as small as possible and, sinking her chin on her chest so her bush-hat would mask the alien-to-that place pallor of her face, commanded her body to absolute stillness and *listened*. Whoever was coming through the wood was making heavy weather of it. The swishing and rustling of his passage grew louder — then, abruptly, ceased altogether. The wood lay silent about her except for its own esoteric life sounds and the whispering of leaves as a small breeze ruffled the foliage above her head. Listening but hearing nothing, Miss Ridley shrank yet further into herself. It's so quiet he'll hear me breathing! she thought in panic — and opening her mouth she drew in shallow wisps of air making no sound at all.

Then she heard him moving again and realized *he was going away* from her! He was going on down the slope towards the pond — he hadn't seen her, she was safe! For a few seconds, her feeling of relief — of liberation, deliverance! — was so intense that a faintness came over her and she simply relaxed, pushing back her hat and raising her face to the sun. But then swiftly her wonted self-confidence — together with a modicum of natural suspicion and curiosity — returned to her. I wonder just what's going on here? she thought. Those were definitely gunshots I heard over by the road, and now here's this man making off cross-country, away from the scene? His back must be towards me at the moment, I'm going to risk having a look at him.

Scrambling to her feet she focused her glasses on the figure now making its way down the slope in front of her towards the pond — and at once was seized again by horror and dread. Stifling a scream she steadied herself, then watched as the last act of a truly wicked crime unfolded before her eyes. She kept her nerve. Once — as she saw the hurled body of the victim hit the water and smash down through it — she gritted her teeth and threw back her head, shuddering, eyes clenched tight shut, gasping at the sheer evil of what was being done. When she opened them again she saw that the big, dark-haired man had turned and, *facing her now*, was wading ashore — so with the speed born of terror she sank down on her heels, tilted her bush-hat again to hide her white face from the murderer who was coming her way . . . By the time she dared open her eyes and rise to her feet once more, he was no longer in her field of vision: the pond, the grassy slope down to it and the fields surrounding it lay smiling under the sun and she could see nothing and no one moving there. The burly, dark-haired man in a dark sweatshirt had walked out of the peaceful country scene within fifteen minutes of entering it.

But she could still hear him. He was going back through the wood the way he had come. He's running away, she thought. He can't get away from this place fast enough because he's done murder here. And she stood stock still because if she moved he might come back looking for *her*, witness to his crime.

The noise he was making grew fainter and fainter and then ceased. Still she stood rigid, finding it difficult to cleanse herself of mortal terror. Then, suddenly, she heard a car start up over on the road. The engine idled for a moment, was revved up, then the vehicle drove away. Slowly, silence moved back through and over the wood, re-establishing itself swiftly and without difficulty because the man and the car had been aliens within it, itself was the true world. And by the same alchemy Miss Ridley drove out fear and became *her* true self once more: Hope Ridley, good citizen, firm believer in justice for all mankind and a brave and determined woman. The vehicle had been driven off towards Dunham, she had noted. Making her way swiftly across the wood, she searched the nearside verges and road surface around the point the two gunshots seemed to have come from for clues as to what had happened there. Her diligence was rewarded: she discovered smears of blood on the grass in that area and spots of blood on the pale, gritty soil. The bloodstains were fresh: where the sunlight caught them they gleamed jewel-bright.

'The bastard. The murdering *bastard*.' Miss Ridley straightened up and cursed him aloud. Then she returned with all possible speed to Hawthorn Cottage and telephoned the local police.

★　★　★

Wall to wall carpeted in a dark shade of red, the hall at Innisfree allowed near soundless movement. Coming out of the sitting-room, Steve crossed to the window on the left of the front door and took cover behind its green velvet curtains: from there he had a clear view of the gate into the property and the path leading from it to the front door.

He looked at his watch: it was just after seven o'clock, but still there was no sign of Cooper and no call from Traven either. So what the hell was happening? he wondered.

OK, sure, Traven had bigger fish than Cooper to fry that day, but —

His mobile buzzed and he answered it. 'Yep?'

'Traven. We've picked up Cooper's trail and there are things you should know. One, he's still carrying his handgun — '

'How come you can be sure if you haven't caught up with him yet?'

'He's used it. Shot a bloke dead with it so he could steal his car. Proof enough for you?'

'Christ! How — ?'

'Leave it, it's being dealt with. Your idea re Rebecca looks like being right. I believe Cooper's heading for Innisfree now, so keep focused. I've contacted high-level clout covering that area: a couple of Specials will be detailed to assist you in Cooper's arrest. They should be with you within the next hour.'

'Right. We mustn't frighten Cooper off, though, so tell them to park well away from the bungalow when they get here, they must not park anywhere near here — *must* not! They *mustn't* close in on us — '

'Calm down, Steve. Your point's valid, and I have already covered that angle; I've briefed the officers concerned to that effect. I'll give you their call number now.' He did so, then asked, 'All right?'

'Sure. You said there were two things you'd

got for me. What's the other?'

'You're not going to like this, Steve — '

'Shit! Just tell me.'

'It's about Hanna — ' Traven heard Steve trying to interrupt but he shut out the sound of it and went on grimly, forcing out the dreadful words, his voice raw but emasculated of all emotion. 'Cooper beat her up,' he said. 'She didn't have a chance to just give him the address like we planned, he went for her straight off, thrashed her and then — ' But he broke off because what he had yet to say was so . . . so *obscene*.

'She's . . . not hospitalized?'

'No, thank God. She's at home, and her own doctor's with her.' But I have to be absolutely honest with him — he loves her. 'There's something else, Steve. She gave him Rebecca's address and he took off then but he . . . took certain precautions before he left.' Christ, I can't say the words to him — *he loves her*.

But Steve knew Cooper well. 'What did he do to her?' he asked, quite quietly.

'It seems he suspected she might somehow be double-crossing him, was sending him into a trap.'

'What did he *do*?'

'He set it up so she would die if it turned out she'd betrayed him — '

'Traven.'

'Yes?'

'Just tell me what he did to her.'

Hang on to your sanity, Steve — like I had to do earlier on, when I got the story. 'He tied her to a chair and put a time bomb in her lap,' Traven said. 'Told her he'd set the thing to blow at eight o'clock, and he'd got an agent of his in cover outside her house with orders to stay there until one of two things happened: either Cooper called him and gave him orders to go into the house and immobilize the bomb, or — '

'Or it would get to eight o'clock without his call and the bomb would detonate. Yes, I read Cooper in that.'

'But my blokes were there by six forty-five. She's safe, Steve. The bomb was taken away and she's no longer in any danger. Keep your mind on arresting Cooper.'

'It's on him. Just one more thing, sir: going by what happened at Hanna's, what time d'you reckon he'll turn up here?'

After a slight pause, 'That depends on too many unknown factors to be answered with any precision,' Traven said, 'but I'd put it around seven thirty.'

'And it's nearly seven twenty now. Good. Not long to wait.'

Something in Steve's voice caught at

Traven's mind — it was too quiet, for one thing, given the circumstances. There was something more, though. But the right word for it eluded him.

'Anything else?' Steve's voice came across the line to him, quiet and gentle.

'No. I'd like you to report back to me every hour from now on until we get a result. And keep your cool, Steve,' he added, then cut the call.

Steve switched off his mobile. From the cover of the green velvet curtains he looked out again at the path leading up to Innisfree's front door, the path along which Cooper would come.

No witnesses bar me and Rebecca. The words he had thought earlier came into his mind for the second time and he smiled thinly: I wasn't sure about it then but, by God, *I'm sure of it now!* A time bomb, on the lap of a woman you've tied to a chair . . . I'd like to pay Cooper back in his own coin, but there won't be time to do so. Sadly, it'll have to be done fast. Fast and clean.

★　★　★

As he drove to the address Hanna had given him, Cooper found his mind unable to disregard the very possibility which — even while himself not really crediting it, advancing it simply in a vicious desire to add to the fear Tregorian was enduring — he had used against her. Namely, that the rumour his agent had recently reported to him was in fact true: Tregorian was a double agent working *for* Traven *against* Desert Wolf. That *was* a possibility and, as such, one he'd be wise to guard against — that is, take care of number one! Accordingly he pulled into the next lay-by he came to, sat back, and revised his plan of action at the bungalow called Innisfree. No way was he going to lay off the Remmick bitch, but instead of working her over there he'd abduct her at gunpoint and cart her off to some place where he could safely take his time about it. Using his mobile, he contacted a couple he could rely on to provide him with such a hideaway — the bloke owed him, seriously owed him . . .

18

'I heard you on your mobile.' Rebecca came into the hall through the sitting-room door. 'Who was it?'

'Traven.' Steve did not turn his head to look at her. As he watched for Cooper now there was a great hunger in him. *No witnesses bar me and Rebecca,* he was thinking as he answered her. 'You've got what you have to do when he comes absolutely clear in your mind?' he asked sharply. 'You're sure of it? Dead sure?'

'I'm sure.' Rebecca halted just inside the hall, staring across at him, frowning. There was something different about him now. She sensed in him a savage malevolence that had not been there before and it frightened her. Going across to him she laid a hand on his arm. 'Don't worry, Steve, it'll be all right,' she said, misinterpreting the reason for the change in him. 'I can do it. I *will* do it, and I'll do it right, I promise. I'm scared, yes, but — believe this, *believe me*, please — I can and will play this out with Cooper exactly the way you've told me to.' She gave his arm a little shake and then, as he turned and faced her, produced a small grin. 'The way we play-acted it through a bit ago until I got it perfect, you making me do it over and over till I could do it fast and smoothly. I got pretty good at it, didn't I?'

'You did.' Steve raised a smile: briefly, bleakly, smiled down into the tense face of Rob's widow. 'We make a good team, you and I.'

'What did Traven have to say?' Her unease about him assuaged, Rebecca moved away, back from the window. 'Is there any news about where Cooper is?'

Scowling, Steve swung round to watch the gate again. 'There's news of him all right. This afternoon he shot a man dead so he could steal his car. Murdered the bloke — a total stranger who had the bad luck to be in the wrong place at the wrong time.'

The words died. Silence fell in the red-carpeted hall. Rebecca stood rooted to the spot, struggling to come to terms with what he had just told her. Steve became aware of her silence and, wrapped up with her inside it, intuited the shock and terror gripping her — and realized it was going to either make or break her. Nevertheless he did not regret telling her about the murder because if she *was* going to break he'd rather it happened before Cooper came, not when she opened the door to him.

'It's OK, Steve.' Suddenly her voice cut through the silence and now it was bright and hard; he sensed a new confidence in her and was glad. 'It took me a minute to get my head around what you said — Cooper murdering a man — but it's all right now, *I'm* all right now. Better, actually. Cold-blooded killing like that — it's vile. I'm not going to let myself be spooked by a bloke like that. As I live and breathe, I will *not!* So don't worry: I won't fall apart when I open the door to Cooper.'

Now, at last, Steve truly believed her. He told her so.

'Good,' she said, and smiled at him. 'Was there any other news from Traven?'

'From information recently in, he reckons it's likely Cooper will arrive here soon now — any moment, even, so we better get ourselves in position straight away.' He did not tell Rebecca what Cooper had done to Hanna — not because he was afraid knowledge of it might unnerve her again, but because he felt it was something that, for the moment, belonged to him alone. And to Traven, surely? Yes, to Traven also.

Quickly then, they took up their planned positions: Rebecca at the window, watching from behind the green curtains for Cooper to arrive; Steve on the other side of the hall from her, standing just inside the open sitting-room door, opposite the front door and facing it. Placed thus he would be six or seven yards away from Cooper when he came in through it — and would have a clear line of fire to him.

Steve stood alert but relaxed, right arm alongside his body, handgun against his thigh. Wrapped up again in the silence filling the hall, he ran his mind over the necessarily basic security measures he had taken in the bungalow. Back door locked, bolted top and bottom; all windows closed except for one in the kitchen and another in the sitting-room; all interior doors open so that should Cooper opt for forced entry the sound of it would travel through the bungalow and give him, Steve, fair warning; and front door locked — who doesn't these days? Especially a woman living alone. Steve shifted his feet impatiently, flexed his gun arm. Come on, Cooper! Come *on*, for Christ's sake! he thought. What's keeping you? If —

'There's a man approaching the gate.' Rebecca's whisper splintered the tension in the hall — but then she breathed a sigh of relief. 'He's gone past. Sorry.'

'Keep watching. It should be soon now, if it's going to happen.' Should be — but what if it isn't? If Cooper doesn't show up soon Traven's Special Forces blokes will be here and —

'It's him, Steve! He's got his head down but it's him. It's Cooper! He's opening our gate! Oh God, I can't — '

'Do it like we practised, love. Come on. When the bell stops ringing, count up to ten then go for it! Quick, cool, *decisive*, remember? You and me against him.'

Warmth and a jaunty élan in Steve's voice — and to Rebecca it seemed as if Rob were speaking to her. Resolve and a fierce excitement surged through her and, hyped up, mind and body alive with controlled energy, she ran back from the window to stand beside Steve.

A few seconds later the doorbell rang. At once Steve set himself ready for fast action, his gun held out in front of him, both hands gripped round the butt and its muzzle centred — chest height to a man — on the locked front door.

Three times in quick succession the bell was pressed. As the ringing died away, Rebecca counted up to ten inside her head, metronomic steady and her lips moving soundlessly; then she walked across the hall to the door and called through it, 'Is that the insurance man?'

371

There was a brief pause, then answer came. 'Yes, madam. I've got my ID here ready to show you.'

'Oh, good. You're late, but never mind. Hold on a moment, I'll open up.' And with the slick speed of recent practice, Rebecca slipped off the safety-chain, turned the key in the lock, then flung the door wide open and, moving in sync with it, got in behind it, pulled it back close to the wall and crouched down low, her chin tucked into her chest and her hands cupped over her mouth *please God don't let Cooper get me.*

As the door swung wide Cooper barged inside fast, his Larsen in his right hand searching the room for its prey — but then he stopped dead. 'Christ, *Steve?*' he gasped, eyes dilating with horror as he recognized the man facing him across the hall aiming a gun straight at him — a gun which even as he spoke *spat two bullets at him.* Striking him full in the chest they drove hard into his vital organs and as the impact rammed him backwards his life was draining from him. Gun falling out of his hand he keeled over, fell heavily to the floor and . . . died there. Lay sprawled on his back just inside the door.

Beside him in a flash, Steve bent down, checked eyes and pulse for signs of life. Finding none, straightened up. 'OK, Rebecca.

Come out now,' he called. Heard her move a little, scuffling sounds coming from behind the door. Anger against her rose up in him then because time was pressing — Traven's Specials would soon be calling him on his mobile to report themselves arrived nearby, and before they did so there were certain things he had to do here. But he reined in his anger because Rebecca's help — her *connivance* — was essential if his plan was to succeed. 'It's safe to come out now,' he went on quietly, 'there's nothing to be afraid of. But there's one or two things I must do, so come on, love. Come out, and close the door.'

Rebecca came out of hiding then. As she sidled out from behind the door her eyes went straight to Cooper's body. She stood staring at it for a moment. Then, without taking her eyes off it, she closed the door and went to stand at Steve's side. 'He's dead?' A cold curiosity in her voice. 'You said you were going to arrest him.'

'Yes, he's dead.'

'I heard two shots — '

'Both were mine.'

'You mean you . . . shot to kill?' She looked up at him. 'Straight off?'

He nodded, holding her eyes. 'I shot to kill, yes. In a situation like this between you and Cooper — *with a man like Cooper* — it's the only way. Believe that, Rebecca: *it's the only way.*'

'Only way to what?' Still there was nothing in her voice but cold curiosity.

Watch your step here, Steve told himself. You've got to work at this if you're going to get her co-operation — which is absolutely vital to you. 'The only way to make sure you're safe to live your life. The only way I know of, anyway.'

'But it's . . . murder.'

For a moment then he could not meet her eyes. Turning his head away, he looked down. But what he saw then was Cooper lying dead, and for a second it seemed to Steve Remmick that even in death the traces of a malignant, triumphant sneer lay on that lifeless face. You're not going to get out of this one, Remmick, the half-open mouth seemed to say, you've done murder here and — well, there ain't no fucking way out of it that I can see, you're stuck with *murder*, chummy. They'll send you down *for life*, you bastard, so I reckon the last laugh's mine, eh?

'Steve?' She touched his arm — and jerking round to face her he saw in her eyes that he was losing her again. 'It's murder. They'll know it, and I can't . . . I see what you mean: if he'd stayed alive he'd have kept after me till he got me, how even from jail he'd have set

374

his agents to find me, but I can't — '

'Rebecca.' No 'love' now, kids' stuff days are gone for ever. 'Don't think too deep, don't question too deep; there isn't time. I said I'd killed him so you'd be safe to live your life.'

'But I — '

'Quiet.' He did not raise his voice but there was an intensity within it which caused her to fall silent. 'Listen to me. It's not only *you* Cooper would have punished. He knew about Donna — knew all about her, where she's living, everything, and he'd have made sure *she* paid for Liam Kidd as well as you.'

'But she's nothing to do with — '

'You think that'd have mattered to Cooper? Then you don't know him. I do, and — *believe this* — he would not have stopped at killing you. He'd have carried his vendetta on to Donna, knowing you'd care about her because she's Rob's daughter, and before he killed you he'd make sure *you knew* he was going to do that. If Cooper had lived, Donna would have paid the price, as well as you.' Steve stopped there. I haven't put it very well, he thought bleakly, but at least it's the simple truth.

Still Rebecca said nothing, simply stood there looking up at him, her face without expression. Then anger rose up in him again, and this time he let it rip. 'So you wish I hadn't killed him, do you?' He slammed it at her, his voice suddenly loud in the little hall where Cooper lay dead. 'Wish I'd let him live, so the sanctimonious Rebecca Remmick didn't have to look fair and square at murder — murder done to protect her and Rob's daughter — and decide whether or not she'd agree to be party to it? Wish I'd left him alive to bring Donna unremitting misery?'

'No!' Abruptly, Rebecca came to life again. 'My God, no! To think of Rob's daughter . . . Simple, really, isn't it? I couldn't, mustn't let that happen, knowing I could have — '

'So you'll help me?'

'I'll do whatever you say, Steve.'

'You don't have to actually do anything,' he said, giving her a quick, reassuring grin. 'Your part in this is simply to give out the story of what happened here the way I tell you to. Will do?'

'Will do.'

'Then wait quiet while I do the necessary. It won't take long.'

Putting aside his own weapon, Steve wrapped his handkerchief around his right hand, retrieved Cooper's gun from where it had fallen, and set about creating the scenario he had thought up. Taking firing stance close to the right side of Cooper's body he raised the gun in his wrapped right hand, aimed it chest-high-to-a-man at the wall behind the spot on the far side of the hall from which he himself had faced Cooper as he came in — and fired two shots into the wood-panelling there, hearing a half-smothered 'Oh God!' from Rebecca as he did so. Then, without pause, he reached down with his left hand, raised Cooper's right, eased the butt of the gun snugly into its palm then clasped the lax fingers around it.

Rebecca watched him — and understood what her part in this was to be.

'You get the idea?' Steve straightened up as he spoke, looked her in the eye.

'Yes. When questioned I'll say that I heard Cooper fire first, and he fired two shots. Then following close on them I heard the reports of your two shots. *Heard* all the shots only, since I was behind the door. Didn't see anything.' Her face was white, her voice matter-of-fact.

'That's right. Because of your position you only heard; you *saw* nothing of it.'

'And up till then, till the time of the shots, I just . . . tell the truth?'

But Steve saw fear rising in her again — saw it clouding her eyes and quickly sought to disarm it. 'It'll be all right,' he said. 'You won't have to face hostile questioning. I can set it up so the only person you'll have to tell it to face to face will be Traven. Apart from that, there'll only be sworn affidavits.'

'It's all right, Steve.' Rebecca had blown her doubts away: she knew with absolute certainty that in this there was one thing she wanted above all and that to get it she would, quite literally, do *anything at all*.

The blue eyes met Steve's steadily, and he perceived the fear that had been in her had been overpowered by something even more elemental. Rob's wife is back in business he thought, she loves him still, so —

'You don't have to spell it all out to me,' she said. 'When I look at it straight, I know I'd take Cooper's life myself, any day, to keep Rob's daughter safe from him. Later on, you'll tell me about her, like you said, and — ' She broke off as Steve's mobile beeped.

Fairly certain who it would be calling him, he answered it at once, giving only the arranged code word. 'Reception'.

'Parcel to deliver. OK to come round now?'

'OK. Situation here in hand, no special security measures required. Remmick out.'

19

As Steve came into his office, Traven pushed back his chair, opened the bottom drawer of his desk and took out a half-bottle of Scotch and two glasses. 'Whisky?' he asked and, on Steve's nod, poured the two drinks and handed one to him. It was eleven o'clock the same evening and at 11.30 both of them were due at a debriefing session with co-ordinating officers from MI6. 'I read your preliminary report,' he said.

Standing side-on to the desk, Steve tipped his glass to his boss, took a much-needed sip of whisky. 'And the one from the senior officer you detailed to Innisfree?' he asked then. He had talked with Traven over the radio twice since the fatality at the bungalow, the first time soon after his MI5 back-up men had arrived there, the second time from another office in this HQ building where they now were, but this was the first time he had spoken with him in person since Cooper's death, and there was a deep unease in him.

Traven nodded. But then to Steve's surprise — he had expected Traven to wade in straight off, hard, with close questioning about the Cooper killing — he changed the subject entirely. 'I had a call from Jane Coates just before you came in,' he said. 'She reports Rebecca and herself settled in at the safe house.'

'Jane Coates?' Disorientated, Steve found himself unable to fit a person to the name.

'The MI5 officer who'll be her minder for a while, remember?' Traven gestured impatiently. 'Come on, Steve, get a grip,' he said. 'As far as you and I — also quite a few others around here and elsewhere in the United Kingdom — are concerned, the night's young yet, so get some whisky down you and sharpen up. I told you about Rebecca because I knew you'd be concerned about her. Now you know she's in good hands, forget her for a while. You'll need your wits about you at the debriefing.'

'Will that cover Cooper's death only?' Steve had pulled himself together. A second swig of whisky had indeed helped.

'No. Since you and I last spoke on the radio its agenda has been broadened.'

'Christ, what's come up now?'

'Mansoor's broken free.'

'Mansoor? But we had him — '

'I led you to think we had. At the time it seemed best; I wanted you concentrated on Cooper.'

'But how the hell did we come to lose him?'

'At the airport. Partly an outside job, but I don't have much information on it yet. Ramadan had got hold of a gun somehow, he opened and sustained fire, covered Mansoor's line of escape. Mansoor made it, Ramadan was shot dead at the scene.'

'You should've told me. The controllers — they were part of all I was working for.'

'There was no need for you to know.' Traven stared at him coldly. 'Your mark at the time was Cooper. The big picture was for me and others to deal with.'

So you're no better than me, Traven, Steve thought with a touch of bitterness but fuller understanding. In our different ways you and I each had an agenda of our own, each kept secret from the other certain areas of our thought and intention. Brothers under the skin we are, you and me — we lied to each other, Traven. OK, yours was a little lie and by way of omission only, a negative thing in intention and in result. While mine was and is — and always will be? Yes, I'm committed now — a lie of commission, a positive act, an act which was in fact a crime but which I dressed up in such a manner as would make it appear legal. Then I set my lie in stone by affirming it in both spoken and written word

381

. . . Still, it's a fact that we each lied to the other, isn't it? The deception was only in the matter of degree.

'There's a couple of questions I have to ask you, Steve.' On his feet now, Traven spoke with quiet authority.

'Wouldn't it be better to keep them for the debriefing?'

'I would prefer to put them to you here, and now.'

'Why? What's it matter?'

'I'll tell you why, then you'll see it matters. At least, I hope you will.' If you don't, then I've wasted a great deal of valuable time and effort — also my freely given trust — on you, Steve Remmick, Traven thought, his face grim. 'It is because I wish to put my two questions to you in the secrecy of me and you alone, with no witnesses — and on my promise that *whatever your answers to them may be* I will never disclose those answers to any other person without your permission to do so.' Traven was silent for a few moments then, allowing time for the implications of his words, together with the personal commit-ment contained in them, to be fully comprehended and then weighed in the balance of Steve Remmick's values. When he went on, his voice was devoid of all expression. 'So, may I go ahead and ask them? It won't take long. You and I have been working together in this for a long time now, so all you have to do is answer 'Yes' or 'No' and I'll accept it as the truth without further probing, whichever it may be. Therefore you have to tell the truth to me now.'

Crunch point, thought Steve, turning to face Traven. Because I'm fairly sure I know what he's going to ask me — and I can see that if I lie I might get what I've come to want very much indeed, a permanent job with Traven in MI5; whereas if I tell him the truth ... Well, he's hardly likely to want a confessed murderer on his staff, is he? Not easy, though, to lie to this man face to face like we are now.

'Well?' Traven's eyes held his and they were black as coal. 'Do I ask my questions?'

His mind made up, Steve gave him a quick grin. 'Go ahead.'

'Did Cooper fire first?'

'No. I took him before he had time to get his gun up.'

'Question two. Did you shoot to kill and then arrange matters to support a theory of self-defence?'

'Yes. Rebecca's my witness to it being self-defence. She didn't see any of it, she only heard.'

'Enough. We'll go into it all some other

time . . . Like I said, what you've just told me will remain strictly between you and I.'

'For ever?'

'All my life.'

'Christ. I wasn't — '

'Cooper fired first, you returned fire: the factual evidence at the scene confirms those facts, and they will be sworn to at or for the enquiry by you, by Rebecca Remmick, and by the senior MI5 officer who was on scene within — what was it? — ten minutes of the shooting.' Having got what he wanted, Traven turned and headed for the door. Watching him, Steve saw him moving with a new spring in his step — and recalling Traven's face on hearing Steve's answers, it seemed to him there had been in it a quiet satisfaction, almost a sort of renewal of self-belief?

'Steve.' Halting by the door, Traven faced him again. 'This seems to be a good time to ask you one further question.'

Steve felt nervous tension rise in him — quelled it and prepared for trouble. 'They say things go in threes, some sort of natural rhythm or something,' he said wryly. 'Ask away.'

'Would you be interested in signing on with my crew? Undercover missions again? Permanent staff?'

Steve could not believe what he was

hearing. It was too good to be true. 'But — I killed Cooper! Shot him dead in cold blood, planned it — '

'And have now admitted that crime to me.' Traven smiled one of his rare — and very self-contained — smiles. 'I've got a lot of time for that sort of courage and that sort of trust. I value it in my agents; I value it very highly indeed . . . Well? Are you up for the job?'

'There's nothing I'd like better.'

'Good. That's settled, then.' Traven turned and opened the door, saying over his shoulder as he went out, 'Come back here to the office after the debriefing, then, and we'll talk.'

★   ★   ★

Glancing sideways, Steve saw that Hanna's eyes had closed. Sitting on the ground a couple of yards away from where he lay stretched out in tree-shade, she had her back propped comfortably against the smooth grey trunk of a beech tree at the edge of Badgers' Spinney and she had fallen half asleep, dark hair falling loose over her shoulders, her strong, broad hands resting on the ground beside her, curled loosely in on themselves on the thin, sun-dappled grass. It's good to see her so relaxed, he thought, and got to his feet and strolled out into the afternoon sunshine and then on down the field to the brook below. It flowed dream-quiet, and so clear that the shadows of the small fish darting about in it played *doppelgänger* to them on the sandy bed below.

Hunkering down on the wild-flower bank, he ran his mind over the six days which had passed since he shot Cooper dead. A lot had happened during them, but now life was settling down to something approaching normality, on the private-life side of things at least. Rebecca was safe and happy, engaged in sorting out her business affairs — she was putting Roberta's on the market — and, with Traven's help, acquiring a new ID as advised and subsequently authorized by him. Hanna, recuperating under Jocelyn Hargest's care, was recovering fast, the worst of the physical pain was over now and although the mental trauma engendered by the hours she had suffered under the threat of Cooper's time-bomb still haunted her, she was winning free of it . . . Thank God for the Hargests, Steve thought. When he had telephoned them on the afternoon following Cooper's death with news of Hanna's 'car accident' Bill Hargest had not wasted time in asking questions. 'Bring her down to us right away,' he'd said at once. 'Joss is in the garden, I'll tell her now. Can do, your end?' So Steve had driven Hanna to Herne's Hill farm and left her in their care, being himself under orders to return to London immediately to continue working with Traven on dealing with the complex and internationally sensitive aftermath of the smashing of operation Desert Wolf, and to be on hand to attend the ongoing enquiry into the Cooper fatality, if called.

Nevertheless, since then he had managed to visit Hanna four times — often turning up at the oddest times, but that had not seemed to faze the Hargests one bit. And on one of those occasions — almost midnight it had been, he recalled now, hunkered down on his sunny bank — he and Hanna had become engaged. He had not yet told her about his coming full-time job with Traven at MI5.

I really must tell her soon, he thought. Thank God her working in with Traven was just a one-off thing — like she said, just some minor jobs during Double Talk. I can't imagine her being involved in big-time undercover stuff; she's not like that, too straight by far . . . Lost in thought, he was running his hand over the ground beside him and his idling fingers, encountering a smooth round stone, picked it up. He looked down at it — and grinned. Perfect! Just right for ducks-and-drakes, he thought — and turning it edgewise between his fingers leaned to his right and sent the stone streaking out over the water. But instead of skimming and skittering bravely across the surface as it was meant to, it struck it edgewise on and sank straight down. The waters of the brook closed over it and then he saw it lying hard and dark on the bed of the stream, water holding it down there, drowning it.

— like water drowned the body of that motorist Cooper shot dead then dumped in a pond so he could steal his car. *Christ!*

'Ste-eve!' Hanna's voice from behind him, and turning his head he saw her standing at the edge of the Spinney. Scrambling to his feet he ran back up the slope towards her. 'Sorry, I fell asleep,' she said, going into his arms as he joined her. And when finally she broke free of his embrace she said, 'Let's go back to the house now. I promised I'd do a bit of weeding; Jocelyn says the kitchen garden's a disaster area . . . Was there any news from Traven, before you left London this morning?' she asked, as they set off side by side along the grassy track through Badgers' Spinney.

'They've got Mansoor. He's under arrest. He was informed on by one of his own, so they were able to take him by surprise.'

Walking close at his side, Hanna looked

down at the path. 'I'm glad I'm out of it all — and that soon you will be, too.'

'Did Traven ask you to go on with it? Working with him?' A shiver of disquiet stirred to life within Steve, but he kept his voice neutral.

Hanna nodded. 'He didn't press me, though.' She kicked idly at a stone lying on the path, and smiled. 'He understands. He's known for a long time how deeply I hate terrorism and anything and everything to do with it. He's got good reason to know.'

Something in her voice — a particular softness, a tinge of sadness even, perhaps? — needled Steve, and he stood still, turned to her sharply, asking, 'How d'you mean, Traven's got good reason to know how you feel about terrorism?'

Hanna too had halted, wishing she had watched her words more carefully. 'I thought you knew — '

'Knew what?' He threw it at her angrily.

Her chin went up. 'It's got nothing to do with you.'

'Everything about you is to do with me — '

'Really?' she cut in, colour flaming her cheeks. 'Then I'll tell you. Traven and I were very close a few years ago, and he wanted us to marry.'

Sensing her totally gone from him, Steve

was appalled at his own crass assumption of ownership of her. 'I'm sorry,' he said. 'I'd no right to say what I did. I don't really think like that, forgive me.'

'Of course.' Surprised and a little shocked at the violence of her own resentment, Hanna spoke quietly. 'Don't be jealous, Steve. I don't . . . I never have loved Traven. But I do like him very much and — back then — I came close to marrying him. But . . . really, I knew I couldn't. No way, not ever. I couldn't live my life with a man whose life revolves round terrorism.'

'Even though he's working against it?'

She nodded. 'Even then.'

'But — why not?' Steve's world was crumbling to dust around him. 'I don't understand. You yourself — you've just spent around two years working against it — OK, on the sidelines, like you said, but that doesn't alter the *principle* of the thing. So why can't you live your life with a man working in anti-terrorism? For God's sake, *why*?'

Hanna had turned away from him, was looking around her, taking into herself the tranquillity of Badgers' Spinney: to her, it was a place suddenly arrived at as a child of terrorism, a place where she had rediscovered childhood, playing cowboys-and-Indians with the Hargest boys and their friends, building tree-houses, gathering holly. A place she had run away from once, when she'd been bad. A place she had come to love.

'*Why not*, Hanna?' Steve's voice was urgent from behind her, asking his question for the second time.

'Because to fight against terrorism — in any *active* sense, I mean — you have to live in the world of the terrorist. And it . . . rubs off on you. If you work in close contact with it for any length of time, it . . . stains you. I've seen it happen.'

'Go on. I need to know *why*.'

'Because of my life in Lebanon before my parents' English friends brought me here!' she interrupted passionately, her eyes fixed on a broad patch of sunlight lying across the path. 'Because of my relatives who were terrorists there, because of my brother who was *brought up to be* a terrorist! . . . To you my brother — Shaheen's courier on the night of the car crash in the hills — was just another terrorist who'd come over here to ply his trade. But he was brainwashed all through his childhood — he was *impregnated* with hatred for 'non-believers', then sent here to work for Shaheen . . . That's the real answer to your 'why', Steve. It's a long, long story. Even though I was lucky, was pulled free of it when I was fairly young, memories have stayed with me: I was scarred, even at so early an age, I guess. I went into Double Talk with Traven because I had to prove I wasn't like my brother — '

'Prove it to Traven?'

She turned on him then. '*To prove it to myself!* To *myself*, don't you see?' But this man she loved still stood silent, staring at her and frowning in seeming bewilderment; so she forced herself to be quiet inside and to speak to him from the head, not the heart. 'You should know, Steve,' she said. 'You've done much the same thing yourself, haven't you? You've been working undercover for Traven to prove you've rejected — *repudiated* — the terrorism you and your brother Robert aided and abetted in the past. So surely you understand? Steve — Steve darling, you *must* understand!'

Steve Remmick understood. Listening to her words, and now looking into her face, he understood the totality of her hatred of everything in any way whatsoever related to terrorism — and also realized what he himself would have to do, would have to *give up*, if Hanna and he were to live their lives together. So it's no contest, Traven, he thought. For me it's showdown time now, and it's no contest; I shall go back on my word to you. I'll find me a straight job and go do it, I've got some useful talents, haven't I? Doing so hurts and it's going to go on hurting — probably it'll hurt you also, but only a little, and briefly, because you're a very self-contained man. Besides, knowing Hanna as it seems you do, as well as she's just told me you do — you will understand . . . I suppose each one of us — Hanna, you, me — made our own choice. About loving, and its place in our lives — about other things also, of course, but they're all tied in with that.

'Steve?' Watching him, Hanna had realized he had been resolving something big in his mind, and now she saw that, whatever it was, his decision had been made and he was happy with it. 'It's all right now, isn't it?' she went on, and then as he nodded and moved closer to her, put his arm round her shoulder, she walked on along the path and he fell into step beside her.

Neither spoke again until they came to the edge of the Spinney; but by unspoken mutual consent they stopped there, stood looking across the garden. Steve dropped his arm, moved a little away from her. 'When I was down there by the brook, I suddenly thought about Cooper,' he said, his eyes on the farmhouse in front of them.

'What a waste of time.' But she had

shivered at the name.

'There's a thing about him I think you ought to know. Traven told me, but when I asked him if he'd told you he said he hadn't, and wasn't going to. But I think it's something you ought to know. In a funny way, Cooper's got a sort of *right* that you should. May I tell you?'

'If you really think I ought to know it, yes. I don't much like talking about him, but — yes, tell me.'

'It's this: that bomb Cooper put on your lap — he didn't set the timer on it.'

'*What?*' Hanna swung round and faced him, a wild, lost look in her eyes telling him that she was remembering what it had been like then, the *waiting*.

'It was a bomb all right — he took it from his car outside Ashburn, he'd got grenades in there too — but he didn't set the timing mechanism going before he left you.'

She stared at him, still adrift in past terrors. 'You're saying the thing . . . would never have gone off?'

Steve nodded. 'Yes. And he hadn't put an agent of his outside your house, all of it was just bullshit.' Slowly, her face cleared, she relaxed. And Steve saw that — strangely — she was truly and entirely free of Cooper now, her gut-fear of the man was gone. 'Why, though, Steve?' she asked, frowning. 'He certainly wasn't averse to killing, was he?'

'Maybe for once in his life he . . . saw things differently? Sometimes you think you know people, but then they do something totally at odds with your perception of them.'

'Cooper, suddenly beset by compassion? You do him too much honour. Most likely he simply forgot, was in too much of a hurry to get to Rebecca . . . I'm glad you told me. I don't quite see why I should be, but I am.' She slid her arm into his. 'Come on, let's go in.'

But Steve stood still. 'So I was right, to tell you?' he asked.

She looked at him then; and intuiting the whole question in him she answered that, and not simply the bit of it he had put into words. 'You were right about me, and Traven was wrong,' she said.

'Sad, for Traven. Perhaps?'

'I don't think so. He can leave me behind now, get on with his life without' — Hanna gave a quick grin — 'without personal baggage to bother with. Travel light and you travel faster, it's said.'

'Probably miss out on one hell of a lot of splendid things on the way, though, I guess.'

CRIME IN HEAVEN

Jane Morell

When Isabel Armstead meets quiet, unassuming Gemini during her final year of college, it simply does not occur to her that he could be involved in violence. Gemini knows of the shady past which Isabel's father David is desperate to hide now that he is a respected surgeon. Through Isabel, he is determined to exploit that knowledge. Then too, there is the mysterious Hanna Fraser who is equally determined to achieve her aims. Drawn ever more deeply into a web of deceit and violence, Isabel must make a terrifying choice between two evils.

IN THE MIDST OF LIFE

Roger Silverwood

A savage murder in a hospital for the criminally insane twenty years ago marks the beginning of a gruesome trail of enquiries to find a missing nurse. In spite of obstruction from the Chief Constable, the quirky Inspector Michael Angel stubbornly ferrets out the suspects, and reduces them to one, by resorting to an unusual strategy. A dead woman wearing one stocking inside out, an American class ring, a missing videotape of the lovely Lola, and two dead cats all play their part in the scramble to find the killer in a south Yorkshire market town at the foot of the Pennines.

THE WORLD IS NOT ENOUGH

Raymond Benson

Greed, revenge, world domination through the power of oil, high-tech terrorism . . . This latest 007 adventure begins outside the Guggenheim Museum in Bilbao, Spain, and continues with a spectacular, high-speed boat chase up the Thames and an avalanch in the Caucasus Mountains before Bond faces a murderous enemy in Baku and a potential nuclear explosion in Turkey . . . Sir Robert King, a wealthy oil tycoon, is murdered in a bombing at the Secret Intelligence Service's London headquarters. M takes the attack personally and sends James Bond to what was once the USSR to protect King's heiress, his beautiful and fiery daughter, Elektra . . .

SEA FURY

James Pattinson

It was an oddly assorted company of passengers that boarded the S.S. *Chetwynd* in Hong Kong and Singapore to take passage to Fremantle. The old vessel, operated by a line that had a poor reputation, was the kind of ship that could hardly attract the finest of officers or crew and was patronized only by the least demanding or affluent of passengers. In this company, living in such close quarters, there was inevitably a certain amount of friction. But human passions would prove insignificant by comparison when the indescribable fury of the storm hit.

THE WRECKING CREW

Mark Chisnell

Pirates used to kill with cutlasses and cannons, but now they use sub-machine guns and the Internet. The result is the same - a murderous reign of terror . . . Phillip Hamnet left port at the helm of the MV *Shawould,* apparently master of his vessel and his destiny — but others had a different agenda on that evil night in the South China Sea. Drug warlord Janac has turned to piracy to fund his battle for control of the Australian narcotics trade, and Hamnet is faced with a fatal decision. As Janac forces one brutal choice after another, Hamnet is drawn deep into the nightmare world of a man who thrives on psychological terror.

DEATH OF A SUPERTANKER

Antony Trew

The *Ocean Mammoth* was among the latest and finest of the monster tankers, yet in a time of falling freight rates and dwindling cargoes it had no useful part to play. It had to die. But the death of a supertanker is not easily contrived if it must appear to have been an accident. The conspiracy to take *Ocean Mammoth* to her doom involved meticulous planning and ruthless execution. But who was responsible? The formidable, withdrawn Captain Crutchley? Freeman Jarrett, the flamboyantly handsome chief officer? Foley, the colourless navigation officer? Or was it some other crewman who had access to the complex electronic system?